ERRANT

JUSTICE

By R.H. Bishop

For evvy garrett

Visit: rhbishopbooks.com

"Who is happy? He who cooks his own food."
                              --Mahabarata

1

The white cardboard shipping box containing our copy of the file in *People v. Domingo Torres*, arrived at our office via an early morning courier delivery. That same morning, I happened to get fed up with my boss, and quit my job. Looking back on the *Torres* case, and how it played out, I get there's a rhyme to those two things happening on the same day. I also now see it might've been better if I'd stayed quit a while longer, like long enough for the case to be over. It would've spared me some embarrassing regrets. On the other hand, there were some definite up sides to my being part of it all, even though the process wasn't always pretty. I guess I should just tell you about it and let you be the judge.

At 8:30 on the dot, clutching my Starbucks, I shouldered through the office door, kicked the white box containing *P. v. Torres* out of my way, dumped my messenger bag on my desk, and greeted the boss.

"Happy Friday, *Abogada*! Ready for the weekend? 'Cause I sure am." I sat at my desk and powered on my computer.

Lucy was sitting in our front room, where she often sips her morning tea and reads the legal newspaper or goes over her files for the day's court appearances. The Law Offices of Lucy Sanders, Esq., takes up the first floor of a converted Victorian house on the eastern edge of downtown San Diego. I have a desk facing the door in the large front room, which was originally a living room. Now it's a waiting room for clients and storage space for our many file cabinets and bookcases. In front of the fireplace is a big oval coffee table, flanked by a nasty and uncomfortable puke-green sofa and a plush armchair, on a big Turkish carpet. I've told Lucy I would even have sex with her if she would just replace the sofa with a buffed, English-style brown leather sectional, the kind with brass studs, or something similar, but she still won't do it.

"Happy Friday to you, too, Armando," she said. "But no, I'm not ready for the weekend," she said. "We're behind in our work. I'm going to have to ask you to come in tomorrow."

"Um. That would be a 'no'," I said.

I reminded her I was leaving for Las Vegas that evening, and was going to be gone through the coming Monday. She denied she'd agreed to give me the day off. As the discussion progressed, I may have raised my voice a little.

Her eyes flashed blue at me. "Oh, and now you're getting upset. Honestly. What are you going to do, quit on me again?"

"Try me," I said, rolling my chair back from my desk. "Just try and see."

She was sitting with a file open on her lap, her reading glasses on the end of her long nose. At the end of the day, she'll have her long nyloned feet up on the coffee table, but now she still had her black Povia loafer pumps, which I helped her pick out, planted side by side on the floor, ready for the day in court.

I admit Lucy had already made a name for herself as one of San Diego's top criminal defense attorneys when I'd started working for her. She'd been somewhere between forty and death, a successful attorney in spite of her dismal work attire. I was a nineteen-year-old homeless community college dropout with a smooth tongue and impeccable fashion sense, one of a long string of young men she'd hired as eye candy for her front office. We still live in shock our relationship has lasted five years. It couldn't have gone on if she hadn't let me give her occasional fashion advice. Today she'd done OK. Her fitted black suit was not yet wrinkled from the workday. Her smooth helmet of grey blonde hair swung back and forth as she shook her head at me.

"Really, Armando, making faces won't help. We're too busy, especially with this new murder case just delivered. I'm due in court in half an hour. I can't waste any more time talking about it.... You know I never agreed to give you the day off, I only said I'd see. Well, I do see now, I see a client facing possible execution, who desperately needs our immediate attention. Exhibit A."

She gestured at the white box just inside the front door.

"Need I say more? .... Really, you.... client in jail... Blah...file to be organized.... prepare for preliminary hearing... Right to deny your... be a team player.... Blah, blah...and I'm going to need you to re-do that.... This is such a busy day for me... having friends over for a home-cooked dinner, well technically it'll be more of a home-served dinner...pick it up at Zolezzi's.... walk my dogs.... a fatal poisoning of a young attorney... sympathetic victim.... days off simply not possible...."

"Lucy," I interrupted her, "this isn't, um, negotiable. I really need to get away and have some fun."

She took a deep breath, and her lips started moving again, but I was too pissed off to hear more than one out of ten words.

"...work ethic... Really. ...never agreed... ...rush to the store, chill the wine.... Blah, blah... can't do it all myself.... acting like a teenager.... unprofessional.... ...client accused of killing his girlfriend.... an attorney.... ...just came in from the DA's office...extremely poor attitude.... Blah, blah...."

I stood up.

Her eyes narrowed.

"That's it. I quit!" I told her. "Handle your new case without me!"

***

The needle on my '78 Chevy El Camino moved up to ninety as Slim and I hit the straight desert highway. Our other vacation buddies still had to finish their workdays before leaving San Diego, but Slim had been free and we'd been able to leave by noon.

I'd told Slim the story of my unfair morning. He'd laughed at my Lucy imitation, but rolled his eyes and slouched back into his seat as I continued my rant.

"Her being some kind of legal genius is no excuse," I said. "I don't need no more of her trying to manage my life! Not for the tiny salary she pays me. I'm done with her bullshit! Right?"

Slim yawned and turned up the radio. His Aztec profile looked like an ancient rock carving, his long sloping forehead, hooked nose, and fauxhawk highlighted against the car window. I had on my new lavender V-neck over black skinnies, all Victoria Beckham in my giant sunnies. Slim rocked an oversize tank over loose cargo shorts, showing off his smooth dark limbs. He'd already posted some selfies, and we looked goo-od.

I shouted over the music. "Lucy's all hot 'cause she's got a new murder case. Some loser poisoned his lawyer girlfriend. At first the cops thought it was suicide, but then they must've found something on our client. He must be pretty stupid, if he couldn't even fake a suicide. What is she going to do? I don't care! This time, yeah, this time, I mean it. I quit! Bam! Riiight?"

Slim had his eyes closed and was dancing in his seat to Lady Gaga.

Miles of road unwound, pancake flat desert separating the scene of my work life from the pleasures of a long Las Vegas weekend. My nerves started to settle.

"Did I tell you this new client might be facing the death penalty? Even though it sounds like a crime of passion? Domingo Somebody, *un mojado*, a wetback. So Lucy's gonna need me to translate, and guess what, honey? Yeah, too bad, I won't fuckin' be there!"

Slim and I pulled in to Vegas while there was still daylight ahead. The big black pyramid of the Hotel Luxor, our vacation destination, pointed to the big open sky, excitingly simple and classic in the busy clutter of castles, palaces, towers, and volcanos. We'd chosen the Luxor 'cause the pool is open late in the summer, and because Slim's latest obsession is with all things Egyptian.

We'd booked a single room to hold the two of us plus three friends who would drive up from San Diego after work. Slim and I filled most of the closet.

"This is a high-end place," Slim advised me. "They'll send up more hangers if our friends need them."

"Yeah," I said. "But remember the Luxor doesn't know we have extra guests staying in the room."

"Right. We'll have to keep a low profile."

Forty-five minutes later, we walked down to the big pool. Slim had on nothing but his neon orange Speedo, and a towel around his neck. He'd put his room key on a matching elastic band around his wrist. I wore my new J. Crew leather flip flops, a Hawaiian shirt Mom brought me from her vacation to Maui, and my Quicksilver trunks. We zeroed in on deck chairs that faced across the pool, with a view of the great pyramid, tall palm trees, and the skyline beyond it. A row of giant columns spanned the length of the pool on one side.

Slim and I played like kids in the pool until the sun set in an explosion of orange and magenta, finally turning into a neon-lit night.

"What do you think life was like in Ancient Egypt?" Slim mused, looking up at the Luxor pyramid. We were lying on still-warm cement, our legs hanging into the Jacuzzi.

"I dunno.   Our ancestors had pyramids too.   Yours were probably those Aztec long distance runners, taking messages along the old Camino Real, or whatever it was called before the conquest."

"I would've liked that," Slim said. "Runnin' through the pines, up into the cloud forest.   Maybe carrying loads of chocolate in a basket on my back. But I was probably a worker, probably a pyramid painter. It's in my genes."

"You won't always be a housepainter, Slim. You'll find something fun to do with your life."

"What about you?   What would you have been, 'Mando?"

"A dancer. A temple dancer. Did they have those? I wonder if they got good pay. Except, do you think they were respected for their art, or were they more like prostitutes?" I sighed. "But realistically, I prob'ly would've been a, what do you call it, a scribe. It's my fate.... Hey!!! Rodrigo, stop!"

Water splashed in my face and we were surrounded by laughter. Our friends had come to collect us for our first night of partying. For a three-day nirvana, Lucy Sanders and her desperate new client were nowhere near my mind.

Driving home late Monday night, after all the neon had faded into black, my head started to ache. Slim was slouched in the passenger seat, his head resting on my shoulder, eyes closed, hands open palms up in his lap. I stuck my arm straight out the window and tried to catch the soft cool nothing of the night air like I could hold it forever in my hand. But, of course, I couldn't.

***

I got to the office early, despite having arrived home from Vegas at four in the morning. Lucy was there ahead of me, planted in the comfortable armchair, a file folder open on her lap.

"I opened up the Torres file yesterday," she started, the moment I walked in. "I want to review it with you. We have to get up to speed. I'll need you to translate when we visit him at the downtown jail this afternoon."

"*Abogada Chingona!*" I cried, clutching my second Extra Energy Monster as I sank into the sagging green sofa. "Kickass lawyer, let's get down on it!"

With Lucy, her reviewing a file with me means I sit there for a long time and try to be awake when she hits the important parts. Lucy's reviews always remind me of a term I learned in my literature class: "stream-of-consciousness narrative." I admit this disorganized process does somehow lead her to brilliant solutions. I'll know all the same facts she does, but only she connects them to figure out the optimal defense for our client.

The Torres case had been assigned to Lucy Sanders, a private criminal defense attorney, due to an overload of cases at the public defender's office. At first it looked like the same sad-ass story. Oscar Wilde said, "each man kills the one he loves." I'm not sure I believe that's true, even in the, like, symbolic way he meant it. Still, there's a lot of cases where it's literally true. Mr. Domingo Torres, age 38, a Mexican national, had been charged with the premeditated murder of a woman he'd been dating. But in this case the victim, Patricia Taylor, 29, hadn't just been his lover. She'd been his attorney, too, representing Torres in his application for political asylum.

"The police and DA are often quick to charge undocumented immigrants," Lucy said, pursing her lips in disapproval. "This case is weak on evidence, but unfortunately the jury will also likely be anti-immigrant, and the DA knows that...."

My knee started to jiggle. She was ready to get on her soapbox and waste my time. "We can't help that right now," I murmured.

Lucy's bright blue eyes reproached me. "Really, it just hurts my heart to see such apathy in a young person." She went on: "Taylor's body was discovered at 12:45 on a Tuesday afternoon in her apartment by the police. A friend of Taylor's became concerned because Taylor had been distraught over a fight with her boyfriend, and she hadn't shown up for work that day. The police went to Taylor's home, broke in, and found her body.

"The coroner's report states Taylor died of poisoning from alcohol combined with an overdose of…" Lucy paused, shuffled through several file folders, extracted a page from the bottom of a file, and read: "Fentanyl, for which she had a prescription. The pills had been ground up and mixed with her drink of sherry."

"Fentanyl?" I exclaimed. "Isn't that a heavy duty anesthetic? How'd she get a prescription for that? Was she a druggie?"

"Well, we should definitely look into that," said Lucy "But it's really not that surprising. This was a three-year-old prescription, and it's only recently there's been a crackdown on overprescribing of addictive pain medication. Some doctors still hand these things out like candy. If she had been a druggie, would she have kept the medicine for the past three years? No, she would've used it up.

"To continue. Based on *rigor mortis* and the victim's body temperature at the time she was found, Taylor died no earlier than six o'clock Monday night and no later than four o'clock Tuesday morning. She would have become unconscious five to fifteen minutes after taking the Fentanyl, and died within an hour. She was last seen alive ten-thirty Monday night, when she Skyped with her aunt, who lives in Oakland. So her time of death was between ten-thirty and four a.m. Monday night."

Lucy tossed the page to the opposite side of the coffee table from the file, and paused to sip tea out of her favorite cup.

"Pills and booze, huh?" I said. "Sounds like a suicide to me."

I reached over and placed the page back into the proper file. As I did so, I saw the large color photo pinned to the facing page, and felt a chill down my spine. She was lying on her side, on the edge of a bed, her face mostly hidden by a mass of long, light brown hair. She could just have been sleeping, except somehow she'd got her arm wedged under her body at an odd angle, and it was sticking straight off the bed. The hand pointed upward, fingers curled towards the camera, like even in death she was pleading for help. Her arm was livid blue. I stared at the picture as Lucy continued talking.

"Does it sound like suicide?" she asked. "Well, that will be one angle. Unfortunately, there's more."

Circumstances at first suggested suicide, but the homicide team learned our client, Torres, had been seen with Ms. Taylor earlier that evening, going in to her apartment. The upstairs neighbors had overheard the sounds of a heated argument between a man and a woman at around seven o'clock Monday evening.

Torres admitted he had been at the apartment for dinner that evening, but denied there had been a quarrel. He told the police he'd left at about seven o'clock, and had not seen the victim after that time. Unfortunately, another neighbor, a teacher, reported seeing Domingo Torres leaving the apartment building at six thirty Tuesday morning. When interviewed a second time, Torres admitted he had come back to see Patty early Tuesday morning, but she had not answered her door. Not having a key, he had left without seeing her.

"It still sounds like it could have been suicide," I said, as Lucy stopped to pour herself more tea. "Maybe she was already dead, and that's why she didn't answer the door. I mean, would he really stay in there all night with her dead body?"

"That's not all," Lucy said. "Based on the neighbor seeing Torres leaving the victim's apartment that morning, the police were able to get a search warrant for Torres's hotel room," Lucy said. "In fact, we will need to draft a motion to challenge that warrant. I wrote a similar motion in a case I had about four years ago. I don't know if you remember, let's go look at our brief bank…."

"Whoa! I'll find the brief later," I said. "What did the cops find when they searched Torres's room?"

"They found a key to the victim's apartment in his dresser drawer. If he really did go home and then return to the apartment Tuesday morning, as he claims, he could have let himself in when she didn't answer the door."

"Shit. Well, what did he say about that?"

"What do you mean, what did he say? I haven't talked to him yet. Ideally, as you know, I like to meet a client in a big case like this before reviewing the file, to hear his story from him first. But I decided to wait, because I'm not sure how good Torres's English is, and I want you to translate. Now that you're refreshed from your four days of larking, of course."

Larking?

"Boss, we weren't larking, we were barking. Barking, and howling at the moon. That's why I'm now so totally ready to investigate the shit out of this case. Let's go talk to Torres. How did he explain not using his key to get into Patty's apartment that morning?"

"Why would the cops have asked him to explain, Armando? I just told you, he'd already lied to them twice, first saying he wasn't there at all and then saying he didn't have a key. By that time, they were all over him as a suspect. After all, he'd lied to them about the fight, about being there that morning, about the key, and, of course, there's the problem of the sherry glasses."

"What?"

"That's how she was poisoned, as I already told you. They were drinking sherry. His glass was in the sink, unwashed, with his prints still on it. The victim's glass was on the kitchen table, with traces of sherry and Fentanyl at the bottom. Torres's fingerprints were on her glass as well as hers."

"So he poured the sherry for both of them. He wouldn't have left his fingerprints on the glasses if he'd poisoned her, would he? What about the sherry bottle? What about the pills?"

"His prints were on the sherry bottle, but not on the empty pill container. The police will say he was very clever. He left his prints on the bottle and the glasses, since he admits he was there that evening and they had drinks together."

"Whose prints were on the pill container?" I asked.

"Only the victim's. But he could have wiped the container and then put her fingerprints on it after she passed out."

"Oh. So, our guy fought with the victim that night, lied about being there early the next morning, and his prints were on the glass of poisoned alcohol that killed her."

"Right." Lucy licked her lips. "Here's another odd fact. The victim's wallet is missing. That suggests she didn't commit suicide, that someone was there and stole her wallet."

"Why would our client steal her wallet? Was he desperate for money? Why not just take the money, or the money and the credit cards?"

"I agree. Still, documents in her wallet might have had value, to our client or someone else. Her social security card and her driver's license could be sold to someone who didn't have legal papers or wanted a fake ID."

This was the kind of case Lucy loved to get her teeth into. Her eyes were shining, her reading glasses were almost falling off the tip of her nose, and a strand of grey blond hair fell over her forehead. If she didn't have her work, what would she even do?

"Here's the first thing I want you to do," she said picking up a file folder. Her lips pursed as she failed to find the document she was looking for. "Oh, Lord, where did it go?" I leaned forward to see what she was looking at.

"You'll have to reorganize this, Armando.   It is astonishing to me, how poorly the District Attorney organizes these files. They do it deliberately, to waste my time, I'm sure."

Lucy finally handed me another file. "Here's the statement from Christine Fernwood, Taylor's friend. She told the police Taylor had been depressed recently and may have committed suicide. That opinion will be helpful, so you should interview her right away. And the best thing is, she's apparently some kind of psychotherapist."

2

I looked up at an ornate white building, all 1920's art deco, on Sixth Avenue, a few blocks south of Balboa Park, where the victim's friend, Christine Fernwood, Phd., shared a suite of offices. The building, and the surrounding area, needed a facelift, but the area already showed signs of heading upscale. Now it probably still provided affordable office space. The name, "Embassy Arms," was scripted on a maroon awning. Big potted plants framed the elevators in the lobby. On the third floor, the door to the suite had a bunch of square brass plates announcing "Wellness Center," with the names and degrees of the practitioners below. The reception area was a small room with four chairs, and a small table with magazines.

I shuffled through the Wellness Center's business cards and brochures, which included Fernwood, another psychologist, a psychiatrist, and a group of licensed massage therapists. Massage offerings included cranial-sacral and visceral massage. Ooooh, nice.

Fernwood's cards were on thick card stock that was a yummy cream color. Elegant script declared: Christine Fernwood, PhD, and contained an address and two phone numbers at the bottom, one for emergencies. Putting one of the cards in my pocket, I turned to the magazines. Swallowing my disappointment at there being no *Vanity Fair* or *Vogue*, I was just opening an outdated *Time* when the door opened.

"Mr. Felan?" A stocky woman who looked to be around thirty, with short brown hair and a face like a plain madonna, smiled down at me. She looked at the magazine in my hands, and laughed. "You like our tasteful reading material? I'm always so disappointed when my dentist's office doesn't have *People*, since that's the only time I get to read it. I should really break down and get some better reads. Hey, come on in. I'm at the end on the right."

She followed me into her office and gave me a firm handshake. "Nice to meet you. Please, sit down. Over here, on the couch, if that's OK with you, so we can be comfortable. Thank you so much for coming to my office, I know you must be incredibly busy. Please, sit."

I parked myself on a buff-colored leather couch, which I coveted for our own office. I wished Lucy was there to see her how much class it added. Next to me was an end table with a box of Kleenex. Never having been in a therapist's office, I deduced this was the spot where the patients would sit, or lie, and let it all out. Dr. Fernwood sat in a plaid armchair, all neo-Americana with a built-in footrest and sliding rocker, placed at a slight angle across from me. I looked around. On the wall across from me were a couple of framed abstract art posters in uplifting but relaxing colors. The carpet was the color of a light Starbucks mocha.

After a minute or so, I realized Dr. Fernwood had stopped her welcoming chatter and was looking at me with her head cocked slightly to one side, smiling like she expected me to do something entertaining. I smiled back. She smiled back and waited. I suddenly really wanted to swing my legs up on the couch and tell her about my messed-up childhood.

"Let's see," I said, pulling myself together and handing her one of my cards. "Here you go. First, thanks for making time to see me today. I'm really sorry about your loss of your friend."

"Thank you. Yes, it's been hard." She took my card and glanced at it. "How can I help you, Mr. Felan?"

"You can call me Armando. Maybe you could start with that morning. You were the one who called the police?"

"Oh, thank you for being so focused. And please, call me Christine." She took a deep breath, lifted her shoulders, and let them down with a deep sigh. "I was actually out of town at the time she...died. Her office left a message on my cell phone, saying she hadn't shown up for work that day. I was her emergency contact person for work. When her office called, I was presenting a paper at a conference up in Santa Barbara, so I didn't pick up the message right away. I checked my messages at the lunch break, tried to call Patty on her cell and at home, but didn't get any answer.

"When I got the message from Patty's office and then couldn't reach her, I got worried. It wasn't like her to miss work without calling in. I called my husband. We decided to call the police so they could go check on her. Brad hung up and called 9-1-1. He called me back an hour later with the news."

"What did you think when you heard she was dead?" I asked.

"I was shocked. You know? I felt guilty. You know how you think you're in tune with your friends, and then suddenly you're wrapped up in your own life and maybe you aren't there when they need you? I didn't expect...." She stopped and her eyes watered.

I nodded.

Christine swallowed and continued. "I'd been impatient with her the night before, because I'd been trying to get ready to drive up to the conference and prepare myself mentally for, you know, the stress of the conference, networking with other people, giving my presentation, and I resented her calling and needing the attention. The paper I delivered there, it was like the start of my career, you know? Now I feel bad."

"You shouldn't feel bad. You had a lot going on."

"You're so nice. Thank you. Because I have been feeling guilty. I should have gone to see her or something, before I got on the road. I'm a licensed therapist, for God's sake. When they told me Domingo killed her, I was relieved because I felt less responsible. That sounds awful, doesn't it?" Her eyes teared as she looked at me.

"Sorry." She suddenly smiled at me through her tears, then made a fist and pretended to bang her forehead with it. "Here I am, whining at you. I guess I needed to talk to someone. My husband, Brad, his way of dealing with emotions is to deep-six them and stick his nose in a book. He doesn't want to hear about it."

"That's rough," I said. "She was a close friend, right? I can't imagine losing my best buddy like that."

"Yes, we'd been close in college and through her law school and my graduate school, and our first year or so of work. Then, Patty and I moved to San Diego from Oakland around the same time, just a year ago. We were both so excited about making a new start in a new town. But we hadn't seen each other as often lately. I have a six-month-old baby at home, so I've had less time to go out. I keep wondering, if we'd been closer, like before, whether I would have seen this coming."

"Seen what coming?"

At first, Christine looked puzzled. Then she said, "Oh, well, I meant the depression, of course. Sorry, I'm still having trouble wrapping my mind around the possibility she was...killed. I guess I just mean...well, Patty had gone into a different sphere from mine. I thought Patty just wasn't into spending her free time sitting around with me and the baby. She was spending a lot of time with Domingo, of course, and she'd made a friend at work. I realize now, she was depressed and isolating herself from me. I feel terrible I missed it. Me, the therapist, right?"

I detected an undercurrent of anger towards her friend, but maybe that was the natural resentment of a new mom stuck at home with a baby while her friend was out on the town. I looked at my notes.

"Well, one problem with a suicide theory is that Patty's wallet was missing," I said.

"That's right, the police asked us about that. Isn't it possible she had just lost it recently? I'm always losing things when I'm feeling stressed out. You know, leaving my purse somewhere...."

"That's a good point," I said. "Let's go back to the timeline the night Patty died," I said. "Domingo Torres says he left her around seven o'clock. You talked to her around seven, is that right? Did she call you at home?"

"Yes. I was still in San Diego. I was multitasking when she called, making sure Brad had everything he needed for the baby, and getting together my materials for the conference. This was the first time I'd left Ethan, my baby, overnight, so I was nervous about that."

"Tell me about that call."

"Yes. I keep going over it in my head. I think we talked for about ten minutes. It should have been longer, but I was rushing to leave town and had to cut her off."

"What did you talk about?"

"Well, the fight she'd just had with Domingo. He'd gone over there for dinner and they'd gotten into this fight and he'd stormed out. At first, she was almost hysterical, and she said she wished she was dead. Then she calmed down and told me about the fight. They were having issues over her control of his legal case. Something about potential witnesses who were members of the gang that was threatening Domingo. Domingo thought it wasn't safe for Patty to talk to them, but she did it anyway, or she was going to do it. I forget. Anyway, he said it was no job for a woman.

"I met Domingo a couple times. Brad and I went out to dinner with him and Patty. No offense to your client, but I could have told her he's a very controlling man, and that wasn't going to change. You know how it is, though, when your friends make bad choices in their relationships. It doesn't help to say anything against the person.

"Anyway, I just let her talk, without telling her what I thought of Domingo. She sounded to me like she'd already had a drink or two, and she wasn't going to listen to reason. She wanted to vent. By the time we hung up, I thought she was feeling a little better. "

"Do you think she might have taken too many pills by accident?"

Christine wrinkled her nose. "She would have to have been really drunk to do something like that. She might have taken the pills recklessly, trying to make a dramatic statement but thinking somehow she'd be able to throw them up or someone would find her before they killed her. I've gone over and over whether she expected me to play that role. But it doesn't work—she knew I was going to be four hours away in Santa Barbara and I wouldn't be there to rush over to save her."

According to my notes, the homicide investigators had verified Christine had checked in to her Santa Barbara hotel around one in the morning, and received a wake-up call in her room at five o'clock the next morning. Christine seemed to have a solid alibi. Santa Barbara is a good four-hour drive from San Diego. She couldn't have been at Patty's after Patty Skyped with her aunt until ten thirty, and checked into her hotel in Santa Barbara by one in the morning. Unless she'd had access to a private airplane.

"So you got a wake up call at five a.m. That's really early," I said.

"Yes. I like to get up and have an early workout. With the baby at home, sometimes it's hard to make the time to exercise. I start to go buggy if I don't move."

I couldn't help smiling.

"What?" She cocked her head at me.

"Sorry. It sounded funny, a psychologist saying, 'go buggy'."

Christine laughed. "Ah, yes, a highly technical, politically correct term we learn in our first year of psychologist school."

"I didn't mean to interrupt you."

"No, no, it was funny. I need all the laughs I can get right now."

She closed her eyes and slowly shook her head from side to side.

I waited until she opened her eyes and gave me another wry smile. "God. Sorry. What else can I tell you?"

"What was Patty like as a person? I know it's got to be hard for you to talk about her, but it would really help us."

"That makes sense, Armando. Your job must be a lot like mine in some ways. If you're really good at what you do, you want to get a lot of information and then let your intuition start working on it. Is that what you do?"

"I definitely believe in intuition," I told her. "My boss, the way she works, when we get a complicated case, she likes to talk my ear off in a really disorganized way and it seems almost random some of the things she focuses on at first. But then everything seems to come together for her, and then she's brilliant. I think I do the same thing, but it goes on in my head and I'm not even conscious of it."

Her eyes lit up. "So part of your job is to be a sounding board for your boss? Your job really is like mine, then. You must be a good listener."

"Not really. I block out a lot of what she says. I try to get the important parts and do something else with the rest of my mind."

"Armando, I'll let you in on a little secret. You are a very good listener. That's exactly what I have to do when I'm dealing with a client whose mind works like your boss's. Or should I say, their mouth?"

I snickered.

"I mean, seriously," Christine continued, "if you can do what you just said, that's a real gift. How long have you been working for Attorney Sanders?"

"About five years," I told her. We talked a little more about my work. Christine told me about something called "listening filters." In the kind of work she and I did, we both needed to listen without "filters;" in other words, being aware if we're having any prejudices or preconceptions that color our perceptions. But sometimes filters have an important function of protecting our psyches from barrages of unnecessary information, like ads on the radio.

"You're saying I don't need to feel guilty when I zone out on my boss?" I said. "Well, you made my day."

Chris laughed. "Thanks for letting me get on my hobby horse," she said. "It was a nice distraction for me. Now, you wanted to know about Patty. We met in college, in our junior year. She'd just moved to Oakland, California, from Idaho, where she'd finished community college, and she'd gotten together some grants and scholarships so she could finish her degree at Mills College. She had a two-bedroom apartment near campus, and was looking for a roommate. I answered her ad. It's funny, we probably never would have become friends if we hadn't been thrown together as roommates. Patty was a homebody. Even when she had a date she would just want to study or stay home and watch a video. We did well as roommates, and lived together through her law school and my master's degree. We didn't get our own places until we were out of school and started working.

"Close relationships, in the end, to me, really can be built on shared experiences, don't you think? Patty might have disagreed with me on that, she would have said you have to have some kind of shared values, too. It definitely helped that we had the same politics. It doesn't matter to me, so much, I mean, how could it? My husband's a Republican, and I'm about as far left as you can get. Patty and I even went to a few Socialist Club meetings together when we were undergraduates, if you can believe that. We both had kind of a rebellious streak.

She used to say she could never be close to someone who didn't share her politics.

"What else should I tell you? Before she met Domingo, Patty dated guys who were immature, not ready to get serious. She was afraid of getting involved with a guy who could really hurt her. Her parents were alcoholics who had a destructive marriage."

Christine shook her head and her eyes filled with tears. Then she bounced back and smiled at me. "I, on the other hand, always went for the more serious, nerdy guys. Don't get me started on why. God, I've been talking more about myself than about her. You really are a great listener, Armando. Is this helpful at all?"

"Definitely," I replied. "Keep going. What was her work life like? Why did she move to San Diego?"

"Patty liked being a lawyer," Christine said. "But her first job, with a business law firm in Oakland, was not a good fit. She knew almost right away it wasn't what she wanted. They were a bunch of stuffed shirts. When Brad had the opportunity for a promotion to work in his firm's San Diego office, he and I encouraged Patty to move down and try to find a job down here. She was really excited to get the job as an immigration lawyer because she thought she'd be helping people in real need."

I stood up to go. "Thanks for giving me so much time," I said. "So, in your opinion, Patty committed suicide?"

"I think Patty was depressed and took the pills herself. I admit, I didn't think Domingo was good for Patty. If he'd done any violence to her, I would have expected something more macho, like slapping her around a little, not poisoning her. But fundamentally, I see him as a user. Possibly a misogynist, although I did get the sense he respected Patty. She was sweet and unthreatening, and I don't think it was in him to kill her. He's a very self-centered and narcissistic man. Which is understandable." She looked at me and hesitated. "You've seen him, right?"

"Not yet. We're going to see him this afternoon."

"You'll see for yourself, then."

"See what?"

She smiled. "I'll just say, if he didn't do it, I hope you can get him off. I thought he would manipulate her, dump her when he got what he could get from her, but kill her? Not the scenario I would have picked."

***

Back at the office, I didn't have time to type up my notes from the interview with Christine, because *La Abogada* had returned from court and was ready to go visit our client. I filled Lucy in as we walked to the trolley stop and took the short ride to the downtown jail.

"Christine's our new best friend," I told Lucy. "She's totally on our team. She thinks Patty killed herself, and she should know. I mean, Patty's best friend, and an expert therapist. The jury's gonna love her, too. She's smart and funny."

As we waited for our client, I looked at his background file. Domingo Torres had been a newspaper reporter in Juarez, Mexico, up until eight months ago. Then his life had been threatened after he had published an article about the popular Mexican singer Rudolfo, linking Rudolfo with the infamous Cantara cartel. Torres had gone underground, crossed the border into El Paso, Texas, and found his way to San Diego. He'd rented a room at the Hazard Hotel and engaged the victim, Patty Taylor, to represent him in an application for political asylum.

Domingo walked into the interview room in his orange jail suit. He was six-and-a-half feet tall, and moved with the lumbering stiffness of a former athlete. But his size wasn't the shock that made my head jerk back. I glanced at Lucy reproachfully for not preparing me for his appearance. Oh, ho, yes! Ice Queen Boss was actually blushing. I couldn't blame her. The man had a face and a smile that could make you forget your own name.

Later I told Lucy, "It's a stroke of luck you brought me along to translate. Girl, I was afraid you were going to faint. Maybe we should agree right now, we'll only interview him together, as a team. I actually now think he did do the murder. The victim looked at him for too long and died and went to heaven."

But enough of that. For now. Our client was a magnet. He had a chiseled nose, cleft chin, and crazy-long black eyelashes. Oh, and short dark hair that curled in tiny ringlets like you see on those ancient statues of Greek gods.

After Lucy and I introduced ourselves and shook our client's huge, shapely hand, Lucy asked, "Do you have everything you need?" It was always one of Lucy's first questions to her incarcerated clients.

"Everything except perhaps my sanity." When Lucy's eyes widened, he smiled wryly. "I apologize. You don't need to hear me being sorry for myself. I mean to communicate to you I have been feeling crazy with grief. I need you to believe I did not poison Pa-tree-cia." Domingo's voice caressed the victim's name, using the sing-song Mexican pronunciation. "She was the finest lady I ever knew. She was so generous, so cultured, and passionate about making a better world. I asked her to marry me." He had a fine newscaster's voice, although his English was spoken haltingly and with a strong Mexican accent. I didn't need to translate, except when he couldn't think of a word or a phrase in English, or when Lucy wanted to be sure he understood a complex or important point.

"You were engaged to marry Patricia?"

The eyelashes fluttered and the skin on his face seemed to tighten. He turned his head and treated me to a view of his perfect profile. "Patricia said she loved me, but she couldn't agree to marry me yet. She said there were complications."

Yeah, I thought. Like, she was your attorney and should not have been dating you.

Domingo insisted Patty would not have committed suicide, apparently clueless that our suicide theory would be his best defense.

"She was quiet, and a little bit delicate, but she very much loved life. We were going to make a life together. She loved to dream about the future. It is true she did not like her work very much. But she would not have killed herself over that. Patricia knew I was going to take care of her, as soon as my legal issues were resolved."

"You and she had an argument the night before, is that right?"

"Yes. It was about my legal case. Her law firm had allowed her to help me prepare my petition for asylum, without charge. I could not afford the cost. After she finished the legal forms, she wanted to help me get written evidence to support my case. I need to prove it is dangerous for me if I have to return to Mexico. I told her I'd get that evidence myself, that it would be too dangerous for her. I have to get information from people who know about the Cantara cartel, who know the cartel still wishes to kill me.

"Patricia was very angry with me. She said she was a lawyer and it was her job and I was not letting her do her job because she was a woman."

Lucy tapped her pencil on her pad. "Was that true?"

Domingo raised his sculptured jaw and blinked several times. "Of course, it was true. The gangs are very dangerous, I would not let any woman of mine to go near to that world."

"I see." Lucy said. "And Patricia didn't agree?"

"She didn't see I was just trying to protect her."

"Did you fight about anything else?"

Domingo looked irritated. "No. Well, except Patty said our relationship was keeping her from doing her job. That it was *antiethico*, not right, for her to be with me and be my attorney. She said perhaps we should stop dating until the case was over. There is no reason for such a stupid rule, and I told her so. I got angry and left. It was a little lover's quarrel only."

"You went back later."

"Yes, the next morning, I went back to try to talk to her before she went to work, but she did not answer the door. The police said, well, why didn't I use my key to get in. I told them I did not have the key with me, it was at my apartment. I didn't think I would need it, because Patricia would be home.

"When she didn't let me in, I thought she was still angry with me. Or maybe she was still sleeping. She loved to... how do you say it?... 'sleep in.' Even on a workday, she would stay in bed until the last possible minute. So, I left and went home." Domingo spread out his two huge hands in front of him, staring at his fingers. "If I'd gone back with my key, I might have found her. I might have saved her. But I was too proud."

Lucy sighed. "Well, if Patricia didn't take the overdose herself, what do you think happened?"

"Possibly it was an accident. Maybe she didn't know how many pills to take. I didn't know she had a problem with sleeping. She never had a problem when...I mean...." The long dark eyelashes fluttered over high cheekbones. He shook his head back and forth slowly, running his hand across a two-days' growth of grayish black beard.

Lucy gave him a minute to recover. Then she asked, "She never used the pills when you stayed with her? Did you ever see the bottle of pills when you were over there?"

"In the month before she died, I stayed overnight maybe half the time. I never saw the pills, but I never looked in her medicine cabinet."

Lucy started to tap her pencil on her pad again. "There was an empty bottle of the prescription medicine in her name.

We can look into the possibility of an accident. But the police think you put the pills in her drink. The pills were crushed and mixed in with the alcohol. That looks suspicious. You need to help us out here. Is there anyone else you can think of who might have done that?"

"No, no, who would want to harm her?"

"Well, that's the question. Did she seem to be afraid of anyone?"

"No, she was not afraid."

"Was she angry at anyone, did she tell you of any disagreements with anyone?"

"Not that she told me about."

"What about her other friends, or people she worked with?"

Domingo shrugged his broad shoulders, which had started to sag. He did share with us that Patty's boss, Frank Slattery, was a "crude and venal man," who told Patty she was spending too much time on Domingo's case. He had met Patty's friend Christine and her husband Brad. Christine he described as a "big talker, liked to brag about herself." Brad was "a very quiet man, like he was not really there."

As Domingo was led out, he turned back to look at us. The suffering in his eyes was familiar. I realized I'd already seen it once today, watching Christine grieve for the loss of her friend.

Lucy and I didn't talk much as we took the trolley back to the office. Leaving your client behind in the jailhouse always gives you pause.

3

"It's nice to have you back home, *m'ijo*." Mom said, clearing the dishes from our table. I moved over to a bar stool at the kitchen counter to flip through the newspaper and keep her company. She was graceful and unhurried as she rinsed the dishes, loaded them into the dishwasher, and used a sponge to clean the countertops with a slow, circular motion. I hadn't seen her since my return from Las Vegas. I live in the poolhouse of our family home, which has its own entrance along the side of the house. She and I still had dinner together a few nights a week.

Over dinner I'd told her about our new case with the criminally handsome client. Then, I'd shown her the striped gondolier shirt Rodrigo had given me as a souvenir of our trip to Las Vegas. I also told her the latest on my ongoing battle with Lucy over our different ideas of what is good for me.

"Well, I respect Lucy's opinion," she said. "Perhaps I haven't pushed you enough. So, you're considering going back to school?"

I cursed myself for bringing it up. "Hey, Ma, what's this?" I picked up a leaflet that was mixed in with the newspaper on the kitchen counter. It was written in Spanish. Translated, the caption said, "Spend a Day in Lovely Tijuana."

"Oh, I brought that home for you to see. When we had lunch at the Country Club last week, Italia gave it to me. Read it, it's funny."

The leaflet, photocopied onto pink paper, was a fake ad for a day tour of Tijuana, making a joke of all the recent gang-related violence in the border community. "Enjoy a lunch at downtown 'Plato de Oro' and see the best looking, best-dressed bodyguards in Mexico." "View decapitated bodies hanging from the famous Puente de Estrellas in our beautiful downtown area." "After tea, experience the thrill of a genuine kidnapping from your own Lexus SUV."

"Very funny, Ma. I hope you drove the old car down to TJ."

She rolled her eyes. "I drove the Lexus, as always. The Volvo probably wouldn't make it there and back. Anyway, these kidnappers won't want me. Our family doesn't have that much money."

I laughed. I didn't really worry about Ma. Other than her weekly visit to lunch with friends at the TJ Country Club, she lives most of the time here in our home in Chula Vista. She loves to work in her garden, and be near my niece and nephew to baby-sit them four days a week. Occasionally, she stays in Tijuana with my father. He runs his business there and stays mostly in his beach house in Playas de Tijuana. Dad rarely comes across the border any more. Thank God. Because he and I have not really spoken in the past seven years, ever since he reacted to my coming out by booting me out of the family home, leaving me homeless for my last year of high school. It was a year of couch surfing and desperation and occasionally waking up places I really hadn't wanted to be. When Dad comes to stay with Ma, I keep to myself.

"So, *m'ijo*," she gave a final slow swipe of the dishtowel over the counter, and spread it to dry along the edge of the sink. "How much do you think I would be worth?" Her smile brought out fine lines at the corners of her eyes, but she was still beautiful to me.

"Gee, Ma." I said. "For you I might even sell my car."

***

"Lucy, Lucy, Lucy." I gave my best Ricky Ricardo imitation when I entered the office the next morning, and found my boss installed in her Alpha chair in the front room.

"Nice of you to roll in before noon." Lucy looked at me over her reading glasses. "So, it took a day for your long vacation to catch up with you?"

I looked at the clock on my desk. 8:44 a.m. "Not at all, *Jefa*. You know my well-deserved little breaks always refresh me. No, you should be proud of me. I was giving my work ethic a workout." Lucy always forgets Wednesday is the day I teach the early Latin Craze Hip Hop class at Frog's fitness, which usually makes me a whole fifteen minutes late for work. Minutes I always, yes, always, make up by working late that day.

I slid into my desk chair and pulled up my schedule and "to do" list on the computer screen. The trick was not to get Lucy talking. I hoped to make a start on the tasks we had set out last night after our meeting with Domingo. These included calling my friend Rodrigo at the DA's office to see if he could get me some inside information on the investigation, and organizing the file for Domingo's case. Then I'd print out some boilerplate motions from our computerized brief bank, which I have organized simply and clearly but which Lucy cannot seem to get her brain around. I also needed to get up to date on our client billings.

I reached for the telephone to call Rodrigo. Maybe he could see me for lunch.

"Er, Armando?"

I left my hand suspended over the telephone receiver, wiggling my fingers.

"Before you make any plans for today, I thought of some other things I want you to do."

So it was that at nine thirty, I was not rocking my "to do" list. I was down at the County Law Library, copying some obscure internal Department of Motor Vehicles regulations. I delivered these documents to Lucy, and left right away to be on time for my eleven o'clock appointment downtown.

I needn't have busted my butt to get there on time. At eleven thirty five, I was still slumped on a cheap vinyl chair in the reception area of the Slattery Immigration Law Center, where Patty Taylor had worked. In the seat next to me was a middle-aged Latino who looked like he'd spent his life doing hard labor. He wore the impassive, stoic expression of one who no longer expects anything to be easy or quick. I wondered how long he'd been there staring at the blank wall in front of him. After about five minutes, I'd intuited that it was going to be a long wait, so I'd pulled out my iPhone and was killing time watching YouTube videos and texting with Slim about this bro' he'd met in Vegas.

I had not been impressed by the outer appearance of the office. Located in a small, older building on a side street across from the downtown jail, it was a narrow storefront sandwiched between Sweet Freedom bail bonds and a *Notario*, which took immigration photos and cashed paychecks for a fee. The waiting room was dumpy, a ten-by-ten square with a reception desk and a row of four small chairs which was barely cleared by the front door when it opened. The front windows were weathered, blurring the view of the trolley lines and the side of the jail across the street.

A showy Latina in heavy make-up sat at the reception desk multi-tasking between answering a busy telephone, typing something on her computer screen, and carrying on a text conversation on her personal cellphone. A nameplate on her desk identified her as Denise Jackson.

Denise finally looked over at me. "Sorry, Mr. Slattery is running late, Mr...," she glanced down at my business card, "Mr. Felan. Can I get you a cup of coffee?"

"No, thanks. Do you have some idea how much longer it will be?"

After answering an incoming call and putting the caller on hold, she picked up another line, and spoke in a low tone. "Mr. Felan is still waiting....yes, oh,...right. I will." Denise looked up at me. "Someone is coming out in a minute."

Five minutes later, a side door opened and a gawky kid in a cheap suit came out to greet me. He looked about fourteen years old, had white skin all over freckles, and his heavy mop of dark red hair made his head look too big for his body. As he held out his hand, I tried to conceal my horror at his unfashionably wide puke-green and mud-brown striped tie, which totally clashed with the blue pinstripes of his rumpled suit. I expected his contrast with my impeccable attire might shame him, but the clear brown eyes meeting mine were direct and unconcerned.

"Mr. Felan? Hi, I'm Mr. Slattery's law clerk, Justin Bloom." He gave me a light handshake. "Sorry, Mr. Slattery is running late. Why don't you come on back and we can get started."

Justin led me back to a large room divided into ten cubicles, most of which appeared to be occupied, judging from the noise level and what I could see. A back corner had been walled off to make a separate room, probably Slattery's private office. Eyes tracked me like a wave down the corridor as I followed Justin to a slightly larger cubicle at the back of the room.

"We can talk here," he said, running his fingers through his mop of red hair, leaving a sort of crest across the top. "Sorry, Mr. Slattery is running late." The phrase appeared to be something of a mantra around this office. Justin cleared a chair for me by removing some files and placing them on the floor. I took a seat and he sat behind a small desk, which was also piled with files and papers.

"So," I asked Justin, "did Mr. Slattery tell you our office is representing Domingo Torres?"

"Right, he did. Are you the attorney who will be handling the case?"

"No, that would be my boss, Lucy Sanders. I'm her assistant." I handed him my business card, which doesn't give me a title. Just, Armando J. Felan, Law Offices of Lucinda Sanders.

He looked at the card and nodded. "I've heard of Ms. Sanders," he said. "You're her paralegal?" His tone was not unfriendly, but something about the brisk, confident way he raised his eyebrows and fixed his eyes on me, made me feel I was being judged.

"I guess you could say that. I conduct most of the initial investigation interviews, draft pleadings, organize files, do legal research, you know...." I stopped myself, repelled by the pompous and defensive tone I could hear in my own voice. Mentally slapping myself, I said, "Did you work closely with Patricia Taylor?"

He pulled on his tie, messing it up even more. "Most of the time, I didn't work with Patty. I'm a law student and I've been working directly with Frank, Mr. Slattery, for almost two years now. Patty had only worked here for, um, about nine months, since last November. A couple of our paralegals worked more closely with her. I can introduce you later."

"That would be awesome." I gave him a friendly smile to see if he would lighten up.

Justin hesitated, intertwined his hands and pressed them together. "I did work closely with Patty on one case. Frank let me help her out on Domingo Torres's asylum case, which she was handling *pro bono*. So I actually know your client, as well as the victim in this case. It's an interesting legal issue whether we can continue representing Domingo in his asylum case, given a possible conflict of interest as witnesses in his criminal case." He looked at me with a pleased expression that reminded me of Lucy when she has a juicy legal bone to gnaw on. The kid's a born lawyer, I thought.

"Wow, you got two connections to the case. Maybe I'll have to interview you twice!"

"That would be fun," he responded, and then blushed.

"Oh," I thought. Surprise. I looked at him with new eyes. He was the worst-dressed boy I'd ever met, although you might make a case his wide tie had a 1970's retro thing going on. My eyes widened at him and he blushed again.

"Well, let's talk about the day of Patty's death first." I said. "Someone from your office called Patty's friend Christine that morning. Was that you? Did you suspect something like this had happened to her?"

His clear brown eyes met mine again. "You mean, did we suspect she'd been killed?"

"You tell me. What did you think, when she didn't come in to work?"

He frowned. "I wasn't working with Patty that day, and I was busy with my own work. Linda, the paralegal who worked with Patty most closely, asked me if I knew where she was, because Patty had a client waiting. She also asked Annie, one of the other paralegals, and Annie said she should try Patty's cell. Linda had already done that. That's when Linda called Patty's emergency contact."

"Did you notice anything unusual about Patty or Domingo's behavior?"

"I didn't. I didn't know they were...dating, until after Patty died." Justin lowered his voice. "Annie once asked me whether there was anything between Patty and Domingo, and I told her not that I knew of. You've seen Domingo, so you can imagine how it was around here. The women who work here were always speculating about his love life. Annie kept volunteering to work on the case, hand-deliver documents to him at his hotel, that kind of thing. Denise, our receptionist, says now she'd always suspected there was something going on between Patty and Domingo. You can talk to her.

"I did notice that sometimes when we were meeting with him, Domingo said things that were sexist, and he could be bossy and interrupting, kind of a stereotypical macho Latino man." He looked at me and blushed. "No offense to you."

I gave him my best smile, just to see him blush yet again. "Oh yeah?" I said.

His face reddened and he knit his red-brown eyebrows together. "Anyway, at first I could tell Domingo's, uh, bossiness irritated Patty. But I think she decided to let it go. In this business, most women learn pretty quickly to hide their reactions and pick their battles."

In this business, or in this office? I asked myself. "Did you observe anything about Patty to make you think she would commit suicide?"

"No."

"Can you think of anyone who might have wanted to kill her?"

Justin brushed his hair back from his forehead. "Well, I've been thinking about that, and I …"

"Waatcccch out!" A door slammed and a steamroller barged in, swinging a wide leather briefcase. "Felan, right?" The steamroller strode duck-footed between the rows of cubicles, grabbed my hand, and shook it. "In here, in here." He threw open the door, literally gave me a shove into his office, and turned around to yell: "Justin, get Jeff the discovery requests from the Hernandez file…no, the amended one…no, don't revise it again, he needs it in that other case, he doesn't know what he's doing. Show him…right. Yeah."

Frank Slattery was short and swarthy. He wore a blue pinstriped suit like Justin's except for it had set him back at least a thousand bucks more. Like Justin's, the suit was rumpled and the tie was loosened.

Slattery appraised me. He raised his eyebrows and sighed to show me he wasn't impressed with what he saw. "So you guys are defending Torres. Stupidest thing I ever did, letting Taylor take that pro bono case. So what do you want from me?"

"Well, we...."

"You work for Lucy Sanders, huh. I heard of her, she's that publicity-hungry cow. She got off the dummy in that arson case. How old is she, anyway? So you guys think you have a good defense here?"

"Well, that's why I wanted to--"

"Yeah, well, here's my advice. Do a plea bargain. Taylor screwed her client, and he killed her. What did she expect? Maybe you could get it for manslaughter, yeah, hot-blood homicide...no, wait, he poisoned her, didn't he, that doesn't fit. Ha! He shoulda stabbed her or strangled her or somethin'."

"You think he did it?" I slipped in the question while he paused to consider other theories.

"Don't ever ask that!" He shouted, loud enough for the whole office to hear. "Do I think he did it??? That's the wrong question! What does it matter what I think?"

The telephone on his desk rang and he answered it in a normal voice. "What? Yeah, OK, put her through."

Slattery covered the receiver with his free hand and turned to me. "Sorry, I gotta take this. Patty Taylor was weak, a pushover type. She didn't know what she wanted. Maybe that's why she was killed, like she let a situation get outa control. That's all I can tell you. You can find your way out."

I was totally sweating as I left his office. Justin was standing at a desk in the far corner of the office, leaning over a file folder with another young man. I stopped in the reception area to talk to the showy receptionist, Denise. Fortunately, things had slowed down for her, possibly due to the lunch hour. A pale woman about my age was standing next to the reception desk, holding a box of mail and chatting with Denise. She looked at me curiously and Denise introduced her as Annie. She and Denise were sympathetic to my cause.

"We were soooo-o shocked when we heard Domingo had been arrested," Denise told me. "You know, all the women in the office would try to be around when he came in for an appointment. He was kind of old, but, you know, wow! Right? We called him 'the bomb.'"

Annie nodded. She had a round face, big eyes, and a tiny, round mouth, like a comic book picture, and bobbed dark brown hair that was held back from her face with a hairband. When she spoke, her voice was high and squeaky. "I told Linda there was something going with him and Patty. The way he looked at her, and then she would try to be so cool. She was his lawyer; she shouldn't have been seeing him. She should have let me have him."

I looked more carefully at her, to see whether she was kidding. Her face was serious, as far as I could tell. I glanced at Denise, who looked at me and rolled her eyes.

"So, Annie," I said. "Justin told me you and Patty were friends. Patty never told you she was dating Domingo?"

"No, and I don't know why she didn't. I mean, I guess I do know. She wasn't supposed to be seeing him because he was a client. She and I were friends, though. I was hurt when I found out, 'cause I told her, you know, stuff about me."

"Uh-huh. I totally get how you feel. So Patty didn't even tell you she had started seeing someone?"

"Well, she kinda did. She told me she'd met a guy, but she didn't know if it was going anywhere so she didn't want to talk about it. Sometimes I'd ask her 'have you seen your guy?' and she'd say she had. I wondered if she might be seeing a married man. Patty was kind of private. We mostly talked about other things."

"Like what?"

Annie looked nervously at the door. "I gotta go," Annie said, slipping around me and heading back into the office.

Denise smiled at me. "Annie can be a little strange," she said. "She's been pretty upset about Patty and about

Domingo. She really did go gaga over him. I'd tell her, like, 'Annie, he's a total magnet, he could have anyone he wants, he's out of our league.' She'd just keep looking at him with puppy eyes."

"Hmmm. Were Annie and Patty very close?"

"I don't know about that. They were both single, and Patty was new in town. They'd go out together on their lunch hour."

"How did Patty like working here?"

"For Mr. Slattery? Maybe I shouldn't say this, but he goes through associates pretty fast. At first, she was all jazzed but by the end I don't think she was happy about coming in to work every day. It's a high pressure practice."

"Did she seem depressed, to you?"

"Well, maybe. I thought she was just kind of fed up with the job." Her black eyes appraised me. Despite the heavy purple eyeshadow and clumpy mascara, her bold look reminded me of Frank Slattery's. Unlike Frank, she seemed to like what she saw. "I mean, would you be depressed if you were hooked up with a guy like Domingo?"

"Yeah, girl. I see your point."

***

"Frank Slattery's an asshole," I reported to Lucy, when she got back from her afternoon court appearances. "I'll go back later and interview some of his office staff. When he's not around." This made me remember the red-haired law student Justin's reaction, when I joked I would have to interview him twice. Hmmm.

I summarized my visit, including Slattery's pushing me into his office and his advice on how to represent our client. I left out Slattery's personal remarks about Lucy.

Lucy said, "I made some calls about Slattery's firm. It's a high-volume immigration mill. Slattery himself has a lackluster reputation as an attorney. He's been through three wives, two of whom were his former employees."

At 4:30, as I was getting ready to pack up and head out for my appointment with Rodrigo, my friend from the DA's office, I got a call on my cell phone.

"Armando-cito!" It was my older sister Consuela. "Where have you been? I left you a message like two hours ago."

"Oh, wow, yeah. Sorry, I was working and forgot to check my messages," I lied. Most of Connie's calls are to get me to babysit my cute but spoiled niece and nephew. If I wait long enough to return the call, she's usually found someone else.

"Listen, have you talked to Mom today?"

"No, I left early this morning. I haven't seen her since last night. Today's her day to have lunch at the club."

"I know, but she should be home by now. I called her at home, and there was no answer. I left a message on her cell and she hasn't called me back. I hope she's OK. She should have called me. I need her to babysit."

My big sister hasn't quite figured out that she isn't the total axis of the universe. I sighed. "Maybe she had something else to do today."

"She should have left her cell on," Connie said. "What if I'd had an emergency at work today and had to go in? I would have needed her to come over."

"I guess you'd have to think of something else."

"Oh. Well, can you come and watch the kids tomorrow after you get off work? Some people at my office are going out for happy hour. Marco really wants to see you."

"Sorry. Tomorrow night I have to go work out. Some other time, for sure."

"O.K, then, how about--" she began.

"Uh-oh, I got an appointment right now," I told her. "We'll talk about it later." Hopefully she'd reach Mom first and get her to do it.

***

The Bar Bar was dark and cool and almost empty when I walked in at five minutes to 5:00. I sat in a back booth and nursed a mojito and watched the after-workers start coming through the door until Rodrigo strolled in, ten minutes late for our appointment. He and I met a couple of years ago at a training on forensic photography. He's so my type, a total bro', with light blue-green eyes, a brooding face, and cut muscles. With his shaved head, and the collar of his form-fit work shirt loosened, he looks like his fellow Cubano, Pitbull. We had a really long affair, almost four months. I only broke up with him because I wasn't ready to get serious with just one person. It's really important to me to have as much fun as possible while I'm still young and cute, which is why I don't want to settle down with anyone or grind away in school right now. Or maybe ever.

Rodrigo is sexy and he can be funny, but it's not in him to lighten up. An ex-Catholic ex-cop, he's really put off by the corruption and hypocrisy of both institutions. Sometimes he feels like he's just landed in the fire in his position as an investigator at the DA's office where the suits just bring the brutality to a higher, subtler level.

"Ooooh, so sorry, Mr. Ocampo is running late today." I lisped in my Marilyn Monroe voice.

"Miss Felan is lucky Mr. Ocampo is here at all," he snapped. "Mr. Ocampo had to sneak away to avoid an office meeting. Did you order me a drink?" Rodrigo slid into the booth across from me, and I shoved my half-finished mojito at him.

Rodrigo inhaled my drink, wiped his mouth on his shirtsleeve, and told me a long boring story about favoritism in a recent round of promotions in his office. "I can't believe it," he concluded finally.

"I love how you still get so surprised."

He shrugged. "When I don't, that's when you can shoot me."

"Stay here," I said. "I'll get us some more drinks."

When I got back, Rodrigo looked more relaxed. He'd pulled the mint leaves out of the mojito and was holding them between his thumb and forefinger and sucking on them like he was inhaling on a J. When I put his beer down, he dropped the mint into the empty glass. Then he used his little finger to slide his mug of beer slowly along the table, tracking it with his eyes until it rested in front of him.

"So let's talk about your new case," he told me. "Your Lady Justice is back in the big leagues on this one. Word is, your new client Domingo Torres is a heavy in one of the cartels down in Juarez."

"Oh, really? Do we need bodyguards?" I pictured a big, ripped guy, staying close to my side 24-7. He'd have on a well-tailored blue suit and there would be a gun bulge under his arm and a cord coming out of his ear, like those guys have who watch out for the President.

"Sorry, I doubt the cartels will be gunning for you. Maybe your boss can play up the cartel angle to confuse the jury and get your client off. She's good at that. Anyway, I talked to this cop, Eric, who was part of the initial investigation. He's not sure they got the right guy."

"Why does he think that?"

"Alan Shaw, the Deputy DA who has the case, and that bastard Burke, who's the head of the homicide team on the case, they didn't like Torres. As soon as they found out he was an immigrant without legal papers, they really didn't like him. When they found out he lied about being at Patty's the morning she died, they decided he was good for it and stopped investigating other leads."

Score one for Lucy. "But Domingo is here legally, for now. His paralegal told me he was even going to get a work permit while his asylum case is pending."

"Whatever. This guy Eric and his partner were the first two cops on the scene, and Eric wanted to follow up on a couple other leads." Rodrigo pulled out a small spiral notebook he carries with him everywhere. "Let's see. Eric interviewed the victim's friends who'd made the call. A man and his wife."

"Christine and her husband, Brad?"

"Right. Eric thought the husband, Brad, was hiding something. Brad was very nervous and defensive. Eric wanted to do a follow-up interview to learn more about Brad's relationship to the victim, but that was nixed by his boss."

"Did he say anything about Brad's wife, Christine?"

"Yeah. That was the other thing. She tried to do all the talking for her husband. She had an alibi, though, she was out of town."

"Did Brad have an alibi, too?" I tried to remember.

"Well, sort of. He said he was at home with the baby all night, after his wife left town for her conference."

"That's not much of an alibi," I said. "Maybe this Brad guy's good for it."

"Well, they latched on to your client instead."

"Hmmmn. So is that all you got?"

"No, *guapo,* I saved the best for last. Eric also went to Patty's workplace and talked with her employer. You're gonna love this. Her boss is a lawyer by the name of Frank Slattery."

"Yeah, I know."

"Well, apparently, that office is a pretty weird scene. Eric went and talked to these co-workers of Patty's, Linda and, ah, Annie. So, as you might expect, the ladies were both crying after they heard the news. Slattery came in to the office and went off on the cops, like an out-of-control explosion, screaming at them that they were harassing his staff. Then, get this, he screams at his staff, 'Linda, did you kill Patty? Annie, did you kill Patty?' Eric says when Slattery screamed at the younger woman, Annie, she looked like she was about to confess. Then Frank started yelling at Eric again, telling him he didn't know how to do his job. Then Frank said he wouldn't let any of his staff speak to the cops without an attorney present."

"That's very interesting," I remarked.

"Right? If the homicide team hadn't taken over and glommed on to Domingo Torres so fast, you can bet they would have been all over Slattery. Eric said he thinks the guy really couldn't control himself, like he's got a screw loose."

"Or he's a very good actor, and he had something he didn't want his staff to tell," I said. "Thanks for the scoop, bro."

"My pleasure. How's Lady Justice doing?" Rodrigo asked, leaning back against the dark leather booth.

"Still being a Numero Uno Shrew, Mother of all Bitches. Remember, I told you she tried to keep me from going on our Vegas trip."

"Yeah, you'll never leave her, baby. You were made for each other."

"This is boring. We're off the clock now, *amigo*."

His eyes got hot. "OK. Talk to me about when I get to see you in that shirt I tore off that gondolier in Vegas."

I left the Bar Bar on the early side and called Mom on my way to my car. "*Mamacita*, what's for dinner tonight?"

"Ah, *m'ijo*, sorry, I just got home. Italia and I went out for a drink, after our lunch."

"OK, I'll pick up some Thai food on the way home."

"*Gracias,* my beautiful boy. We'll take a swim after, yes?"

"Sounds good. By the way, did Connie reach you?"

"She tried, *m'ijo*, she tried." Ma said.

4

The next morning, Lucy left for court and was scheduled to go out to lunch afterwards with an old client, a doctor she'd successfully represented many years ago on a DUI charge, and who'd been a great source of referrals to our office. I worked unmolested at my desk, my gold happyplugs pumping my newest playlist into my ears. On my screen was my report on last night's interview with Rodrigo. As I wrote up Rodrigo's description of Frank Slattery's behavior when the police came to his office, I started thinking about how I could re-interview Slattery's law clerk, Justin, without going back to that office.

The bell that rings when our front office door opens, barely gave me enough warning to get my feet off my desk.

"Oh, it's you," I said, pulling out my ear buds.

"I hope you don't mind I didn't call first," Justin said. "Frank's in court all morning, so I thought I'd take a break and see if you wanted to follow up on our, um, interview." He was wearing the same suit as before, but he'd taken off the jacket for the ten-block walk to our office. His rumpled shirt was a pale pink that clashed with his dark red hair and white skin. The walk in the noonday August sun had flushed his face and brought out copper-colored freckles.

"Sure, come on in." I stood up, and he entered and took in the front room with frank curiosity: the fireplace and waiting area with the shabby rug, big armchair, shameful green couch, and my tiny reception desk. There is a small chair next to my desk, which I use to meet with clients, but I decided to take Justin into Lucy's office. "We'll be more comfortable in here," I said.

"Your boss has a great reputation, Armando," he said. "Last year she gave a lecture to my Criminal Procedure class. She's won some big cases."

"Yes, she has." I settled myself into Lucy's chair. The leather was soft and glowing, and the long seat back hugged and supported the curves of my body. As I reclined by rocking the chair back gently, I imagined this was my office, my chair, my desk, my diplomas on the wall. My kind-of-cute, red-haired law student studying the diplomas behind me with respect and admiration. Maybe I should consider going to law school after all.

"We were interrupted when your boss came in yesterday. Is there something specific you were going to tell me?" I asked.

"Right. Sorry, I was distracted. I really am in awe of Ms. Sanders. You're lucky to work for her."

Lucy's reputation for vindicating the oppressed in hard-to-win cases is deservedly stellar. I hear she's also a great lecturer in the classroom. Her reputation for being a major pain to work with, while quite big among my family and friends and the criminal bar, is not so well-known in the broader legal community and the general public. Justin must not have heard that his own law school had stopped sending students to her, after several students complained she was unreasonably abusive in her criticism of their work.

Now, I just deadpanned to Justin, to see if he'd blush again, "Honey, you have no idea."

He didn't blush, but his eyebrows shot up and his clear brown eyes met mine as he waited for me to elaborate. When I didn't, he said, "Well, anyway, where were we? Yes. Why I'm here. Well," he gestured with his hands, "you had asked me whether I could think of any reason Patty would…kill herself, or someone would want to kill her. I can't, specifically, but I do think I should let you know more about what we were doing in Domingo Torres's political asylum case. I went and saw Domingo at the jail last night and got him to sign a waiver to allow me to tell you about it. Domingo didn't know how far we'd gotten in the investigation. He told Patty he didn't want her following up on the more dangerous parts of the investigation, so Patty hadn't told him what she was doing." Justin paused. "I don't know how much you know about political asylum."

"Not much. Just you have to show that you would be subject to persecution, some serious danger, if you returned to your home country."

"That's the basic idea, but it's a lot harder to prove the specific elements than most people think. You have to show that the persecution is based on..." Justin counted on his fingers as he listed, "race, religion, nationality, political opinion, or membership in a particular social group. That's the tricky part of Domingo's case. He received death threats from a drug cartel called Cantara, which is active along the northern border of Mexico. We can prove those threats occurred, because there were letters sent to Domingo personally and to the editor of his newspaper. We'll argue the danger still exists, that the cartel hasn't forgotten about him, so it's still dangerous for him to go back. The death threats came after Domingo published an article about Cantara and its links to the singer, Rudolfo. The hard part of Domingo's case, from a legal standpoint...."

As my eyes started to glaze, our front bell rang, and I stood up quickly and went to the front door. "Excuse me."

Lucy was striding in, her face flushed with annoyance. "Dr. Bibber called to cancel our appointment," she said, "but I didn't check my phone until I'd gotten to the restaurant, and... had to miss... waste of time...."

"Hey, Lucy, glad you're here," I interrupted. "Frank Slattery's law clerk, Justin Bloom, is here. I just showed him into your office. He got Domingo's OK to discuss Domingo's asylum case with us."

Lucy raised her eyebrows at me and then silently entered her office. As she arranged herself in her fine chair, I decided I didn't want the law degree enough to go through so many years of school.   No amount of education would make me develop an actual interest in the fine points of law that appeared to give such delight to Lucy and Justin. I should probably also rule out developing an interest in this nerdy law student. I eyed Justin's clashing pink shirt and red hair speculatively and smiled to see him blush again when our eyes met.

I took the chair next to Justin, facing Lucy's desk. "Lucy, Justin was telling me Patty Taylor had done some investigation in the case that she hadn't told Domingo about," I told Lucy.

Justin stood to shake hands with Lucy. "It's a real honor to meet you, Ms. Sanders. Patty and I were working on trying to establish that Domingo would be in danger of persecution for his political opinions if he returns to Mexico. Legally, the statements Domingo made in the articles he wrote can't be characterized as political opinions, unless we can show Cantara has a political component to its activities. We were working with a professor at San Diego University who studies the activities, including political activities, of the cartels in this region. He referred us to a former Cantara gang member, Paolo Sanchez, who's now doing some kind of gang prevention work. Patty actually interviewed Sanchez, the day before she died. If we can show Cantara is still a threat and that it has political affiliations, this would then allow us to argue--"

"Domingo was being persecuted based on his political opinions," Lucy finished. "Sounds like a bit of a stretch to me, but immigration law is not my area."

"Well, no, Ms. Sanders, I'm afraid your analysis may be right..." Justin said. "Case law on this point...."

***

"Armando," Lucy said, after Justin had left, "you didn't need to yawn so openly while Justin and I were discussing Domingo's asylum case. Your obvious lack of interest was unprofessional."

"Well, shit, there goes my plan for a hot date with a budding star attorney."

"Really?"

"God, no. Not my type. What a geek." Once Lucy had entered the room, Justin had been all business, and failed to blush even when I gave him one of my better smiles.

"You could do worse," she said. "He's a bright, ambitious young man."

"You could be right about that," which is what I say to her when I really mean, "you couldn't be more wrong."

"The part that is of potential interest in our case," Lucy was saying, "is the factual investigation. Patty had gone behind Domingo's back and interviewed that former Cantara gang member, Paolo Sanchez. You and Claude go interview him, after you look at Patty's notes on her interview."

Claude Washington is an investigator Lucy uses frequently in our more complex cases. I'm pretty sure they have some kind of after-hours thing going on, but I can't get either of them to admit it.

"I don't need Claude with me," I told her. "I can handle the little gang-banger on my own."

"I'll call Claude," she said. "Now, unless you're planning to spend the rest of your day in my office, why don't you get back to your own desk."

5

Early Friday afternoon, punchy from paperwork and ready to get out of the office, I decided it would be a good time to go interview Brad Fernwood, the husband of Patty's friend Christine, and the one who had been with the police when they discovered Patty's body. The police had thought Brad seemed suspicious and nervous. Maybe if I got him off guard, I'd learn something.

Brad worked at SimCo, a software company in Black Mountain Valley. If I set off right away, I could avoid the rush hour traffic. I put the file I needed into my messenger bag, left Lucy a note, and took off.

The sun was hot, and there was a cool breeze coming through my open windows. As I opened the Camino up on the freeway, the wind and the sound of my tires on the road pounded out a rhythm and my mind put a sound to it: "OK, OK, OK...."

I parked my car and put on the clear, heavy-framed glasses I wear sometimes to disguise myself as a more serious kind of a guy.

SimCo's office occupied the fifth floor of a posh building in a business park just off the freeway. It was a different world from downtown San Diego. Although the land must be worth a million dollars per square foot, the area has a feeling of wide-open space, with a view of unmolested nature in the rolling hills and canyon to the east.

As I walked through the business park, I looked at the people around me. I was surprised how many of them were very young, my age or younger. The ethnicity was about evenly divided between White, Asian, and Indian. No brother Latinos that I could see, although in my Calvin Klein business casual attire I was up there with the better dressed in this crowd. Were these people happy? What did they do for fun?

The reception screening at SimCo was, as I had hoped, somewhat lax. I breezed into the reception area, saying, "I'm here for Brad Fernwood. Sorry, I'm running a little late. I forget, he is....?" I gave a friendly smile and gestured left and right, with open palms, indicating the two corridors that led to the inside offices.

The hip-looking young woman at the front desk returned my smile and pointed. "On your right. Third door down."

"Thanks."

I gave a quick tap on the door marked with his name. "Brad?"

"Come in."

Brad was a mushroom, with a really high, square forehead, small hands, and thick glasses that distorted his eyes. He was at his computer keyboard when I opened the door, and he looked at me impatiently. I expected his tie to have an arrow and turn up at the end.

I entered and came up to him at his desk, handing him my business card. "Hi, I'm Armando Felan, our office is representing Domingo Torres. Sorry I didn't call first, but we're on a tight schedule. Hope you have time to answer a few quick questions."

Brad took my business card and stared at it, then looked at me, then looked back at the card, like a store clerk checking your picture ID. He looked like he hoped it would give him a reason to reject my credit.

"This, this is, uh…not a good time," he said. "I'm working on a project with a short deadline." He adjusted his wire-framed glasses.

"Dude! I can relate to that," I said. "Our client has a preliminary hearing at the end of this week, and there's about six more witnesses I got to interview before then. I'll try to make this quick, get it over with, OK?"

"All right, I guess so. Give me a second to close this down."

I sat and looked around while he did something on his computer, hunching over the screen like I was going to steal his valuable work. The window behind him had a view of the hills. There was a bird of prey hovering over the hillside, its tail flashing red as it angled towards the sun. Brad's office was neat, with no documents or files lying around in view. The art on the walls was more of the large framed nature photographs I'd seen in the reception room. The only signs of the occupant's personality were a desk photo of a smiling Christine holding a square-foreheaded baby, and a large brass paperweight bust of Napoleon Bonaparte. A clear plastic rack held his business cards, which identified him in a plain font as Brad Fernwood, Senior Software Engineer, SimCo Medical Technologies. I took a card, which was on a cheap-looking smooth white card stock. These techies probably mostly just bumped their iPhones together to exchange personal data.

"OK." Brad finally looked up from his computer. "What do you need to ask me?"

"Just a few routine questions. Gosh, this seems like a great place to work. I've never been to Black Mountain Valley before. Seems like a community of bright, science-minded people. Kind of the opposite of downtown, where I work, where it's more law, business, advertising, financial-type minds."

"Is that so? Maybe that's why I feel comfortable here."

"Right? Hey, if I had a good brain for science and tech, I'd be right here. Sometimes in my job, I get so sick of dealing with people's craziness, you know?"

A smile crept onto his pale face, and he nodded.

"So, what do you do here, anyway?"

"Me, personally? I do research and development. I'm designing a software program related to development of artificial intelligence. I don't know whether you're familiar with the state of the research in this area, but we're designing computer-based intelligence that can go beyond just sifting through data and calculating probabilities. Some day you'll be able to have a conversation and not know whether you're communicating with a human or a computer."

"Me?" I asked. "As in, in my lifetime?" I raised my eyebrows.

Brad nodded. "Assuming you have an actuarially typical lifespan, yes, I would say so."

I thought about it. "Psychologically, that makes sense," I said. "Don't you think most of us tune other people out anyway, and hear only what we want to hear, based on our assumptions about the other person? So I could be chatting away with a computer and not know it, 'cause I'm so into myself. You know, like people falling in love over the Internet and they never see the other person."

"Well, we aren't relying on human neuroses," he said, looking at me like I was a neurotic. "On the scientific end of it, there are specific probes we use to gauge the human qualities in a conversation. We'll be able to fool even those people who are looking for any lapses in humanity." The flourescent light overhead reflected off of his glasses and I got a bit of a chill. How could cool Christine be married to this guy?

"I guess the psychology would be more in your wife's area of expertise," I said.

He nodded. "Yes, she would have that perspective. She's interested in how people relate to one another."

"Well, it sounds like you're both in professions that are a good fit."

He was silent for a minute. "Yes, we are. My wife is very happy in her work. So, how can I help you today?"

"Yes, down to business. Tell me about your relationship with Patty." I watched him closely.

"My what? What do you mean, my relationship with her? Where did you... I wasn't having...." He stopped himself. "Oh. You mean, like me and Christine, our friendship with Patty. You made it sound like..." Brad gave me an accusing stare. His small white hands gripped the edge of his desk.

"Sound like what?"

"Nothing." His face had closed up. "You've already talked to my wife. I don't know what else I can say."

"Tell me about Patty. How did you know her?"

"Through my wife. They were friends."

"Did you like her?"

He looked like I'd asked him what color underwear he preferred.

"Is that really relevant? I liked her OK."

"What was she like as a person? Did she ever seem depressed?"

"My personal impression of her was...." He hesitated, one of his small hands fidgeting restlessly on his desktop. He took his glasses off and wiped them with a pocket handkerchief. "She was a gentle, quiet person, who was genuinely nice. I did like her, very much, all right? She was very unassuming, almost withdrawn sometimes, but she was never afraid to stand up when there was something she wanted. I thought going into the law would be good for her, but I don't think it was making her happy. She was hard on herself sometimes, so maybe she did take her own life. I'd rather think it was an accident. And, it's unbelievable to me that anyone would want to kill her." His voice shook a little on the last sentence.

So you are a little bit human after all, you scary mad scientist guy, I thought to myself. I asked Brad a few more questions, and his story corroborated the timeline Christine had given me for the events of the night of Patty's death and the discovery of her body. Then he became impatient and kept referring me to Christine for further information. He actually opened up his computer and started to log back in, while I was still asking him a question.

I was preparing to go when I was seized by a coughing fit, which turned into coughing mixed with hiccups. This happens to me sometimes, and the only thing that helps is to drink water backwards from a glass.

"Are you OK?" Brad asked.

"Could I have...a glass of water?" I coughed out.

"Sure, wait here." Brad went out.

Holding my breath to try to suppress the hiccups, I looked at the Napoleon bust on Brad's desk. I picked it up and saw the piece of green felt glued to the bottom of it had come loose on one edge. I peeled the felt off past the middle of the base and saw some writing. There was an inscription: *To Brad, all my love, Patty.* I replaced the bust back on the desk before Brad came back with my water. I no longer needed the water to cure my hiccups.

***

"If he hadn't been so rude, I might not have sneaked a look at his paperweight," I told Lucy back at the office.

Lucy was less excited about my find. "That is a potentially helpful fact," she admitted. "You must have been psychic to look under that paperweight. But what does it mean? Are you sure there was no date on the inscription?"

"Positive. But now we have proof there was something going on between Brad and Patty. Maybe he went to see her while Christine was out of town, found her with Domingo, and came back and killed her."

"Or, possibly, it was a gift of friendship."

"Oh, come on, *Abogada*! It said, 'all my love'." That is not just friendship. If it just said, 'love, Patty,' then it could possibly be friendship. But not 'all my love.' 'All' means, like, none for anyone else. In that way, I mean. Poor Christine. Do you think she knows?"

"It's not so clear, Armando." Lucy frowned. "It's an expression that could mean different things to different people. Some people express themselves in more extravagant terms."

I swear to God. Lawyers. Sometimes they just have to argue every point. You say, "It's a nice day out." They turn it into a federal case. Normally I would have argued it out with her, but it was time to go home, so I just said, "You could be right about that."

"Tomorrow's Saturday," she said, "but you owe me some time, for the day you took off. We need to see Patty's work files, especially the ones related to Domingo's asylum case. See if your friend Justin can get you those tomorrow."

"He's not my friend."

6

The front office of the Slattery law firm was locked, so I called Justin on my cell when I arrived. He came to the front door to let me in. He didn't look so clownish in his weekend clothes: nice-fitting Levi's, worn skater shoes, and faded T-shirt. The T-shirt had the logo of a local law school and the slogan: "To Play the Game, You've Got to Know the Rules." Of course. Still, he had a sweet shy smile and I liked the way he brushed his red hair back from his forehead with his hand when he saw me.

"I've been looking at the file again," Justin said, ushering me to a seat in the largish cubicle where he'd met with me on my first visit. He pulled up a chair next to me and leaned in front of me to log into Patty's computer account.

"Here's the one I thought you'd be interested in."

The day before she died, Patty had gone to Barrio Logan, a Latino neighborhood just south of downtown, to interview Paolo Sanchez. Sanchez was the former gang member who had been working with her consultant, a local professor, on study of drug cartel dynamics. Sanchez now worked at an after-school program for at-risk youth. According to this document, which was in the form of a draft declaration to be signed by Sanchez, Sanchez had family members in Juarez, and had had personal contact with members of the Cantara gang. Sanchez stated Cantara had engaged in "political activities," including running members for public office and lobbying. He stated it was likely based on gang culture that recent threats to harm Domingo would still be in effect. Patty had left blank spaces in the declaration, like she expected to get more information to support the statement. I printed the document for later review with Lucy. I also printed copies of the time sheets, which detailed the work Patty and Justin had done on the case, and copied a folder of other documents onto a flashdrive.

I finally gathered up my documents to take back to the office, and went to the cubicle across the hall where Justin was typing on a computer, with stacks of files and books in front of him and on the floor at his feet.

"Thanks," I told him.

"I hope they help," he said, swiveling his chair to face me. "You think you'll be able to use this draft declaration in Domingo's defense?"

"I'll see what Lucy thinks. I'll have to go talk to Sanchez myself, first."

"Well, good luck." His words were dismissive, but instead of turning back to his work or getting up to see me out, he leaned back in his chair. He looked up at me like he wanted to say something. At first, I wasn't sure what was up. I raised my eyebrows a little, and he took off his glasses, rubbed his eyes, and pushed his red hair back from his forehead. His face flushed as he watched me watching him. Ah.

I wasn't sure I wanted anything to happen with this boy, but I didn't feel like leaving just then, either.

"Listen," I said, "if you have a few minutes, maybe I could ask you a few more questions about Patty."

"Right." He shook his head like you do when you're trying to dry your hair. "Sure. You want to bring the chair back in here?"

I went back to the other cubicle and wheeled the chair I'd been using across the wide, quiet hallway of the deserted office. The place had a nighttime-in-the-day feeling, like a movie matinee. We'd been working alone in a narrow pool of light, with darkness behind us in Frank's enclosed office and in front of us over the twin rows of cubicles that went up to the front end of the room towards the street.

Justin moved a pile of books so I could fit my chair in across from him. "I've been thinking a lot about Patty, of course, since she died. First, when we heard she'd taken pills, we all assumed she'd, well, killed herself. I remember thinking suddenly that suicide was a terrible act of violence. I'd never thought of it that way before. I always thought it was something people had the right to do if they needed a way out when life…got too hard. But when I thought about her taking her own life, it seemed brutal, like, well more like a murder." He leaned back in his chair, and frowned. "Sorry. I'm not usually this inarticulate."

"You're not inarticulate. I totally know what you mean. We're still thinking her death might have been a suicide," I told him. "Do you think she might have killed herself?"

"I could see that, yeah. Patty was a very quiet, shy, person, hard to get to know. Some people are just like that, introverted, happy to be alone. But I know she had strong feelings even if she didn't express them. We actually made a good connection over Domingo's case. I'll try and explain it.

"I decided to be an attorney because I want to contribute something meaningful to society. I'll never make a lot of money, but I'll be satisfied I made a difference. Patty was like that, too. She left a high-paying job at a big firm to come do immigration law for less than half what she was making before. One day, after we'd been talking about Domingo's case for the first time, she said to me suddenly, 'Thank you so much, Justin. This is what I've wanted to do for a long time. I went through a lot to get my license, and now I'm finally getting to do something real.'

"I told her not to get her hopes up, because Domingo's case looked problematic to me, and it would be a longshot to think we could win it. She looked disappointed and asked me if I was saying I didn't want her to work on the case. I told her that wasn't what I meant. We talked about how to do your best on a case working within the limitations of the law, and how you can also work to change the laws. Then she surprised me. She smiled and said, 'Do you think it's ever right to take a short cut to get the right result in a bad system?' We got into this kind of radical discussion of how to change our whole system of government."

"Why did that surprise you?" I asked him.

"Well, that's my point. I mean, I have discussions like that with other people, like some of my law school friends, all the time. The reason it was surprising in Patty was she didn't seem the radical type. I don't think she would have opened up to me like that, except that she was excited about us taking on Domingo's case. She was so conservative-looking, soft in her manner, and always seemed most concerned with pleasing others and with getting all the details right in her work, rather than looking at big picture issues. I thought she was going to be more of a religious do-gooder or a social worker type, like some other attorneys we've had, assisting the individual clients but not ever really questioning how the system is set up. Then she turned out to have a rebellious streak. It's cool, when someone goes against type like that." I noticed again how Justin waved his hands in a rolling motion while he talked.

"So, Patty thought the System was messed up. Did that make her depressed?"

"I don't know about that. I didn't work directly with her, except on Domingo's case."

"Did she and Frank Slattery talk about politics?"

"I doubt it. Frank's a good guy, but his politics are, on most issues, moderately conservative. I can handle his ragging, but he would have given Patty a hard time and I don't think she would have had much of a sense of humor about it."

I remembered something. "Did Frank ever sexually harass Patty?"

"I wouldn't bother going in that direction." His eyes lowered and then flashed back up at me.

"Oh-kay," I raised my eyebrows at him, but decided to let it go, for the moment.

I stood up to leave, and he stood with me. "Hey," he hesitated, and brushed his hair back from his forehead. "I'm going to meet some friends for a drink tonight at the Bar Bar, around nine. To celebrate finishing our summer school exams. You probably already have something to do…."

"Yes, I do." I said. I'd been planning on meeting Slim and Rodrigo there later. "Actually," I said, "I might be able to drop by for a little while."

Lucy came in to the office as I was organizing the documents from Patty's files. Usually on a Saturday she wears jeans or a sweatsuit to the office, but she'd put on a suit for a visit to the jail to see Domingo. She looked tired.

"Domingo's going stir crazy," she said. "His preliminary hearing is next week. I wish we could find something to get this case kicked early."

I told Lucy about the draft declaration Patty had written shortly before she died. "When can Claude and I go interview this Paolo Sanchez kid?"

"Let me take a look at the documents first, Armando. Maybe you can go later in the week. The DA's file lists Patty's only surviving relative as a brother, Sam Acres, who lives in Oakland. He'll be coming to town on Monday, and you'll need to interview him. I've been thinking more about Brad's relationship with Patty. Interview him at home with Christine and see if you can get more of a feeling about their relationship. Their subpoenas for the hearing are ready for you to serve. Brad may be more willing to talk to you, if he knows he may have to testify."

"Guess I'll try to catch them tomorrow. There goes my Sunday, shot to hell."

***

Hillcrest was jumping as usual on a Saturday night. The Bar Bar was starting to fill up when I walked in. Justin was sitting in a booth across from two guys, and got up to greet me. After I slipped in on his side, he slid in next to me and introduced his friends, both law school classmates. One looked smart, the other beautiful. Pete was dark and stocky with frizzy hair, and wore thick glasses and a white button-down shirt with rolled-up sleeves. He greeted me with a manic grin and a girlish flap of his hand. The other guy, Daniel, was *muy bien* fine, a pale, tallish, lounging model with cheekbones. He had white-blond hair swept back in a pomp, and wore a blinding white V-neck tee under a blue Lauren blazer with a crest that made him look like a British lord. He gave me a subtle wiggle of the eyebrows to let me know he was all that, but I decided I'd wait and see for myself.

When my drink arrived, Pete said, "Now we can have another toast. School's out!"

Justin laughed. "Pete, what will you do when there's no more school? You thrive on it. When the proctor passed out that Evidence final, you looked like a hungry man being served a big plate of barbeque ribs. You rolled up your sleeves and dug in."

"If it's inevitable, you might as well enjoy it," Pete said. "I guess after two years of this, I'm finally starting to *like* taking tests."

It was unclear to me whether Daniel and Pete were a couple. They were sitting close together in the booth, and Daniel was ruffling his hands through Pete's wiry hair.

"Fuck school, anyway," Daniel said. "I'm ready to go travel around the world. I can go to school when I'm old. Who wants to come with me?"

"Uh-uh, no more traveling with you," Pete said. "You won't plan anything ahead, and you like to put your life in danger for the excitement of it. That's what broke us up."

Justin was watching me. "How about you, Armando? Do you like to travel?"

"I haven't done that much." I took the pink umbrella from my Mai Tai and twirled it around on the table between us. "I went to Berlin a few years ago, for my brother's wedding."

"You recommend Berlin?" Justin asked, in a formal tone. I grinned, because he reminded me of my four-year-old nephew Marco asking me about my preference in breakfast cereals. Justin blushed.

"Oh, my god, I loved it," I said. "There was this slammin' club, called Tresor? It was like my second home there. That joint was so lit. It's in this, like, old power plant and they have the best techno music anywhere. Someday I want to go back there." I described the wild, electric, uninhibited vibe of the place, so transforming and liberating to my inexperienced 16-year old self.

Justin and Pete were smiling and nodding as I talked. Daniel's long green eyes trained on me.

"Tresor's a second-rate tourist trap," he said. "Anybody can get in there. It's passé. I go to Berghain or, for a change, Renate. Renate's so intimate, don't you think?"

"Oh, I don't know," I said, waving my hand dismissively. "I found Renate boring. Stuffy, is how I found it. But that's just me. Maybe that's just because my uncle owns the place."

"Your uncle owns Renate?" His eyes widened.

"Sure. Fritz Felan. His father, my grandpa, he married Hilda Frankfurter. You know, *those* Frankfurters? They wanted to branch out from the steel business, and they got big time into clubs."

Daniel was looking at me with new respect. Next to him, his friend Pete was starting to snicker. Justin looked at me, his sherry-colored eyes dancing.

Daniel looked puzzled. "I hadn't heard of any Frankfurters in steel," he said.

"Oh, did I say steel? I must have misspoken. The Frankfurters only dabble in steel. The bulk of their fortune is actually in sausages. Really big sausages."

Pete burst into laughter, and Justin joined him.

"Ah." Daniel glared at me.

"So," he said, leaning back in the booth and smiling slightly. "Armando. You're a...pa-ra-le-gal? Is that right?" He pronounced 'paralegal' slowly, rolling the word around in his mouth like a hard candy he'd never tasted before.

"Sometimes." I watched him.

"Para—that means next to something, doesn't it? From the Greek, as you probably know. Like para-site? So, then, would you be, like, next to a lawyer?"

"Would you be, like, a spoiled rich bitch who thinks he's hot shit 'cause he can be a big educated man on Daddy's money?"

Justin took advantage of Daniel's brief hesitation to grab my arm and drag me out to the dance floor.

I said in Justin's ear, "You don't need to protect me from your friend. I can go all 'Mean Girls' whenever."

He looked at me, his fine dark reddish eyebrows going halfway up his white forehead. Then he put his hand gently on my shoulder and brought his lips super close to my ear to say, "I could see that. Well done."

He moved his face back so he could watch me respond. Our eyes met and I felt the familiar electric jolt of unexpected attraction. Everything around the two of us seemed to disappear, except the rhythm of Pitbull's "Tonight" throbbing in time to the colored lights on the dance floor.

I whispered in his ear, "Then why did you interrupt us?"

"I interrupted Daniel, because: a) I wanted to dance with you and, b) I'm sick of watching him make an ass out of himself. Can we please talk about something else?"

As we left the dance floor, I spotted Slim and Rodrigo, wedged against the rail that bordered the edge of the dance floor. Rodrigo looked a little dangerous in a black sleeveless vest that showed off his buffed arms. He frowned as he noted my arm around Justin's shoulders. Slim was wearing his pearl choker and a fishnet T-shirt, and a pout on his dark face.

"Rodrigo won't dance with me," he said.

"Come to our booth and meet Justin's friends," I said.

Justin started asking me what there was to do in the desert. The rest of the room disappeared as we spoke into each other's ears. Gaga's "Bad Romance" came on, and I saw Slim and Daniel slip out to the dance floor.

"Do you want to come over?" Justin asked me in a low voice. "'Cause my apartment's just a couple blocks from here." I didn't turn him down.

7

Light was starting to expand through the cracks in the curtains when I woke up the next morning. Justin's studio apartment was vintage '20s, old Spanish-style with thick stucco walls, and old hardwood floors. Other than the bed and a dresser, the room only had a desk, which was surrounded with books and papers, and a long brick-and-plank bookshelf.

Law books and outlines filled most of the side of the bookshelf next to the desk, but on the other side was a small collection of books of different shapes and sizes. I got out of bed and knelt in front of them. There were a few by Gore Vidal, including a well-worn paperback of The City and the Pillar, some non-fiction books about famous judges and lawyers, and a collection of short stories by Mexican and South American authors, in Spanish, next to a well-worn Spanish/English dictionary. On the top shelf, laid flat with the front cover facing up, was a beautiful coffee-table book of recently published drawings by Tom of Finland. It must have cost a fortune, I thought, paging through the artistically idealized drawings of muscular male bodies. I stopped at a full-page sketch of a man with black hair and a slender body with a perfect butt, executed with economical pen strokes in black and white. Nice. Would Justin have spent the money for this book, or had it been a gift?

I got back on the bed and regarded Justin. He was sleeping with his face buried in his pillow. After our active night, he was sleeping hard, grabbing his rest in what I assumed was the sleep-deprived life of a law-student who also worked full-time. With that all-kinds-of-fierce tousled red hair and those big freckles on his white shoulders, he looked about twelve years old. I thought about the contrast between his young appearance and his middle-aged kind of maturity, and how it had caused me to underestimate him. This boy could totally engage me for a while, I thought.

I dressed quietly and left without waking him. On the way out, I wrote my cell number on a business card, leaving it on top of his desk.

Retrieving my car, I headed home to my breakfast date with mom and my sister, Gaby, who was staying with Mom and me for her summer break from UC Berkeley. I updated them on Domingo's case.

Mom said, "You think the cartels are involved in this girl's death, *m'ijo*? It sounds improbable. I would look for the personal angle, myself. Her former lover, that scientist husband of her friend, he sounds suspicious to me. I respect your boss's opinion very much, but she is incorrect on this one point. A woman doesn't give a man a gift inscribed 'all my love' unless there is a romantic connection. And that man may seem cold to you but I believe he is really very passionate."

Mom wanted to go shopping for Gaby's back to school needs. "I've got our charge cards for all your favorite stores," she trilled. "I'm feeling very extravagant today. Armando, you should join us."

"Ma, we did a big shop yesterday," Gaby said. "You spent a fortune, even for you. How much jewelry can you wear?"

"We'll skip the jewelry store today, then. Let's stock up on beauty products, my lovely girl."

I kind of wanted to go, but I also wanted some alone time to relive the highlights of my night with Justin. I put in an order for a couple of the new Raf Simons textured 50s shirts I'd seen at Macy's, knowing Mom would find the best color and fit for me. "I think I could get away with wearing them to work," I told her, "if you can coordinate them with my jacket collection."

I was about to put on my suit and hit the pool, when I remembered stupidly promising Lucy to serve the subpoenas in the Torres case. Mom and Gaby took off for the mall, and I sighed and headed to the office to get the documents.

First, I wasted almost an hour driving to Frank Slattery's booshi La Jolla condo, only to find him not at home, and then headed back downtown to his office, in case he was working on the weekend. Maybe Justin would be there. If I showed up, would he think I was stalking him? Why hadn't he called me yet?

On a Sunday afternoon, the business part of downtown, especially the part over by the courthouse and jail, is a ghost town. Sometimes you see theatergoers coming or going to a matinee, or the odd office worker wearing shorts and a T-shirt and looking totally pissed off at having to work on the weekend, but mostly it's homeless people hanging out, or the poor underclass that has to rely on public transportation, wandering between trolley and bus stops.

There was a black classic Mustang parked in front of Slattery's office, on the otherwise deserted street. At first, I wondered if it could be Justin's, but then I remembered he'd told me that, coming from the Bay Area where public transportation was more of a mainstream thing, he hadn't budgeted for a car when he came to San Diego for law school. Maybe it was Slattery's. I figured him more for a new Jaguar or Mercedes, something in-your-face expensive but not truly fine. I parked behind the Mustang and got out to take a closer look. Holy shit. It was a classic pony with 17-inch radials giving it a resto-mod look. Inside, I could see the front and back seats had been replaced with modern leather seats in cherry condition, and what looked like a Le Carra steering wheel.

I glanced back at my Camino, feeling kind of guilty, like you feel when you walk out of a bar with your date and see someone even hotter walking in. What do you do? Well, I still loved my *pachuco* classic El Camino, and the Mustang was out of my league, anyway. If it was Frank's, I thought a little more of him. But really, though, if he could afford those great digs and this *coche muy classico*, couldn't he have a little bit nicer of an office? I smiled, imagining Lucy saying, "That shows a great lack of respect for his clients and his employees." Hey, I'd have to remember that. I could tell her that crappy green couch in our reception area was a sign of disrespect for her clients, not to mention her hardworking staff. I could see our office with a leather sectional made out of the same creamy soft leather that lined this Mustang.

My hand was shading the passenger side window to get a good look at the Mustang's interior, but there was still a strong reflection and I saw a movement behind me before I heard the voice.

"Yo, that's my car, man!"

I turned to see a beefy *Mexicano* a few years older than me, standing in a macho stance with his legs a couple feet apart, ready for action, looking kinda proud and tough at the same time. The distinctive silhouette of a girl with long stick legs and a round head peered out from behind him. I recognized her right away.

"Sorry, brother." I said, straightening up to face them. "You got a nice ride. Is this a '72?"

The guy relaxed and gave me a nod that used his head and shoulders. "Close. It's a '73. Last year of the classics."

"*Muy pachuco.*"

"Thanks."

"Where'd you get the seats?"

We stood and talked about the car for a couple minutes.

His companion came to stand at his side. "You're that guy who's representing Domingo, aren't you?" she said, in her squeaky cartoon voice.

"Yeah. Armando Felan." I held out my hand to the guy first. Then I turned to the girl. "You're Annie, right? You work for Frank."

"Are you here to see him?" she asked.

"Is he here?"

"No. Nobody's here. I mean, nobody's in the office. I had to come in to do a couple of things Frank needs for tomorrow. Now Carlos is in a rush to go, and I didn't finish what I needed to do." She pouted, the lower lip of her tiny mouth popping out like a child's just before the tears hit. Carlos looked alarmed.

"Baby, I gotta be at work in half an hour. I barely got time to drop you off."

"You were late coming to get me. You knew I had to have at least an hour here. Frank is going to freak if I don't have everything ready for his court appearance on Monday morning."

Carlos hung his head.

"Maybe I can help," I said. "I need to talk to you, Annie. I don't mind waiting around for you, and we can talk while I drive you home." I addressed myself more to Carlos, and gave a jerk of my head towards the Camino to show him I had wheels.

Annie regarded me with her round eyes. Her mouth pursed so it was almost invisible in her doll-like face. "What would you do while I work?" she said.

"I got my laptop in the car. I can write up some notes for my work. Bill my time to the office," I told her.

Carlos looked doubtful, but Annie sent him on his way and took out her key to the office.

"Thanks for doing this, Armando," she said, all business now the boyfriend was gone. "Are you sure you don't mind?"

"No, you're doing me a big favor. I kind of needed to work today anyway, on account of I took time off of work last week. My boss was totally stressing me out and I needed a three-day weekend, you know what I mean?"

"Tell me about it." She rolled her eyes, then turned to open the door, punched some numbers into a box to shut off the security alarm system, and shouldered her way through the inner door into the back office. "Sometimes I just want to go down to the airport, give them my credit card, and tell them, get me on a fucking airplane that goes as far away as possible," she squeaked. "Working sucks." Her high voice matched her looks, with her round head in its hairband, big chest, and toothpick legs, like a cartoon character.

Too lazy to go get my laptop out of my car, I sat at Justin's desk and played on my iPhone while Annie finished her work. His desk was the opposite of mine. I clear off everything every night before I leave work: all the files go back in their drawers, pens and highlighters put away, computer completely shut down. Justin's desk had law books and papers covering the top and spilling over onto the floor. His computer was hibernating, but he was logged off and I couldn't find his password anywhere handy. At first, I couldn't find any personal items, but then I saw, taped to the base of his computer monitor, staring up at me, a little photo, like a school picture, of a cute Latino about my age. OK, whatever. I pulled up my iPhone and started looking at videos of Pitbull.

Annie came over and found me a few minutes later and squeaked, "Let's get out of this dump. You can take me home now."

We drove south, almost halfway to the border, to Annie's apartment in National City. In the light Sunday traffic, it was only a ten-minute drive. Carlos wasn't exactly her boyfriend, she told me, but he was someone she'd known for years and they went out sometimes. He wanted to get married, and she thought maybe someday she might do that, but she wasn't ready yet. "I just don't know, Armando," she confided. "It would be nice to have a guy support me and not have to work. I'm not sure I'm in love with him, though. Maybe I'll never be in love. I get bored so easily."

"I get that," I said. "Take your time and have fun, that's what I say."

Her apartment was in a small, two-story 70's complex, on a tree-lined dead-end street a few blocks west of Highway 5. I parked in front of her building. She didn't invite me in, so I pulled a couple of bottles of spring water out of my trunk and handed one to her. We sat in my car and talked and sipped the water, like teenagers on a date.

"What I don't get," I told Annie, "is everyone says Patty was so nice. Why would anyone want to kill her?"

"Yeah, she came across that way," Annie said. Even her profile was cartoon cute, with a tiny nose turned up a little at the tip. "She was super polite, and she had a pretty face with those big sad-puppy eyes that men love. You know, like, 'please save me.' At first, I was afraid she was too serious, but we ended up having some good times. She was a good listener." Annie turned away from me and looked out the window.

"I'm sorry," I said. "This must be hard for you. Talking about your friend, I mean."

Annie pursed her mouth and nodded. "Yes, it is, but I want to help you find out what happened to her. I'm sure Domingo didn't kill her. I want you to find out the truth. I considered Patty a friend, even though we didn't know each other that long. She didn't know a lot of people when she moved down here. I moved here a couple years ago from Salinas, and most of my family and friends are still up there. Patty and I started having lunch, on the days we didn't just sit at our desks and work through lunch, that is. Then we started seeing each other sometimes after work and on the weekends. We were both still finding out what we wanted in life."

"Wow," I said. "That reminds me of something your boss, Frank, said. He said Patty didn't know what she wanted. So you think that's true?"

Annie nodded again, her shiny hair bobbing up and down. "Yes. It's funny Frank would say that. He can surprise you that way. He acts like such a...wild animal...and then he says something and you realize he has feelings and he notices things. But it's true about Patty. At least...at least, it was true, when she first came, before she met Domingo. She told me she didn't think she'd ever really been in love. But I think that changed when she...got involved with him. Now I know about her and Domingo, I know that when she saw him she realized for the first time what she really wanted. Him."

"You never had a clue about her and Domingo?"

She shook her head. "Uh-uh. Well, OK, I did wonder. It was the way Domingo would look at Patty when he came into the office, especially later on. He sort of ignored everyone else, not trying to be rude but like he really only saw her. I didn't think it was just because she was his lawyer. When guys start to do that, it at least means they have a big crush. That's why I'm sure he didn't kill her. He's not like that."

"Yeah, girl," I said, "I'm glad to hear you say that. Of course, I agree with you about Domingo being innocent, since he's our client. But you have to admit a lot of men end up killing the women they love. We think that's why the police were so quick to focus on Domingo, even though they don't have much evidence against him. They didn't consider other possibilities."

"Exactly," she cried. "What do they have on him, anyway? He's a gentleman. I just know it. I mean, you've met him, right? If he loved a woman, he wouldn't hurt her."

We sat quietly for a moment, thinking about my client. I wondered if Lucy could get a jury that was all women.

"If Domingo didn't kill her, what do you think happened?" I asked Annie.

"Oh, I think she killed herself," Annie said. "I think Domingo broke her heart. I'd kill myself if he broke up with me."

"Why do you think they broke up? Did someone tell you that?"

"I don't remember. Didn't they have a fight or something, that night? I would want to die if a man like that loved me and then broke up with me. I guess she felt she couldn't talk to me about him, 'cause of the work thing. But I wouldn't have told Frank, I would have kept her secret."

"Did you talk to Patty the night before she died?'

"No. I saw her at work that day, but we didn't get to do lunch. She had to drive somewhere to do an interview."

"How did she seem that day?"

"I didn't notice anything at the time, but when I look back on it I think she had something on her mind. She seemed, well, tense. The Saturday night before, we'd gone out to a movie together, and to a club after. We had a really fun time. God, Armando, I feel so bad. I'm afraid I did most of the talking, like I usually do. I talked mostly about myself and this guy I'd been seeing."

"I'm guessing you don't mean Carlos."

She did a Mona Lisa smile and the corners of her eyes crinkled as she looked at me. Then her expression got sad. "Anyway, I went on and on about my little problem. I didn't give a shit about the dude, I was just bored and needed some drama in my life so I was making a big deal of how he hadn't called me in two days. After she'd had a couple of drinks, Patty even said to me, she said, 'Annie, if he does call you, you'll just break up with him anyway. He probably knows that and that's why he's not calling.' Of course, she was right. You see, the thing about Patty was, if she hadn't been a little drunk, she would have been too polite to say that. That's how she was. You know?"

I thought for a minute. "Patty wasn't her usual self that night?"

"That's exactly what I'm saying. Really. Now I look back on it, it's not just that she'd had too much to drink. She was upset about something, Armando. I just wish she'd told me what it was. I bet you anything she was afraid Domingo was done with her. Listen, can you tell Domingo, Annie says 'hi'? Will you remember to do that?"

***

Brad and Christine's house was a craftsman-style cottage with a long front yard in lower Mission Hills, a pricy neighborhood just north of downtown. It looked like someone spent a lot of time keeping up the front garden. By the time I got there, most of the garden was in the shade. There was a car in the driveway and a car out front, which hopefully meant Brad and Christine were both home.

As I opened the front gate and walked towards the front door, Christine came around from the side of the house. She was wearing gardening gloves and a matching apron, and held a pot and a little shovel full of soil.

"Armando!" Even though I was making a surprise visit, she smiled as if she had expected me over for a social call. "How nice to see you!" She put down her things and held out a gloved hand. She laughed when we both looked and saw that her glove was covered with dirt. "Sorry. Come on in! I was just trying to get some gardening done while the baby's napping."

"Thanks, Christine. Sorry to bother you at home like this. I like your garden. My mom is a big gardener, too."

"Oh, your mom likes to garden? How wonderful. Where does she live?"

"Here in San Diego. In Chula Vista, near Eastlake. I live with her."

"She must be so happy to have you at home with her." Christine walked me around to the back of the house and we entered a big, cheerful kitchen. "Is your father still…?"

"Oh, he's still around," I said. "He has a business in Mexico, and since my little sister went away to college, he stays down there most of the time. Mom prefers to stay up here, in the house where I grew up."

"How interesting." Her look made me think she'd gotten the whole sub-text of my life from my three sentences. She walked over to a cabinet and pulled out two oversized mugs.

"It is," I agreed. I again had to resist the urge to tell her my life story.

"Would you like coffee, or tea?" Christine asked.

"Whatever you're having would be great."

She turned the water on under the kettle. "Have a seat. I just want to check on the baby."

While Christine was out of the room, I looked around me. The kitchen felt like it was the center of the household, with a Mission-style dining table and chairs, bowls of fruit and vegetables on the counters, a bookshelf full of cookbooks and art books, and a vase of purple and orange flowers in the middle of the table.

Christine came back into the room talking. "Our eggplant is still going strong. Your mother might like to try this kind." She chatted on as she made coffee and set out some muffins on a plate. When everything was ready, she sat down at the table and smiled at me, with her head cocked to one side.

"Enough about my garden. Don't get me started. It's one of my passions. Now, tell me, how are *you*?"

I wanted to tell her all about the warm, hopeful feelings I was having after my night with Justin, and how they scared the shit out of me. Maybe, sometime after the case was over, if I could afford it….

"Well, we've got a time crunch right now in Domingo Torres's case," I said. "The preliminary hearing is this Friday, and we're still interviewing witnesses. In fact," I said, "I have a subpoena here for you and one for Brad. You've probably also been subpoenaed by the DA's office, but we always need to cover all the bases. Is Brad around?" I got the subpoenas out of my bag, and put them on the table.

Christine took hers, and handed Brad's back to me.

"Brad left. He had to go out of town on business."

"Where is he? Do you have a number where I can reach him?"

Christine gave her wry smile, humorous and apologetic, but there was a look of alarm in her eyes. "All I have is his cell number. I'd give that to you, but he'd get royally pissed at me."

"Well, we don't want that," I agreed.

Her face cleared. "I know. Here's what I'll do," she said. "I'll call him and ask him to call you."

"That sounds good. Where did he go, exactly?"

"Uh, I'm not sure where he is now. He said was going to go to several different cities to talk about a project he was working on. I always reach him on his cell, so I don't get a number for where he's staying."

I really wanted to talk to Brad about his relationship with Patty, but I decided not to raise it with Christine.

"How is your investigation going?" Christine asked.

"Well, we still think the case against Domingo is very weak," I said. "There's no real motive for him to have killed Patty. Your testimony about her mental state, and the way she died, still point to suicide. But we have to look at all the possibilities."

"Why don't the police believe it was suicide?"

"We think it's because they like Domingo for it, and there's no clear motive for suicide. We'll have to look into Patty's background to see if we can find out what really led to her death."

"You know this, of course, but suicide doesn't always have a clear explanation, to people looking at it from outside. Patty had depression, I'll testify to that. She was in denial about it, which can be dangerous because then you don't get treatment or develop ways of managing the condition. I am still so angry at myself for not trying harder to get her into treatment."

"But you didn't know she would take her own life," I said. "It doesn't sound like she was acting all that depressed in the months before she died. For one thing, she was in love with Domingo. I wonder, did she think Domingo was breaking up with her?"

Christine frowned. "She didn't exactly say that, but she was pretty upset. If she thought it was over, that might have put her over the edge."

"I did hear she was maybe getting burned out with her work. Maybe she was too sensitive to practice law."

"No, Patty would have made a fine attorney," Christine said. "If she'd hung in there, she'd have been happy. It was a good place for her. The real problem was, she lost her focus when Domingo came on the scene. Oh, Armando, I just realized the last time I saw her, she came over to visit me and sat right where you're sitting now. This is so sad. It didn't have to happen."

I left with a bag full of eggplant, and spent the rest of my Sunday playing video games with Slim.

8

Monday, I needed to finish serving the subpoenas. Brad had not called, but I didn't really expect he would respond to Christine's request to call me. Finding his business card in the file, I called the direct number and left a voicemail. Then I called back on the general office number.

"SimCo Medical Technologies, how may I help you?" chirped a female voice.

"Hi, I hope you can help me. I'm Armando Felan, Brad Fernwood's financial advisor. He just left me a message to contact him at his hotel because he forgot to charge his cell phone, but the number he left was a wrong number. We need to talk this morning about an investment decision. Does someone there have his travel itinerary with the name or number of his hotel?"

"One moment, I'll ask."

After about a minute, the woman came back on. "Sorry to keep you waiting. I checked with our office manager. Mr. Fernwood is not traveling for business, he's on vacation. We don't make vacation arrangements for our employees. We don't know where he is."

Aha, I thought. Brad had lied to Christine about being out of town for business, or Christine knew but she had lied to me about where he was.

Around lunchtime, I decided to walk the ten blocks to Slattery's office, to serve him before my appointment to meet

Patty's brother Sam.   Denise, the friendly receptionist, was there, and told me Mr. Slattery had just left for court, and Justin was at the law library. "Do you think I could talk to the paralegal who worked with Patty?" I asked. "Justin suggested I talk to her."

"Sure, that would be Linda Chappell. You might also want to talk to Annie, Annie Haskins. Remember, you met her? She's the one who was friends with Patty. Annie and Linda both kind of hung out with Patty, they would know the most about her."

I opened my mouth to say I'd already talked with Annie, but for some reason I didn't. Our time over the weekend, in the peaceful deserted office, felt like a secret.

"Let me see if Linda's available," Denise punched some buttons with her turquoise-blue fingernails, and spoke into the phone. "…yeah, the hot one, who was here last week about Domingo…, yeah, OK."

Denise turned to me. "You're in luck. Linda and Annie were just going out to an early lunch, but they'll talk to you if you walk out with them."

The door to the office opened and two women came out. Linda was probably ten years older than Annie, wore too much make-up, over-sprayed her hair, had cheap but on-trend work clothes, and carried what was probably a good quality knockoff Coach bag but might have been real.

While I thanked Denise, Linda and Annie walked out the door to the street. As I caught up with them, they were giggling. Linda gave me a knowing look, from which I realized that Annie must have told her about our interview that weekend. From the look Linda gave me, you'd think Annie'd told her we'd had wild sex on Frank Slattery's desk, instead of a heart-to-heart about Annie's love life and her dead friend.

"Sorry," Linda said. She had a bold stare, and a short, voluptuous figure.   Her voice was loud but husky, like she smoked or screamed a lot. "It's just that this case, um, well, first we have Domingo Torres, and now, you."

Annie elbowed her friend and said, "Lin-da! Stop!" I'd already forgotten how high and squeaky her voice was. She made a perfect O with her little round mouth.

"Riiight?" I said. "Girl, I almost fell over when I saw Domingo. Even in those jail clothes, he looks really fine. My boss, she was, like, speechless, and that doesn't happen very often. I mean, wow, right? How tall do you think he is? So, Linda, what was Patty like to work with?"

"She was cool. Even though Patty was already a professional woman, an attorney, she had this kind of humbleness in her manner. She was...unpolished, if you know what I mean. Even her looks, you know, she had a great figure, all tall and leggy, but she wore like no makeup, and boring clothes. I told her she was like an undiscovered fashion model. I offered to fix her up, give her a free makeover. She would've been gorgeous, but she just laughed at me. Now with her work, she was different. She was really eager to learn, not like most attorneys I've trained who already think they know everything."

"She was the same with me," agreed Annie. "There's a lot of pressure in our work, because we do such a high volume of cases. She definitely got overwhelmed sometimes, but she never took it out on us. Patty was eager to learn immigration law. She was really ambitious."

"No, I disagree with that," Linda said. "She was in a hurry to learn to be a good attorney, but not to make a lot of money or be famous or whatever. She was dedicated, like a nun, like what she wanted more than anything was to help people. Especially when she first started. The last couple of months, she seemed to be getting a little frustrated. Believe me, I know the early signs of burnout. You start getting disappointed in the clients for the stupid things they do, like when they tell lies to Immigration before they see an attorney, or don't follow through with the simple tasks you assign them.

You have to have a sense of humor about that kind of thing, since you have no control over it. I don't say she was going to burn out, but she probably needed a vacation."

"Have you seen a lot of attorneys burn out at your office?"

"Oh, yeah." They both said at once, and looked at each other and laughed.

"I'm thinking Frank isn't the easiest guy to work for, either," I ventured. "Especially for women? Did Patty have any problems with him?"

The women looked at each other, and finally Linda spoke. "I guess it's no secret. I'm going to tell you this because I think it's the right thing to do. But can you agree this won't get back to Frank, or get around, unless you really have to use it?"

"Absolutely."

"Like you've probably heard, Frank does have a problem working with women. If you just laugh and tell him to knock it off, he'll back off. He's a screamer anyway, so you just ignore the harassing remarks along with all the screaming abuse he gives to everybody.

"With Patty and with some other woman attorneys, it's been different. It's like Frank has to prove something by getting them to go out with him. Two of his past wives were attorneys who worked for him before they married him. He's more subtle about it, too, with the ones he, um, targets. Instead of making crude remarks, he sends flowers, says nice things, you know."

"Was Frank asking Patty out?"

Linda and Annie nodded.

"For the first few months, he kept asking her out, in front of everybody at the office, and she kept saying no," Annie said. "Everyone could see it happening, and she tried to just laugh it off like it was a joke between them. She had a very soft manner, so it didn't come naturally to her just to tell him to…"

"To fuck off," Linda finished for her.

"Right. Anyway, it seemed to us like he was doing it less, after a while. But then, a couple of months ago, she came out to lunch with Linda and me. She told us Frank was still asking her out, but only when they were alone together."

Linda added, "He sent her notes and flowers and made her go with him to some Bar functions as part of her job. Patty said one time Frank even went over to her apartment on a Sunday morning, with a bottle of champagne."

Annie broke in, "I told her she should just tell Frank she had another boyfriend. Like, she could say there was someone else from her past and they had gotten back together. That way Frank wouldn't take it so personally and he'd leave her alone."

Linda said, "We joked she could say her boyfriend had just gotten out of prison for murder, and he was moving in with her."

"Now that seems kind of...." Annie hesitated.

"Ironic," Linda finished for her.

"Yeah."

"Did she consider filing a sexual harassment complaint?"

"That's what I suggested," Linda said. "But she said she didn't want to rock the boat."

On the way to meet Sam Acres at Patty's apartment, I crossed Broadway and walked down Fourth Avenue to the Hazard Hotel, where Domingo had lived at the time of his arrest. The Hazard is one of the few flophouses left downtown. I walked into the hotel. I'd been there several times before to interview witnesses. Every time I go in, the lobby looks a little more run down. In contrast to the size of its rooms, the Hazard's lobby is very spacious, with an old movie-theatre style carpet covering the whole floor, and all the furniture, vinyl chairs and couches in a style of like fifty years ago, placed against the walls. A big glass window spans most of the wall facing the street. Dull, faded curtains are pulled back to let in dirty sunlight which manages to be the opposite of cheerful. The place is like the inside of a neglected fish tank. Nobody is ever in there. Today, though, I felt happy when I saw who was at the front desk.

"Spanky, my friend!" I cried. "Who's the man?"

"Armando, brother! You're the man!"

"No, you!"

"No, you! Hanh, hanh, hanh, hah." Spanky's pumpkin face shows a broad grin with a total of about six teeth. His lack of teeth gives his laughter and his speech a sort of honking sound. He was wearing his usual bandana headband over stringy gray-blond hair that fell to his shoulders. He pointed a yellow forefinger at me, punctuating his laughs.

"How come you're still stuck in this shithole?" I asked. "Every time I go to the Marriott, I think I'm gonna see you behind the desk. You're too classy for this place, man."

"Yeah, this place is getting to be a drag. I gotta call the cops, or the ambulance, or both, maybe four times a week now."

Twenty years ago, Delmar Shuette, a.k.a. Spanky, was a young bass player who played with big name jazz players. He went downhill after his family pressured him to go into the military to "straighten out." Lucy represented him on a possession charge a few years ago, and he and I stayed in touch.

I asked him, "Do you remember a real tall guy who used to live here up until a few weeks ago?"

"Yeah, I expect you're talking about Domingo. Really tall guy. Had hands like fryin' pans. Sure I remember him. Quiet guy, I didn't talk to him much. He got himself arrested for murder. You got that case now?"

"We sure do. Hey, did he ever have any visitors?"

Spanky squinted his face in an effort to remember.

"He got a visit from a pretty young lady, a few weeks after he moved in. I just saw her the once. She was a skinny thing, voice like Betty Boop. Then, maybe a week before he got arrested, there was a kid in a suit. Red hair. Met Domingo in the lobby."

"How long did they stay?" I asked.

"Let me think. When the lady came, it was around dinnertime, and there was a bunch of people coming and going. I just sent her up to his room. Shortly after that, I had to call the cops on a drunk who was botherin' one of our residents. I don't remember seeing the young lady leave."

"What about the red-haired kid?"

"Now him, I don't know if he went up to the room. I think Domingo was waiting for him down here. They might've gone out some place together."

Patty's apartment was in a new building, all black concrete and smoked glass on the outside, with balconies overlooking the bay and downtown. I pushed the buzzer for her place on the sixteenth floor, and after a few seconds was buzzed in. When I got off the elevator, the door to the apartment across from it was wide open, and Sam called to me to come in.

My first view was of a dark, spiky ball, backlit by a sunny view of the San Diego Bay and the blue bridge leading to Coronado Island. The high rises of the Coronado Cays were just visible, bright white against the deep blue water and light blue sky. The view from the big picture window was fine, even though it was cut in half by the shaded black glass of a neighboring high rise. It was like a curtain had been drawn halfway across the window.

As I walked into the room I saw the ball was Sam's head, and he was sitting on a couch against the window. He was stocky and round-faced, with a bad highlight job on his spiky dark hair, and heavy dark-framed glasses. He had on wide corduroy pants, a plaid lumberjack shirt, and big sandy-colored suede work boots, like he was on a deerhunt instead of in an urban condo on a warm summer day. He didn't get up, but held up a hand to greet me. The other hand held a bottle of beer, and there were a couple of empty bottles on the coffee table in front of him.

"You must be Armando," he said. "Take a load off." He flapped his hand at a small armchair across from him. "It's as hot as hell here. This is why I don't live in Southern California." His face was sweating, despite the blasting air conditioning.

I suppressed a shiver, wondering why he didn't take off his heavy shirt.

"Here." Sam reached into a bag at his feet, and handed me a bottle of IPA, a trendy label from a local microbrewery.

"I admit you all have some great beers down here," he said. "Maybe I'll get a chance to go tasting, once I get done with all of this." He gestured towards the rest of the apartment, which contained piles of mostly unassembled moving boxes, a roll of tape, a couple of half-filled large trash bags, a small stack of books next to an almost full, floor to ceiling, bookshelf, but no other signs much packing was in progress.

"Oops, here's the opener. Sorry, I'm having a bad time here. Please, have a drink with me."

I opened the bottle and took a long slug, looking out at the warm view of the sun and the water and the bridge and feeling the cold dark inside the room. We drank together in silence for a minute.

"I'm really sorry about your loss, man," I said.

"Thanks." Sam picked up a framed photo from the coffee table, and looked at it like he needed to finish something before he could talk to me. I got the feeling he had been staring at it just before I came.

Finally, Sam handed me the photo. "She was one of the sweetest people I ever knew," he said, his voice starting to break. "This shouldn't have happened." He reached down and got us each another beer.

The only pictures I'd seen of Patty were the post-mortems, which showed a small, cold face surrounded by a heavy cloud of hair. In this photo, Patty looked like a different person, relaxed, with a half-smile on her lips, unintentionally flirting with the camera. She was holding a small orange cat that rested its head on her shoulder. Her shiny, honey-blonde hair was unstyled, but perfectly framed her face.

"Wow," I said, handing back the picture. "Your sister was really beautiful."

"Yeah, but she didn't know it. A lot of the time she seemed so ordinary, and then she'd relax and be happy and look like this. I actually took this picture. She and Chris were visiting me and she picked up my cat, Pumpkin. She loved animals," Sam said.

"Nice," I said lamely. In the distance, I watched a boat motor slowly by the Coronado Bridge. I wondered whether it was a tourist cruise or the ferryboat that shuttled between downtown and the island. I had a sudden urge to ditch work, get out of downtown, drive over the bridge, and spend the day at the beach. The chair I was sitting in was next to a round table with a coaster and a book on it, and a standing lamp to read by. It was angled to face the part of the view that was not blocked by the building next door. This must be where Patty had sat and read. The cool room, and the looming nextdoor building, gave the illusion I was in a protected cave, safe from the heat and danger of the outside world but still getting to enjoy the view. Had Patty felt safe here?

I picked up the book. It was a bestselling chicklit book Mom had tried to get me to read, but I hadn't been able to get into it. "Did your sister like to read?" I asked Sam.

"Oh, yeah, she was a big reader. Unlike me. I'm more of a TV, gaming kind of guy. Chris always said Patty was an introvert, she liked books more than people. Books were, like, her friends. I started to pack them, to take to the library, and I got stuck."

An hour and two more beers later, I was on the floor, boxing the last of the books.

"You are so solid to do this for me, man," Sam said. After assembling a few boxes for me, he'd collapsed back on the couch and started to talk.

"Why would anyone kill her?" he'd asked me, his eyes watering.

"Maybe, like you said, she did it herself."

"Why do people kill, anyway? What's the point? What is it going to solve?"

"You got that right, brother," I'd said. "We've had clients who said they felt like they had no choice. But look how they end up."

"Want to know what I think?" Sam said. "I think, at the bottom of it, you know, like, fundamentally? It's out of a feeling of injustice. Like an unfairness you have to fix. Think about it, man. Well, take money, right? Someone has it so much better that you, like by an accident of birth or luck, so that's an injustice you gotta make right...."

I placed a paperback copy of *Crime and Punishment* into a box. "Classic motive," I said. "Like you could spend the money better than the rich person would, right? I mean, I'd never kill anyone just for money, but I've felt that before, haven't you?"

"Yeah, or you're in love and they cheat on you—you feel deprived of something that's yours by rights. Not that the person's yours, but your love for them, that's yours. 'Course, you could just keep loving them, I guess." He opened another beer and took a long drink.

"I guess," I said. I'd never been in love like that, where you get jealous and possessive. Thank God.

Sam's eyes were starting to focus less on me, and more on Mr. Alcohol. Fearing I would soon lose his attention, I focused on the questions I needed to ask.

"Hey, Sam, you didn't find Patty's wallet, by any chance?"

"What? Oh. No," he said. "The cops searched for it already. There was a purse she was using, with a hairbrush, make-up, cell phone, but no wallet."

"Were you and Patty close, growing up?" I asked.

"I wouldn't say very close. She was six years older than me, and we had different fathers. Our mom married my father after Patty's dad died."

"That's why she has a different last name?" I asked.

"Yeah. Actually, she grew up with her father's last name, Martin. But some time after she started working, Patty decided to start using our mother's maiden name, Taylor. It was kind of a tribute to our mom, who died a couple of years ago, and kind of a statement as well. Patty's dad, Mr. Martin, was not a good guy." He put his head in his hands.

"Now it's just me and my crazy Aunt Jill. Patty was close to my dad, her stepfather, but Dad was killed in a car crash when I was ten."

"Oh, wow, I'm sorry. That must have been tough."

"It was, for all of us. It was traumatic for Patty because she was in the car with him at the time. After Patty went away to college, we got along when we saw each other, but we both were caught up in our own lives. When mom got Alzheimer's, we'd visit her together, like to make it easier for each other, and we got a lot closer during that time. When Patty lived in Oakland, we'd go together to see Aunt Jill. But I've only been down here to San Diego once since she moved here, and she never came up again. Only that one time, I had to come down on business, and I had dinner with Patty and Chris. They were talking about how they didn't miss the Bay Area at all. I joked with them it was just because they'd both found better jobs. The two of them started laughing and saying, "yeah, we especially don't miss 'Goose-more'." That was their name for Gosmore and Huskins, the law firm Patty worked for in Oakland. I never talked to her again."

"When you were growing up, do you remember her ever having mental health issues?"

"When she was a teenager, my sister went through a hard time and saw a therapist for a while. Once, she told me she had always had to fight depression. It runs in the family. My Aunt Jill is a depressive. God, poor Aunt Jill." Sam opened another beer. He seemed close to tears.

"Jill was so broken up when I told her, man. She'd just had that SKYPE with Patty that very night. How weird is that? What I picture is, Patty might have wanted to say goodbye to Aunt Jill, without upsetting her. They were close, in a weird way."

I was liking it. If Patty's own brother thought she had committed suicide, a jury ought to buy it. I felt I'd gotten what we wanted from Sam. I got up, stretched, and went over to the couch, where Sam handed me my fourth beer.

"Your sister had good taste in books," I told Sam, sinking into the couch next to him. "You know, I love reading, too. Just seeing these books makes me feel close to your sister. I get why you had trouble packing them up."

"Yeah. So, you've read some of these books?"

"Sure. She's got some classic English and Russian literature, and some magical realism, which I love. My mom was the one who got me hooked on reading. My older brother and sister never really got into it, so Ma was real happy when I became a book junkie." I swallowed some beer, which could have been a little colder. Why hadn't Sam put it in the fridge? The packing had been kind of hot work, and the A.C. didn't seem so effective now.

"Yeah," I continued, "I could read all day. When I go out to the desert, even in the middle of summer, I lie around the pool all day and just read. You know? After the classics, when I got a little older, and developed my own tastes, Ma introduced me to more modern writers, you know, Isherwood, Vidal.... Ma and I are real close, you know? She's given me so much. Like you and your aunt, maybe. Anyway, I forgot, you aren't into reading. So what video games d'you like, Sam?"

I finally realized Sam wasn't listening, because his head had fallen against the couch and he was snoring.

I set down my beer and packed the rest of the books. When I finished, Sam was still lying on the couch, but he was awake. "You're my buddy, man. You packed the books for me. You're a good friend...."

Before I left, I handed him the subpoena for the preliminary hearing. That seemed to sober him up a little.

"Yeah, thanks, I think I will go," he said, like it was an optional party invitation. "I'm gonna be down here for a while anyway, taking care of stuff. My firm has a local office down here in Black Mountain Valley, so I can go in there and get some work done."

"Black Mountain Valley? Hey, do you work at the same company as Brad?"

"Yeah, we both work for SimCo. We started working together in Oakland, and he moved down here to work for our San Diego office. That's how Christine and Patty met Brad. They came with me to our big office Christmas party, and Brad was there. Probably the last time the guy went to a party."

"Really?"

"Ah, Brad's OK, once you get to know him."

I remembered something. "Christine told me you were going to stay with her. Is that right?"

"Yeah. I didn't feel like I could stay here, where.... Chris offered to let me stay with her instead. She's easy to hang out with."

I nodded. "What about Brad? Have you seen him since you got here?"

"No. He's out of town. He never says much when I see him. He's super smart and everything, but I can never get him to talk about anything except his work. Patty always liked him. Maybe he just seems quiet because I've only seen him with Christine, and she's usually doing the talking."

"Did Patty ever date Brad, before he married Christine?"

Sam's head jerked back and his eyes rounded in a classic expression of surprise. With his round face, spiky blond hair, and dark-framed glasses, he looked like a character actor. "Wow. Where did you hear that?"

"Why, is it true?"

"No, I'm sure it isn't. You're saying Chris, I mean Patty, might have had an affair with Chris's husband? No... no, she wouldn't do that."

"We're just looking into a lot of possibilities. That's how these investigations work."

As I turned to go, Sam said, "Is there any way the judge at this first hearing will just agree that Patty took her own life, and this case will be over?"

"That would be nice, but the judge is probably not going to kick the case at this point."

Sam's fingers were twirling the tassel. "What would the judge need to, uh, kick the case?"

I shook my head. "At this point, we'll really push the judge to accept the evidence that points to suicide. That's the next best thing to a signed confession from somebody else."

9

Outside Patty's building, I called Lucy to check in. She was on the trolley on her way back from visiting Domingo. I reported the news about Frank Slattery's harassment of Patty, and the little I had learned from Sam.

"Do you need me to come back right now? 'Cause I was going to try again to serve the subpoena on Slattery. It's almost three-thirty, he should be coming back from court."

"Get the subpoena served. He's going to pitch a fit when you serve him." I could hear the satisfaction in her voice. "Don't ask him any questions yet. I don't want him to know that we know he was harassing the victim."

I trekked back to Chez Slattery, stopping at a convenience store for bottled water and a hot dog to soak up the four beers I'd had to drink with Sam. As I walked west down C Street, a kid in a blue suit came around the corner of First Avenue, walking towards me quickly. He had a mop of red hair. I stopped at the door of his office and waited for him.

"Hey," I said, staring at him. The long warm afternoon, the beer, and the memories of our recent night together all hit me together in a wave of attraction that almost knocked me over.

"Hey." He blushed and pushed his hair back from his forehead. "You came back."

We stood on the sidewalk outside the doorway.

"Did you think I might not?" I asked.

He bent his head and his brown eyes flashed up at me from under his eyelashes, which were straight except for on the outside edges of his eyes where they turned up. "I wasn't sure. You just left before I woke up and then I didn't hear from you."

"But I left you my card. That meant that you should call me."

Justin smiled shyly. "I didn't see any card. What did it say?"

"Just my business card. With my cell handwritten on it. I left it on your desk. You were sleeping so hard, I didn't want to wake you."

He threw back his head and laughed. "How subtle of you. That shows how well you know me. My desk is like a disaster area. A black hole for important papers."

"Does that mean my card was important?"

He just looked at me. We were smiling at each other, when I felt an elbow jostle me from behind with strong force. It reminded me of the times I've played soccer with real jocks who are trained to create a big space around them using all their body parts.

"Ow!" I cried.

"Outta my way, you're blocking the door." It was Frank Slattery's voice.

"Oh, it's you, Justin," he said, ignoring me. "Did you find anything on that libel immunity issue?" The tank inserted itself between Justin and me.

As Justin answered Frank, I took the opportunity to open my briefcase and pull out the subpoena for Frank. A moment later Frank, still talking to Justin, moved his arm to open the office door. I held out the subpoena and stuck it in his outstretched hand.

It took him a second to stop talking and register my presence and the paper in his hand.

"What's this shit?" he growled, looking at me and not at the subpoena.

"Just a formality, Mr. Slattery. A subpoena for the preliminary hearing in the Torres case. Attorney Sanders will be in touch before the hearing."

I was really hoping for a reaction, but he disappointed me. Without a word he opened the door and went inside.

Justin stayed outside and turned to stare at me.

"What's going on?"

"Lucy just wants me to get all the subpoenas served early. We got this case on a short timeline...." I stopped. Justin seemed rather shocked. I didn't like that I was starting to justify myself with him again.

As we stood there, the front door to Slattery's office opened. The receptionist, Denise, stuck her head out the door.

"Excuse me," she said, looking uncomfortable. She looked at Justin. "Justin, Frank says to tell you he needs you in his office right away." Denise looked back and forth between us. "Sorry," she said, and closed the door back behind her.

"I gotta go." He turned his back on me and was gone.

Walking back the ten blocks to our office, I thought about my encounter with Justin. Maybe it had been a bad idea to think I could be seeing him while I worked on this case. I decided to stop thinking about him. Tonight I would go to my Hip-Hop class and then see if Slim could hang out.

When I got back to the office, Lucy was in her chair in front of the fireplace, sipping tea and editing a motion. I told her about Slattery's reaction, including his assaulting me before I even served him with the subpoena.

"I bet I'll have a bruise tomorrow." I lifted up my Aberzombie polo shirt and craned my neck to look at the area above my right kidney where Frank's elbow had connected. While I was at it, I scanned my beautiful brown torso for any other signs of imperfection. Was that a tiny blur of fat overhanging the top of my A and F cargo pants? "You should pay me combat pay to deal with that guy."

"Well, when you're done admiring yourself, let's make our plan for tomorrow. We've got a lot to do before the preliminary hearing."

***

A few hours later, I lay on a deck chair by our pool, working on a Mai Tai and watching Slim practicing gainers off our diving board. Mom reclined next to me, knocking back a gin and tonic with extra lime. When I got home from working out, she was just coming home herself. Mom hadn't felt like cooking, so I'd gone for Thai take-out, and we were now pleasantly full. The August night was warm and the darkness had just settled in. The air smelled like a mix of Ma's perfume and the white-flowered vines that grew along our back fence.

Mom fanned her face, blowing a strand of hair across her wide forehead. Her bare toes wiggled on the towel under her feet. "Our Slim, he has a beautiful body," she said dreamily.

We watched as Slim executed a perfect gainer, slicing the water like a knife with his body in a vertical line down to the point of his toes. When he surfaced, his dark hair streaming straight back from his Aztec face, Mom put down her drink and clapped.

"Bravo, Slim!" She pronounced his name, as always, with a Mexican accent, so it sounded like "Sleem."

"Ma, what did you do today?" As usual, we had spent dinner talking about me, and my work.

"I went over to the community college. I signed up for an English class."

I almost choked on my drink. "But your English is perfect. You have a little bit of an accent, but your English is great. Why would you do that?"

"I want to use it more. This is an advanced class, where you read books and poetry in English and you talk and you write about it."

"That sounds cool," I said. I was a little hurt she hadn't asked me to take the class with her. Part of our special bond was our shared love of literature, from the time she first started reading to me, until she could start introducing me to her favorite classics. In middle school and high school, it was a secret pleasure I hid from my friends, but now I was proud of it.

Mom held her hands out in front of her, with her fingers spread wide, and stared down at them, her head tilted to one side. Her short nails held a flawless, dark reddish-brown manicure. As always, she wore her flashy gold wedding ring, which had a huge round diamond with two smaller diamonds on each side and a matching band with little stars carved into the gold. On her other hand she had a ring I hadn't seen before, a flattish square-cut ruby surrounded by tiny diamonds.

I saw she was looking at me and smiling. "What do you think, Armando?"

"The new ring? I like it. It's all neo-*art deco*. Where'd you get it?"

"No, I mean my manicure." Mom wiggled her fingers. "I did it myself."

"But, Mom…" I started to say, when my cell phone rang.

I picked up the phone and answered it without looking to see who was calling. "Gloria's Salon," I said.

"Armando?" It was Justin's voice.

"Oh…hi."

"Hi. I found your number."

"So I see."

"It was right there on top of my desk. I just hadn't seen it."

"Oh, well, that's good."

There was a short silence. I waited.

"Um," Justin said, "Listen, I'm sorry about today. I don't think, I mean, I hadn't thought ahead about how awkward this could be. That's why I was kind of shocked today, when you served Frank with the subpoena."

I leaned forward in my deck chair and hugged my knees to my chest.

"I know. Listen, I'm doing something right now. Can I call you back in, like, an hour?"

"Yeah."

"Sorry, Ma," I said. "What were we talking about?"

I was beating Slim at the new video game he'd brought over, when I saw the time.

"Shit," I said. "I told Justin I'd call him in an hour and it's been almost two. I gotta take a break."

"Go ahead, bitch. I'm gonna practice and get you next game."

I took my cell phone and curled up at the top of my bed and dialed. He picked up after about eight rings.

"Hey, Armando," he said in a sleepy voice.

"Hey. Were you asleep?"

"Not yet. Just doing some work. What are you doing?"

"Slim's here and we're playing his new video game."

"Which game?"

I told him.

"Don't know it. Is it good?"

We ended up talking for almost half an hour. Finally, Justin said, "So, can you come over when you're done playing?"

"It might be late."

"Just come when you're done," he said, and hung up.

I went back and sat down by Slim.

"You're going over there later, right?" Slim asked, still pushing buttons on the console and watching the screen.

"Do you think I should?"

"Follow the fun, *amigo.*"

I woke up in Justin's bed again. I'd gotten there after midnight, and was sound asleep when his alarm went off at eight a.m. I finally reached over and turned it off and read the time. Shit. Justin rolled over and covered his head with his pillow.

I shook him. "Hey, why is your alarm set so late? I gotta be at work in half an hour!"

"Well, go get ready, then. Do you want coffee? Or I have a Monster in the fridge."

"Monster," I said, grabbing my clothes.

By the time I showered and dressed, Justin was dressed for work and sitting at the little kitchen counter eating a bowl of cereal, his head buried in a law textbook. He looked up when I came in.

"I forgot to ask you last night," he said. "How is Domingo's defense shaping up? Any developments?"

I sighed loudly. "I'm not awake enough to talk about work. *Caramba! Bambino!* Is that the only suit you got?" I asked.

He turned back to his book and made a rude hand gesture.

I came up behind him and placed my chin on top of his red head. "I'll take you shopping," I said.

I made it to the office only a few minutes late. Lucy was in the front room, staring disapprovingly at a document.

"Thank God you're finally here."

"What's up?"

"Look," she said, waving the paper. "This is bullshit."

Lucy only swears when she is way pissed about something. I've only seen it happen a few times. When she starts to swear, she's at number nine on her irritation scale. I might have said it's a ten, but one time I was talking about it with our investigator Claude, and he said, "Brother, I hope you never see her at ten."

I sat down. "What is it?"

"It's new discovery from the DA's office. It was faxed over late last night, after we'd left. It's a statement by Paolo Sanchez, the ex-gangster Patty interviewed the day she died. Sanchez says Domingo is a member of the Bustamente-Arias gang, the gang that's fighting with the Cantara cartel. It says Domingo is suspected of killing a woman who was a member of Cantara. Sanchez claims he told Patty all of this when she interviewed him. The DA's going to argue Patty told Domingo what she'd learned, and Domingo killed her to keep her quiet."

"Shit," I said. "None of that was in that draft declaration of Patty's, or any of the other files Justin gave me. What's going on?"

"This is fucking bullshit," Lucy repeated. "It's way too convenient. Someone with the cops or the DA got to this Sanchez person, and is paying him. Or threatened him. He's lying. They're fucking with our client, Armando. They think they can pull this shit with him 'cause he's poor and helpless. I bet they've got something on Sanchez, something maybe from their buddies at immigration. Shit. They know when they lie like this we can't do a fucking thing about it. They were probably laughing when they wrote this. God *damn*."

I took the statement from her hand and read it. If Sanchez stuck to it, his testimony would kill Domingo at trial. The first part was nothing new. The Bustamente-Arias cartel had recently been challenging the Cantara cartel for control of the drug-traffic corridor through the El Paso area. Domingo had published a series of articles linking the famous singer Rudolfo to Cantara. But the rest of the statement was what had my boss throwing a hissy fit.

According to Sanchez, Domingo and his uncle Francisco were both active members of the Bustamente-Arias cartel, and Domingo used his position as a reporter to attack the Cantara cartel and to support his uncle Francisco's attempts to get into political office. Sanchez declared that "word on the street" was Domingo had personally been involved in the shooting death of a woman named Sabrina, a Cantara gang member who had been a girlfriend of Rudolfo's. The Bustamente-Arias gang had claimed responsibility for the killing as retaliation for an earlier Cantara killing.

"This is some serious shit," I said. "He's a gang member and he's been accused of killing another woman? What's a jury going to think about that? And how can we prove the rumor's not true? Sanchez is just saying all this based on 'word on the street!'"

"Blatant hearsay," said Lucy. "They know the judge won't let it in. What are they up to?"

It was hard for me to believe the DA would manufacture such false information. Lucy calls me cynical and apathetic, but I have noticed many times I still have faith in our system and our government where she does not. Nothing cruel or corrupt surprises her.

We talked about what Patty would have done if Sanchez had told her Domingo was a gang member suspected of murdering a woman. Would Patty really have threatened to expose Domingo?

"Wait a minute," I said. "She was his attorney. Wouldn't that information be privileged or something?"

"Possibly. But by getting romantically involved with Domingo, Patty had already crossed some lines. If they were having a lover's quarrel, she might have made a stupid threat." Lucy frowned. She has unlimited compassion for her wayward clients, but hates to see lack of self-control in a professional.

Lucy continued, "If I were prosecuting this case, I'd argue Patty was mentally unstable, she made a threat to expose Domingo, and Domingo thought she would do it and decided to kill her. Now they can say he planned to kill her to cover up his involvement in a gang murder. The really bad news is, they can use this bullshit lie to say that the whole thing was planned in advance. They've made up a case with all of the elements of first-degree murder."

"But if Sanchez had really told Patty that Domingo was a gang member and a killer, why would Patty have prepared that draft declaration for Sanchez to sign? That declaration was written the day before Patty died. And it contradicts this new statement from Sanchez. It looked like she thought Sanchez would be a positive witness for Domingo."

"That's one reason I think Sanchez is lying. Let's go see what Domingo has to say about all this. I'm going to make this stunt backfire on those bastards."

10

I blinked at the change in Domingo's appearance. Even before we told him about the declaration accusing him of the murder in Mexico, he radiated gloom. His chiseled features looked unnaturally tight, and grey stubble darkened his jaw. I'd have to get him busy with a razor before the trial.

When Lucy told him about Paolo Sanchez's declaration, the color drained out of his face. He looked at me and spoke in Spanish.

I translated for Lucy, "Tell the lawyer I'm sorry but there's nothing to be done."

"Tell him if he wants to give up, I can leave right now," Lucy said. "If he wants to fight, he needs to start helping us. I have to hear his whole story."

Before I could translate, Domingo spoke. "Don't go. I'll tell you my story. Of course, I want to fight."

He leaned forward in his seat, elbows on his knees, so he was at eye level with Lucy and me. "My life hasn't been especially... how shall I say, noble? But I am not a bad person like that statement says. I grew up in Juarez. My parents were upper middle class, and they could afford to send my brothers and me to university in Vera Cruz. I was a good student, but what I really loved was basketball. I played for a couple teams in Europe, until I became injured. So I came back to Mexico, thirty-two years old, with nothing but a bad knee and some good memories.

"I started looking for work. I did a little bit of modeling. I tried to get a job coaching, but most schools are too poor to pay their coaches. Then my uncle Francisco got me a job working for his newspaper. It was like a new start to my life. I started covering sports, and then they moved me to entertainment. I met interesting people, and I was good at writing about them. I wrote these articles on Rudolfo. You know him?"

Lucy and I nodded. "I've heard his music, but I don't know much about him," I told Domingo.

"Rudolfo is a singer, but he is more than a singer. His songs are inspirational. He writes songs about the working people, the poor people. Some of his songs are *narcocorridas*, songs that make heroes out of drug dealers. That sounds bad to people in your country, but it's more complicated than it sounds. Maybe you can understand it if you understand your country's Rap music. Or if you like to watch the old Western movies that glorify the outlaws in America's Wild West."

Lucy loves Westerns. She was looking proud and relieved, like a stage mother watching an audition. Domingo's face had relaxed and lit up as he started to talk about his work. If he could do this with the jury....

"My series of articles on Rudolfo was very extensive. While I was writing the articles, I had the opportunity to travel with him and get to know him. He is a charismatic and thoughtful man. There were all kinds of people around him, of course. The people around him included high level-drug dealers, who could buy their way in to any part of society and who peddled their products to the hangers-on in Rudolfo's entourage. In my articles, I mentioned some of these people, but I did not mean to imply Rudolfo was part of Cantara, or any other drug cartel.

"That's where I was so stupidly naïve. A dumb jock, not thinking about the whole big political picture, about what happens when you get anywhere near the gang wars in Mexico. I was a new reporter. My editors should have picked it up. They should have taken out those parts. But they didn't.

Instead they made them bigger, pulled quotes out of place, and made them the focus of the article. Now I know why they did it. The newspaper is controlled by the Bustamente-Arias cartel, which is fighting with Cantara. I was just a *pendejo,* a fool in their little game. Cantara put a price on my head."

Lucy asked, "What about your uncle, Francisco?"

"*Tio Francisco* was part of the whole thing. I don't think he meant to put my life in danger. But he got appointed to be the head of the Culture Ministry. Rudolfo had wanted that position, to help do good in the community through the arts, but my articles killed his chances for that. Francisco helped me get out of Mexico and gave me a little money to live on when I got here."

"Do you know this man, Paolo Sanchez?"

"No. I remember Patty telling me she wanted to interview him, that this professor recommended him as someone who knew about Cantara. I told her not to do that, that I'd have my *Tio Francisco* take care of that angle."

"Why would Sanchez say you were involved?"

"If he is trying to help Cantara make me look bad, or get me in trouble, that would be a good way to do it."

"What do you know about this woman who was killed?"

"Sabrina was killed in an attack at her home in Sinaloa, along with six men, including one of her brothers who was high up in the Cantara cartel," Domingo said. "This happened about a week before I left Mexico. Bustamente-Arias left a note taking responsibility for the crime. I was hundreds of miles away, in Juarez, when Sabrina was killed. I was at a large birthday party for one of the editors of our newspaper, so it is no problem to find witnesses to testify I was in Juarez that night. It is stupid of Cantara to accuse me of this."

"Did you know Sabrina, Domingo?"

"That's no secret, *Abogada,*" he said. "Sabrina was still with Rudolfo last summer, when I traveled with him to prepare my articles. That relationship, I tell you, I could have written a whole novel about how that woman tried to run Rudolfo into the ground. If someone hadn't shot her, she would have done the job herself with drugs and alcohol. She was a holy mess.

"I was used by my uncle and my so-called friends, the publishers at *Commoción,* in their political game. Now I've got a reputation as a puppet for the B-A gang. Or worse." He threw up his hands and gave a wry smile. "But what can I do? Right now I have more pressing problems." His big hands gestured towards the cold cement walls of the interview room.

"Let's talk about Patty," Lucy said. "Why are you still so angry about her wanting to investigate Cantara? She was just doing her job. Do you have a problem with women working?"

There it was, the twitch of the lips and a spark from the beautiful dark eyes. This was the scary look that Lucy really didn't want the jury to see. Quickly, the look was gone and he put his head in his hands. After a minute, he looked up and his eyes were just very sad.

"You have my number, *Abogada.* I am still angry at Patty, but I'm mostly angry at myself, because I failed to protect her. I've been torturing myself over this ever since she died. I should have stayed with her that night. She…I never felt this way about a woman before. She was so gentle and loving, but she was very driven to prove herself in her work, without depending on me. I couldn't believe a woman could have all of those qualities at once. She was... *simpatica.* I was afraid I wouldn't be able to protect her the way I wanted to."

"Protect her from what?"

"Well, the fucking dangerous mess my life was in, to start with."

"Other than that, did you think she needed protecting from something?"

He frowned. "Like what?"

"I'm asking you."

"Well. There was a quality about her. She seemed vulnerable, like she wouldn't see danger if it was coming. Like she was too good."

"Her friend Christine says she tended to be dramatic, maybe emotionally unstable."

"That is a lie. Patty was a sweet and calm woman, a real lady. She could be passionate, but she never dramatized or tried to manipulate people. Christine is a controlling woman. She didn't like Patty spending so much time with me."

Lucy said, "Domingo, we've learned that Patty did interview Paolo Sanchez, the day before she died. Are you sure she didn't tell you about it?"

Domingo widened his eyes and his face darkened with anger. Then he leaned forward and put his head in his hands.

"Domingo?" Lucy waited. "You have to tell us what happened."

He looked up. "My God," he said. "You won't believe me, but I tell you I didn't know. That's what we argued about. I warned her not to touch that part of my case. I told her I would take care of it. Do you know what this means? They killed her, to get revenge on me. She tried to help me and they killed her." Domingo looked at us. "Be careful."

11

"It was too late when he saw the federales. They stood in a row, like the bars on a jail cell. He could see the black holes on the business ends of their rifles. He had walked into a trap. He had to surrender or to die. His life had been a golden trap."

"This isn't your kind of music," I said to Claude. "What's a soul brother doing listening to *narcocorridas?*"

We were in Claude's black Cadillac, cruising slowly along Imperial Avenue towards Barrio Logan. On my previous outings with Claude, his CD player always played soul oldies.

Claude Washington is one of the few private investigators in town Lucy will work with. He's about Lucy's age, medium height, with really black skin and short black hair that is just starting to grey. A scar runs down the left side of his face. He has known Lucy apparently forever, as far as I can tell when I hear them talking about the past.

"I'm doing some research for you, girlie. Lucy and I talked about your case last night. This here's Rudolfo, that singer your case is all wrapped up with. Tell you what. I'll give you the CD. It's not my preferred genre, and I don't speak the lingo."

"Gee, thanks, Claude."

"No problemo. I was gonna bill it to Lucy anyway. What's the song about?"

I translated some of the words for him and then gave him the short version of the story as the song went on. "The guy's a drug lord who grew up poor and joined a gang when he was young. It was his way out. He traveled all the way to Spain. He became a hero in his community. When he went back home to see his old girlfriend, the federales were waiting for him. He figures out his girl has tipped them off. Instead of surrendering, he starts shooting and the soldiers kill him."

Claude and I listened for a couple of minutes. "Not my style, but this Rudolfo has quite a voice," Claude admitted. "I like the long, high notes. So, Lucy says this Sanchez kid was helping your client with his immigration case. Then the DA talked to him and he went sideways on you. Lucy figures the DA got something on him and told him what they wanted him to say. I hate to tell you, but it could be even worse than you think. It might not be the DA that's got to him."

"You mean, who, Immigration?"

"Get real, girlie. I got news for you. The Mexican cartels are all over this side of the border. If this Cantara gang is really after Torres, they could be using this kid to get him. It might be hard to do a hit on Torres in the jail, but once he gets to prison it'll be a piece of cake."

After Claude's scary talk, the Barrio Connection after-school program was an anti-climax. Teenagers played games, ate snacks, and worked on homework on long cafeteria tables. As they looked up when we came in, I saw the familiar hard stare I remembered from high school.

While I was looking around, Claude had zeroed in on our target. He detached a big young man from a group of kids playing Wii on a large flat-screen TV. They walked over to me.

"Paolo, this is Armando Felan. He works with Domingo Torres' attorney."

Paolo shook my hand with a firm grip. He was tall, over six feet, with a heavy build like a rugby or football player. His hair was cut to about a half-inch long all around, and he had a plump, pretty-boy face with perfect skin and girlish lips.

"Hey, Armando. Nice to meet you. Let me show you around?" Like he was sure our main interest in being there was to see the important work he was doing.

"Sure," I said. Claude nodded.

Paolo took us on a circuit of the big room, stopping by each station of kids and talking about what they were working on. He shared some of his program's success stories, and explained the program's outreach efforts in the schools. He seemed more like a used car salesman than the tough gangsters I had met. We played along with his act as we circled the room.

Claude, who had been following us and looking around the room in silence, took over the questioning. "OK, Paolo. Let's cut to the nitty gritty. What gang do you claim?"

An angel's smile played on the boy's red mouth. "Oh, no, I'm all done with that, man. I've been out of that scene for two years. I'm getting my GED and going to college."

"That's BS, man. You told the DA that you know what's goin' on inside the Cantara cartel. You gave the DA real specific information that only someone in that gang would know. So you claimin' Cantara?"

Paolo smiled sweetly. "If I was still in the gangs, why would I be working here for a lousy ten bucks an hour?"

Claude shook his head. "If you wasn't in the gangs, your ass would be dead by now. What are you getting for your testimony?"

Although Claude had kept his voice low, some of the kids in the room had sensed the tension between him and Paolo. A couple of them got out of their seats. Paolo turned his head to look at them.

"It's cool, guys." He waved them back to their seats. "Let me finish my business."

Claude stood and folded his arms as he and Paolo and I watched and waited until the kids got back to their activities. Then Claude deployed his secret weapon. He gave Paolo a stare that made the husky kid start and take a step backwards.

Claude took a step towards him and spoke quietly in a neutral tone. "Listen to me, boy. I can see you been through a lot. I respect that. Maybe you feel safe up here this side of the border, with the DA actin' like they be on your side. But you know the DA's still gonna fuck up your case with the Immigration. After you give them what they need, they'll make sure your ass gets deported."

Paolo hesitated a moment and then he shrugged. "I don't think so. I got a good lawyer for that."

Claude shook his head. "OK., we're almost done with you and your bullshit. Who told you Domingo Torres worked for Bustamente-Arias?" Claude asked.

"I don't remember. It's just something I heard."

"Where did you hear it? When?"

They went around for a while but Paolo continued to smile and give vague answers. Maybe he heard it like a year or six months ago. Maybe at a party or at work. He really couldn't remember.

Claude pulled Paolo's statement to the DA out of his jacket pocket.

"We got a mistake here. It says you told attorney Patty Taylor that Domingo Torres was a killer for the B-A cartel. You didn't tell her that, did you?"

"You mean the lady lawyer who got killed? Sure I did."

"Sure you did what?"

"I told the lady I heard Torres was in with Bustamente-Arias."

"When did you tell Attorney Taylor you heard Torres was a killer for B-A?"

"I told her the day she came to talk to me. She wanted to make a case that Cantara was after Domingo. I said, maybe so, 'cause Domingo was part of Bustamente-Arias. I heard those gangs don't like each other too good."

"How many times did you talk to Ms. Taylor?"

"Just the one time. She came here one afternoon, just like you did today. She talked to me. The next day, she died." His face took on a look of concern. "Poor lady. She seemed real nice. She was very interested in our program."

As Claude drove back to the office, I took the Rudolfo CD out of his player and put it in the CD case. The cover showed a plumpish man with a humorous face, wearing a stylized, bright-red mariachi outfit, holding his guitar up next to his head in a mock power salute. Five of his band members stood behind him, wearing black suits, hands on their hips, with amused smiles on their faces. I put the CD in my briefcase.

The interview with Paolo had been unsettling. Watching him spar with Claude had been like watching people converse in a foreign language. I usually have a good sense of people when I interview them, but I could not get any reading from Paolo. If I hadn't known he was lying, I'd have said he was a nice kid.

"Claude, what did you get out of that interview? Where is that kid coming from?"

"That baby-faced kid is a first class gangsta'. I don't know what he's doin' in that place. Only thing I can figure is Cantara's got him on special assignment. He's gonna get his citizenship and he'll work for them on this side of the border. Maybe recruit kids from his little program. You see how those boys looked at him? Look how he's worked the system."

"Why do you think he's telling those lies about Domingo?"

"Can't say for sure. I still think the Cantara gang could have put him up to it. But did you see him when I brought up his immigration case? My guess is, he ran into some problem with ICE. Probably a prior juvenile or criminal conviction. The DA might have offered to make that go away if he played ball with them."

"That's what Lucy thought when we first saw his statement."

"She's a smart lady."

Lucy was pleased we had gotten Paolo to admit he'd only met with Patty one time. "We can use the declaration Patty drafted to impeach his statement that he told Patty Domingo was a gang member. I should be able to kick his testimony."

I spent the next day working mostly on other cases, although I was able to reach Karen Chang, the head of the Immigration Attorney's Association, to see what she knew about Frank Slattery. I got the names of his two most recent ex-wives, both of whom were practicing attorneys in San Diego. Chang also told me one of them had gotten a restraining order against Frank during some ugly divorce proceedings.

"Do you know why she got the restraining order?"

"The usual kind of reasons," Chang said. "She kicked him out, and he kept trying to get back in the house, and he kept calling her."

"Did he ever hurt her physically?"

"Not that I heard. He can be a bulldog, at least in his professional life. Anyone who's had to work with him knows that."

"No kidding," I said, my hand dropping to the bruise on my back. "Has anyone ever filed a claim of sexual harassment against him?"

"Not that I know of. But he does have that reputation."

By five o'clock, I had set up appointments with both of the Slattery marriage veterans. On my way to meet Justin for drinks, I decided to stop by Christine and Brad's house to see if Brad was back.

As I walked up the path to the front door, I caught the scent of baking bread. The door was open, and I knocked on the closed metal screen. Christine rose from the couch and came to the door.

"Oh, Armando, what a nice surprise! Come in, come in. Sit down."

Following her in, I was startled to see Patty's brother Sam seated on the couch, holding a square-headed baby. He had taken his glasses off, and with his round face and spiky hair, he had the look of a baby himself.

"Oh, hey," he said. "What's up?"

"Isn't Sam good with little Ethan?" Christine said. "I'm lucky to have him here while Brad's been away. Sam's been cooking, and watching the baby."

"Yeah, right, stop exaggerating. I just turned on the breadmaker when you told me to," Sam said. He jiggled the baby and started to make silly faces at it.

Christine looked at me and rolled her eyes, as if to say, "He won't even let me say something nice about him."

"Armando, how are you? Is there any news about the case? You certainly work long hours. You must be tired. Can I get you a drink? A snack?"

"No thanks, I'm going out to dinner in a little bit. I just stopped by to see Brad."

Christine and Sam exchanged a glance.

"He's still out of town," Christine said. "I talked to him Sunday night after I talked to you. I told him to call you and he said he would. But I haven't talked to him since then. Sometimes when he's out of town on business he doesn't call every night. Now tell me about you. How's your investigation coming along?"

"It's getting a little more complicated," I said. "Did Patty or Domingo ever talk to you about the drug cartel that was supposed to be after Domingo?"

"Let me think. I'm sure Patty did, in a general way." Christine pursed her lips as she thought. "Patty told me Domingo was applying for political asylum, and he had to prove he would be in danger if he went back to Mexico. She was trying to work with a professor who was supposed to be an expert on Mexican gangs. He gave her some leads, but she said he was kind of a pompous ass. You know, the kind who talks a lot and says nothing and you have to listen to them because they're the professor. Right? God, how I hated school."

I laughed. "Tell me about it." I did my imitation of a professor from whom I'd taken Art History at the local community college a couple years ago. I'd thought it would be a good idea to go back to school part time, and I hadn't been back since.

Christine threw back her head and laughed. Her laughter was intense and contagious, and she, Sam and I ended up having one of those laughing fits where you really can't stop. Finally, the baby got concerned and started to cry, making Christine stop and reach for him.

Sam handed off the baby and asked me if I wanted a beer.

"Not this time, thanks. I'm on my way to get a drink with some friends."

"Nice."

"So what were we talking about?" Christine said. "Oh, yes, the drug gang that was after Domingo. Armando, could the gang be responsible for killing Patty? At the time, I agreed with Patty that Domingo was being overprotective. I didn't think she might really be getting in over her head."

"Patty didn't tell you about meeting with a former gang member?"

"She told me she'd had that fight with Domingo, but I don't think she told me she'd actually talked with anyone already. Did she? Did she go alone? Patty did say she had a law clerk helping her with Domingo's case. I can't remember his name. She said he was super smart and really wanted to win the case. If it was dangerous, why didn't he go with her?"

Good question. That reminded me it was almost time for me to go meet him. I got up to leave.

"Oh, one more question," I said. "Christine, did Patty ever talk to you about her boss, Frank Slattery?"

"Wow, you are covering a lot of ground. I can't believe how much you have already done in this case. You guys are amazing. You've gone so far beyond anything the police did. Attorney Frank Slattery, huh? Patty found him very difficult to work with. She said he was a real jerk and made the office environment unpleasant by yelling all the time. When she started working there, he was harassing her, asking her out and not taking no for an answer." She frowned. "I'd forgotten about that. Maybe I didn't take it seriously enough. God, this is getting complicated. I wish it could all be over." Christine sighed. She put her finger out and the baby grabbed it.

I said goodbye to Christine and Sam, leaving them on the couch playing with the baby while I let myself out the front door.

12

I got to the Bar Bar before Justin. The booths were full so I sat at the bar and ordered a mojito. As I waited for Justin, I went over the new routine I was going to teach in my dance class the next morning. The fingers of my left hand danced on the bar counter as I sipped my drink.

"*Que estas tomando?*" A voice said from behind me.

"*Que?*" I said, as I swiveled my seat around one way, then the other. There was Justin, smiling down at me. I looked behind him but there was no one there.

I flushed. "You speak Spanish?"

"Sometimes," he said. "So what are you drinking?"

"Mojito."

"Say, Armando," Justin said, sitting down next to me and signaling the bartender for another mojito, "what were you doing with your hands before?"

"*Estas referiendo a anoche?* Are you referring to last night?"

He blushed. "No, this." His long hands imitated my fingers dancing on the bar.

"You were watching me."

"Yeah. You looked like you were working on something, not just fidgeting."

I explained about going over the new steps for my Latin Craze Hip Hop class.

"You're a dancer."

"I was in a little local company when I was in high school. Now I just do some teaching."

"Why did you stop being in the company?"

"I needed to find a job where I could support myself. My dad kicked me out of the house when I was still in high school. I didn't want to wait tables and live poor all my life."

Later that night, Justin was searching his refrigerator for a Monster, for me to take on my drive home. He said, "So. We still haven't talked about the Torres case. Or about Frank. I have questions for you. You probably have questions for me. I think we should go ahead and talk about it. I don't want it to get in the way between you and me."

"I know. That's why I've been avoiding it." I felt the little "bad idea" voice buzzing in the back of my head.

"I understand." He pulled a Monster out of the back of the refrigerator, and held it as he looked at me. "I think it's better to talk about it. You don't have to tell me anything that's privileged. I'm just really curious about how Domingo's case is developing. I'm the one who got you started on looking into Patty's investigation of the Cantara cartel. Patty and I were planning on doing some of that together. Are you still looking at that angle?"

I looked at Justin. He met my eyes and brushed his hair back from his forehead.

"OK," I said. "Yeah, that's become a big part of the case now." I told him about Paolo Sanchez's new statement to the DA. "Obviously," I said, "the DA is going to try and use Sanchez's testimony that Domingo works for the Bustamente-Arias cartel, and argue Domingo killed Patty when she threatened to expose him."

Justin's face darkened as I told him the details of Sanchez's statement.

"That's bullshit!" he said angrily, when I finished. "You've seen the declaration Patty drafted after she met with Paolo. It's completely inconsistent with what Paolo is saying now. What does that dumb kid think he is doing? He's out of control!"

"What do you mean? Out of whose control?" I asked.

"Well, I meant, he's out of control of whoever's pulling his strings."

"Isn't that the DA? They're the ones who got him to make the statement."

"True. I'm just trying to say, don't you think Sanchez is still involved with Cantara? They're a lot smarter than the DA. They wouldn't put him up to this. They would know this statement will just destroy his credibility and his usefulness."

"Oh, wow, I see what you mean."

It was a relief to be talking about the case. Lucy had been tied up in court a lot and we hadn't had much of a chance to talk things out. I told him about our interview with Paolo and he listened intently.

Finally, I took the Monster out of his hand and got up to go. Justin cleared his throat. "Now. About Frank."

I sat back down and sighed. "Your boss."

"My boss."

"What."

"Why did you subpoena him for the preliminary hearing? What could he possibly know about Patty's murder?" He looked at me accusingly, and then down at the kitchen counter.

I hesitated. "Justin, you know I can't do this. Please don't go there."

Justin looked up at me. His dark eyes flashed. "This sucks."

"Frank's asked you to help him make this go away," I stated.

"I also want it to go away so it's not an issue between you and me. I know Frank. He can be rude and obnoxious sometimes, but he wouldn't kill anyone. I can guess what road you're on with him, and I don't want you to waste your time."

"You know this isn't right, Justin. You're the law student."

His head jerked back like I'd slapped him.

"Sorry," I said. "I don't want to hurt you. Maybe we need a break to figure this out." I got up to go. As I left, he was still seated at the counter with his arms crossed and his broad shoulders hunched.

***

The next day, when it was time to start thinking about leaving work, I was agonizing about whether to call Justin and try to make up. Maybe I should just go home. Mom and I could do some catching up over dinner.

Lucy came out of her office to put some paperwork in my inbox. "Tell me what happened today with the ex-wives of Frank Slattery. Hmmm, sounds like the name of a soap opera."

I told her the ladies had not been very helpful. In fact, like Justin, they'd seemed remarkably loyal to Frank.

"I can't understand what that jerk has that inspires such devotion," I told Lucy. "One thing I noticed, though. Slattery definitely has a 'type.' Both women were the same superficial type as Christine: tall, quiet, fair coloring."

"Maybe he considers himself to be a Svengali. It can be hard for some women to resist that kind of attention."

"Yeah, I guess."

"What's wrong?" Lucy said. "You've been quiet all day."

I couldn't tell her about Justin. "It's my mom," I said. "I think I need to spend more time with her. My sister Connie called me this morning, and said mom offered to help her find some childcare. Mom's started taking Community College classes and she won't be able to baby sit anymore. Connie thinks Mom's having some kind of breakdown."

Lucy frowned. "Since when is a woman taking classes a sign of a breakdown?"

"You would say that."

"I'm serious. It's time for her to do something for herself. Your mom's just raised all of her kids and finally gotten them out of the house." She looked at my face and her eyes rounded with that deer in the headlights look.

"Go ahead. Remind me. I'm twenty-four years old, and I'm still living at home with my mother. I'm having a shitty day anyway. Here, here's where Frank Slattery gave me a big ol' bruise." I pointed to the spot on my back. "You can kick me on the other side."

"You said it, not me. But I didn't mean it that way. You're too touchy. I'm just saying, why should she have to spend her days taking care of your sister's kids?"

"Some women love to take care of kids," I said.

Lucy's expression hardened. "So I hear."

"I didn't mean…." Maybe I had, I thought. I just wasn't going to get through another hour of work today, so I let myself get mad. "Never mind. Time for me to go home and see what Mommy's made for dinner."

Great, I thought, as I left the office and walked to my car. I got in the car and sat for a few minutes. I fished in my briefcase and stuck the Rudolfo CD into my player while I thought about what I wanted to do. After my talk with Lucy, my pride kept me from going home to dinner with Mom. And today was Mom's day to have her long lunch at the TJ country club, after which she often neglected to make a real dinner. I'd gotten fuck-all done in my investigation of Domingo's case. The only boy I wanted to be with right now should probably be off limits until we resolved the case, which wasn't going to be happening any time soon. I'd insulted my boss and acted like a petty child. What else could go wrong?

Before I could start my car, my phone rang, and I answered it without looking at who was calling.

"Armando?"

"Oh, hi, Connie. Listen, I can't really talk, I'm…."

"Armando, it's Mom. She's been kidnapped."

13

I picked up Connie at her home in an upscale part of the Eastlake development in Chula Vista. While we bombed south towards the border, Connie filled me in. Dad had received a phone call at his office in downtown Tijuana. The caller said they had taken Mom and they would let her go if Dad paid a hundred and fifty thousand US dollars, in cash, by Friday at the end of the business day. Dad wanted all four of his children at his home in Tijuana at once. Gaby, who had been staying with him for a few days, was already there.

"Is Mom OK? Did Dad talk to her?" I asked.

"I don't know. I didn't talk to Dad. Chuy called me and told me what happened and asked me to call you and get down there as soon as possible. He was on his way to Dad's house. He and Dad were about to get on the phone to their accountants to get the money together."

My big brother Chuy followed in Dad's footsteps, handling most of the international business for Dad's firm. He loves making money almost as much as his wife loves spending it. It was just luck he was in town, since he's out of the country on business a lot.

"I don't know what I'd do without Mom." Connie started to cry. "She should have been more careful. Did she take the Lexus? I told her not to take the Lexus."

"Mom didn't want to live in fear."

"Well, she could have thought about us. She has grandchildren. Who's going to take care of them? She loves them so much." Connie was sobbing. "What am I going to tell my little ones?"

We reached the border crossing. It was seven o'clock, the rush hour traffic was winding down, and there were only about ten cars ahead of us. Connie wiped her eyes and sat quietly as I drove through the inspection area.

Connie and I stayed quiet as I merged onto the straight highway that parallels the border all the way to Playas and the coast. Tall orange lights illuminated the border fence, monolithic against the dark sky. I forced myself to keep my speed down, fighting the irrational thought that when we got to Dad's house, Mom would be there and I could take her home.

"Oh, God, oh God," Connie said, hiccupping a sob. I waited for her to make her point, until I realized she was praying. Connie is the only one of our immediate family who is a devout Catholic. Dad and Chuy still attend church to keep their business networks healthy. My little sister Gaby, who refused to undergo the traditional Quinceñera celebration when she turned fifteen, calls herself an "antitheist." She explained to me this means that she thinks all organized religion is harmful, maybe even evil.

Me, well, it's a long story. Let me just say, for now, that going back to the church would be like eating a watermelon with way too many seeds in it. The amount of bullshit I'd have to filter out poisons the good that might be in it. I wish I could be like my friend Slim. To him, the church is like a perfectly ripe pomegranate, and he relishes every bit of it. Crunching through those nasty seeds just makes him stronger. He likes to go to confession and give the priests detailed descriptions of his frequent mortal sins.

I thought about Mom's relationship to the church. We had not talked about God or the Church for years. Mom would still go with Dad to church events to support his business networking, but she didn't attend church on her own. She had always loved the rituals of the holidays, and making big traditional holiday meals for the family. Where was she now? If she was even still alive, was she turning to God for comfort?

We reached the top of the hill and Playas spread out below us, with the landmark bullring silhouetted in the city lights. I call our family home here "Dad's house," since he is the only one who lives here all the time now. Mom stays here with him sometimes, but it has never really been her home. The family moved to San Diego before I was born, renting out the old home in Tijuana, and buying the house in Playas for Dad to stay when business kept him late, and for the family to stay in on school vacations. When Gaby left for college a couple of years ago, Dad started to live at the Playas house most of the time, with Mom staying home in Chula Vista.

We parked and walked towards the house. That night, as always, the familiar smell of the cool salty sea air and the diesel fumes that hit you as soon as you cross the border combined with the sounds of faraway music, trucks downshifting on the nearby highway, and breaking ocean waves. I associated Dad's house with the hardest days of my growing up, those long family summers when I was still trying so hard to appear to be something I wasn't, and so amazed when people, especially my Dad, didn't see right through me and shun me.

Sr. Orlando Felan was in the living room with my brother Chuy, my little sister Gaby, and two men I didn't know. Gaby and Chuy got up and came over to us and greeted us without words, Gaby hugging Connie briefly and then hanging on to me a little longer. Chuy grabbed my hand and my shoulder for a man-shake, and took Connie's hands and gave her a formal kiss on the cheek. We walked over to Dad, who hugged Connie, and shook my hand, the first time we had touched in many years.

"Connie, Armando, *Gracias a Dios*, you are here safely." His voice shook with emotion. Dad was heavier, and his dark, strong-featured face had more lines in it since I had last seen him, and his thick hair was almost all gray. Tonight he looked very foreign to me, with the heavy gold chain around his neck and the large jade and gold ring he always wore on his little finger.

"Can you tell us anything more?" I asked. "Did you talk to Mom?"

"No, I asked to talk to her but I did not. They called me at the office at about five thirty. It was a man who said, 'Don't hang up, I have your wife.' I asked whether she was OK. He said she was not harmed. He said they would not hurt her and they will set her free, if we give them the money. They will call again Friday with more instructions. I asked how we would know she is OK, and he said, 'She will talk to you, before you bring the money.' That was all."

"What can we do to help?"

Dad said, "I...," closed his mouth, opened it again, and stopped. I had never seen him at a loss for words. There was a long silence. My brother Chuy exchanged glances with the two strangers, who were seated at a card table covered with papers.

Chuy spoke for the first time. "We've brought Sr. Rivera and Sr. Posada, to help us get the cash for the payment. They have been going over our assets. We don't have enough liquid assets to make a hundred fifty K in cash right away."

"You mean we can't pay in time?" Connie squeaked. "For God's sake! It's not that much money! What will they do if we can't pay in time? Did you tell them she has grandchildren? Can't they wait for us to raise the money?"

Sr. Rivera cleared his throat. "If I may say something, Señora." Normally, I'd have written him off as just another one of my dad's business buddies, an oily middle-aged man in a wine-colored polo shirt, wire-framed glasses, too much gold, and a prosperity paunch. But tonight he was the all-powerful God of Industry, potential savior of my mother.

"This may be a comfort to you," he said, in a soft, dry voice. "As you must know, these *sequestros* have become rather common in the past few years. We know what to expect. The people who took your mother are probably members of an organized, ah, association. They won't hurt her. They just want money, to help finance their operations. It's in their interest to give us time to raise the money and to return your mother safely. A smooth transaction, and the safe return of the victim means, from a business point of view, er… well, not to put too fine a point on it, it will be good for their future business if people know that payment of the ransom will ensure the victim's safe return. Having said that, it is in everyone's interest not to delay, and to get the money paid on time. The question is how best to do so."

"Wait a minute," Gaby said. "What you are saying is, by paying the ransom, we're helping keep the kidnappers in business, to do this again."

"Er, yes, you could put it that way."

"Shouldn't we at least talk about going to the police?" Gaby asked. She ran a hand through her short, dark hair. Her large brown eyes narrowed as she looked at Dad's advisors accusingly.

"Uhhhhh…." Sr. Rivera looked at his associate, who turned to Chuy.

Before Chuy could speak, Dad said in a clear, firm voice, "We are not going to talk about going to the police. It is too risky. She's mine, I want her back."

Gaby's pretty face was still puckered in a frown, but she knew enough to let go of the issue. "I still don't understand," she said. "I thought we were rich. We own a lot of property as well as your business. A hundred and fifty thousand must be small change to you, Dad."

"I'm not saying we don't have the money, Gaby. But we don't keep it all lying around in the bank, we have it invested in various places. There are significant penalties for cashing in some of those investments on short notice. Armando, you asked what you could do to help. We are looking at the most advantageous way to raise the money by Friday afternoon. All of you children are listed as part owners on some of the firm's real property and other assets. You may be needed to sign documents here tonight, or at bank offices tomorrow or Friday. The way you can help right now is to stay out of the way while Chuy and I review our situation with our advisors. Gaby, why don't you and Connie go to the kitchen and make something to eat."

I trailed after the women into the kitchen.

Three hours later, Connie and I were driving back across the border. I had spent the evening mostly curled up in a chair in the kitchen, watching my sisters prepare and clean up from a simple meal of sandwiches that no one had had much interest in eating. After cleaning up, Gaby took the chair next to me and we sat in numbed silence. Connie talked to her husband on the telephone, walking him through the process of feeding the kids and putting them to bed, even though I'm pretty sure he usually does all those tasks anyway.

Occasionally, I'd drifted into the living room and listened to discussions involving "cash-out penalty, tax advantage," and "better interest rate on the other side." Early in the evening, I overheard Chuy on the cell phone with his wife. His normally aggressive tone softened. "Ai, *mi amor*, yes, she was driving the Lexus.... I don't know if they will give it back, *Querida*. .... But what can I do?"

After about two hours, Dad had called Connie and me into the living room to sign some papers.

"What are these for?" I asked.

"This is to cash out some investments at *Banco Naciónal*. There's a penalty, but it will be easy to get the cash out quickly if we need it.

"Now," Dad said, "I need you both to be available all day tomorrow and Friday in San Diego, as soon as the banks open. We're negotiating an emergency loan based on some rental properties I have over there. Your names are on the titles as part owners for, ah, tax purposes, and you'll need to sign off on the loan."

"What am I going to do with my kids? Ma was supposed to have them tomorrow. Ah, mama, how she must be worrying. The kids are her life."

Dad's voice rose. "Pull yourself together, Connie. If we can't get this loan, we're going to have to pay a huge penalty to cash out other investments. Bring the kids with you if you have to."

"What about the home in Chula Vista, Dad?" I asked. "Shouldn't we try for a loan on that, too?"

"Your mother's a co-owner of that house," Dad said. "She'd have to sign off on any loan. Anyway, I just got a loan on the property, to finance another purchase. There's not much equity left."

***

I got almost no sleep that night. Connie and I hadn't gotten back across the border until after one a.m. When I got home I showered and crawled into bed and had crazy fantasies of tracking down Mom and rescuing her, or committing desperate crimes to raise the money to pay her ransom myself. I needed to be doing something, but I was afraid of making things worse. Before we'd left Mexico, Dad had called us together in the living room.

"Before you go," he'd said, looking briefly at Connie, longer at me, and settling his gaze on Gaby, "Before you go, I want you to listen to some advice from Sr. Posada."

I had assumed Posada was some kind of flunky for Sr. Rivera's bank, but he spoke with the authority of a man who works for himself. "When your father called me, he wanted to talk about ways to find your mother and, ah, recover her. He asked me whether I had contacts within the police department who could be trusted to investigate this incident. I told him in my experience, which includes assisting over a dozen families in this situation, the only time there was a bad result was when the family, against my advice, tried to track down the kidnappers.

"In that case, one of the family members had associates who were active in a local gang, and the family put the word out in the street they were looking for the kidnappers. The situation quickly deteriorated, and the victim was found killed the next day. I won't tell you the details of what was done to her. What you need to know is the family's attempts to interfere resulted in *Los Badboys*, the local gang, becoming involved in a power struggle with the gang that was responsible for the kidnapping. The larger gang decided to forfeit the potential ransom and kill their hostage, to send a message to *Los Badboys*.

"Your father wanted me to tell you this so you don't try to be heroic. Going to the police could have exactly the same effect as trying to work with the gangs. I strongly urge you not to speak to anyone else beyond the immediate family, until this deal, uh, this matter, is resolved. I recommend you conduct your daily lives as if nothing unusual has happened, in case the, ah, perpetrators, are watching the family."

"Do we know what gang has Mom?" I asked.

"The border area is unstable at this time." Posada said, "It could be any one of several groups that are currently doing this kind of business."

Sr. Posada's warning had done the job. Even Gaby had whispered to me, as she walked me out to the car, "'Mando, promise me you won't do anything to try and find Mom," and Connie had spent a lot of the trip back speculating out loud about exactly what the kidnappers had done to the victim in Sr. Posada's story.

"Why did they pick on Mom?" she sobbed. "She doesn't even live in Mexico. The gangs don't kidnap people who live up here. We're Americans, not Mexicans." I had finally told her to shut up, but now I was torturing myself with the same pointless speculations. At last, I slept for about an hour.

14

I awoke trying to think what reason I would give Lucy for missing work. Then I remembered Posada's advice about keeping to my normal activities.

Like a zombie, I went through the motions of dressing and putting away my clothes from the night before. As I took my towel into the bathroom to hang it up, I saw something pink was hanging from the edge. It was a damp piece of paper, which I recognized as the joke flyer advertising a Tijuana kidnapping experience. The last time I had seen it had been in the kitchen when Mom and I were joking about it. How had it gotten into my room in the poolhouse?

The towel was still damp from my shower the night before. Water had soaked into the paper, turning the top half dark pink. When I pulled the paper off, the top stuck to the towel and tore into shreds. There was some writing on the back. I pulled the scraps of dark pink off of the towel and pieced together the written part. The ink had run in spots, but I assembled the pieces and could make out three words in block print: "*No te ocupes.*"

As I read the words, I froze. Don't get involved? I had a flashback to Domingo's face, two days ago, when he found out Patty had interviewed Paolo Sanchez the day she was killed. Domingo had told Lucy and me, "be careful." I saw Paolo Sanchez's exaggerated expression of concern, when he told me he was sorry about Patty's death. Mom's kidnapping, and this note, could only be a warning to me to stop investigating Cantara's involvement.

I rushed into the house, looking for any signs someone had been there and taken the flyer. Why would they have come to the house? They must have followed me home from my meeting with Paolo, followed Mom to Tijuana, and decided to take her. I didn't see any signs of the house being searched, but I knew they had been there, maybe spying on Mom while I was off at Justin's. Why had I left her alone?

Afraid to change my routine, in case Cantara was watching me, I left the house at the usual time. I drove to the office, parked, and walked to the office.

When I saw Lucy sipping her morning tea in the chair by the fireplace, I realized I wasn't going to be able to convince her call off our investigation without telling her what was happening. I described what had happened, and the warning note, and begged her to withdraw from Domingo's case.

After she realized I wasn't making a bad joke, Lucy looked genuinely shocked. "I'm so sorry, Armando. Your poor mother. That note...do you have that note with you?" she asked.

"No. I left it at home. Lucy, if we don't stop the investigation, they'll kill Mom, like they killed Patty."

"That's not likely. I think your father's friend gave you good advice. Treat this like a business transaction, keep the police out of it, and your mother will be returned to you."

"Don't you get it? They want us to back off!"

"I wonder why the warning was to you, not to me. I'm Domingo's attorney."

"It's because I interviewed Paolo. They don't want me to follow up."

"Fine. We don't need to do any more investigation related to the gang angle, at least until your Mother is back safe. There are several other avenues I want to explore in Domingo's case."

I started to feel relief for the first time that morning. Lucy had court all day, and there were several documents she needed me to file by that afternoon. I forced myself to concentrate and complete the filings, keeping my cell phone right in front of me on my desk and checking it every five minutes, so I wouldn't miss any calls.

I called Connie several times, the last time around 2:30. "No, 'Mando, there's still no news. I just talked to Chuy and he says he'll meet us at the bank sometime tomorrow. Dad's going to stay at his office all day so he won't miss it in case they call. Hold on." I heard her voice, low and intense. "Raffie, mommy's on the phone. Let go of mommy....you need to wait....LET GO!!!! You are getting on MY LAST NERVE!!!!...." Then, a child's loud wail, "Waaaaaah!" My sister's voice again, "I gotta go. Bye."

By three o'clock, I was crawling out of my skin, trying to focus on client billing and obsessing on the idea that I should be trying to sell my car to help pay Mom's ransom. I gave up on work, went online, and put in ads to sell the car for twenty thou or best offer, and gave my cell number for buyers to contact me.

By the time I finished advertising my car, it was three thirty. I hadn't eaten all day, but I couldn't face the idea of food. Lucy had told me I should go home early and rest, but I couldn't face my house either. The worst thing was, I had no one to talk to. Gaby was down in Mexico with Dad and Chuy, it stressed me out to talk to Connie, and I was afraid to tell any of my friends. Mom has always been my go-to person when I have a crisis and need to talk.

Finally, I knew what I really wanted to do. I fished in my briefcase for a card, took it out, and dialed.

"Come in, Armando. I'm so glad you called."

"I felt awkward about it at first. With your involvement in the case and everything."

"I understand. But there's no conflict with your seeing me. Just look at it from a common-sense point of view. We both want the same thing. I don't want to see Domingo wrongly convicted of Patty's murder. Patty was my best friend. I do think she loved Domingo. She would have wanted me to help you fight his case. I have been trying to help you, although I don't think I've been much help. And God knows, if you need a little counseling to help you do your job better, I'm honored you asked me."

"Thanks, Christine."

We were in her office. She had stayed late so she could add me to her calendar. As I sank into the comfortable leather couch, my body felt tense and wound up. Christine sat quietly, her head cocked to one side and that expectant look on her round face. This time, though, she didn't wait for me to begin.

"Armando, I have an idea of how I would like us to start today. One of the issues you mentioned to me when you called was that you are going through a crisis to do with your mother. Can you tell me about it?"

I talked for almost an hour without stopping, except for a few gentle questions from Christine. One of the questions, "tell me about your relationship with your mother," triggered massive tears. I had to reach for the Kleenex box more than once. As I spoke, I realized I had a very deep conviction Mom would be coming back safe and unharmed. I just wasn't ready to lose her, and I wasn't going to. Mom was tough and would do what she needed to survive. Magically, I had just finished unloading what I needed to say, and I was sitting silently with a huge feeling of relief washing over me, when Christine told me that our time was almost up.

"Wow," I said. "Thank you so much. I feel so much better. I had no idea what therapy was like."

"You did good work today," said Christine. "You have a real gift for expressing yourself. I'm sure your mother will come home safely tomorrow night."

I took out my wallet and handed her cash for the fee we had agreed on. She took it gracefully.

"Armando, are you sure you don't want me to bill your insurance?"

"Not this time."

"OK."

I put my wallet away. "So how does this work, usually?"

Christine smiled. "There is no 'usually.' I have clients who come see me on an as-needed basis. Other clients like to come in regularly, usually once or twice a week. It's up to you."

What an uncomplicated way to plan such an intimate relationship, I thought. I scheduled an appointment for the same time the following week.

15

Mom didn't come home Friday night. Friday morning, I went to the bank with Connie and we signed all the paperwork to get an expedited loan secured by some rental properties. I couldn't face the office, and spent the rest of the day with Connie, helping her with the kids and fielding a few calls about my Camino. I even spent an hour with a guy who wanted to see the car and test drive it. It turned out he had a side business in restoring and re-selling cars, and was considering re-tooling my Camino for use in drag racing. I would've sold it to him, but he never called me back.

Dad and Chuy had raised the $150,000, and had the cash at Dad's office in TJ by early Friday afternoon. At 6:00, Dad received a call on his office telephone, and he was allowed to talk to Mom. Mom told him she would be released safely if he did what the kidnappers said. Then a man came back on the line and told Dad to put the money in a briefcase, put the briefcase in his car, keep his cell phone on, and wait for further instructions.

After being told to drive to two different locations, Dad was told to drive to the Tijuana CostCo, park his car at the end of the lot, leaving it unlocked with the briefcase in the front seat, and walk into the store and stay inside for ten minutes. Dad followed these directions and came back to find his briefcase gone. By that time, it was 9:00 on Friday night.

By midnight, we'd heard nothing from Mom. Dad asked

Connie and me to stay in the U.S., in case Mom was dropped off near the border and decided to cross to this side.

I'd spent the early evening with Connie at her house. Connie thought it was likely Mom would come straight to Connie's house to see the grandkids, and she urged me to stay the night with her.

"Connie, Mom will want to come home first thing," I told her. "I want to be home when she gets there."

I spent a night of hell, camping out on the living room couch, calling local hospitals, and checking with my siblings for news. Around 8:00 a.m., I was on the phone with Connie and heard the sound of our automatic garage door opening.

"Connie, hold on, I hear something." I dropped the phone, opened the door connecting the kitchen to the garage, and saw Mom's Lexus come into view as the garage door rose. The windshield glinted in the sunlight, and then I saw Mom at the wheel, pulling into her space like any other day. She saw me, smiled, and waved.

I wanted to hug Mom and jump up and down, like a puppy. Something about the way she got out of her car, slowly and deliberately, made me slow down and help her out gently.

"Mom, are you all right?" I asked.

"I'm fine. Fine. Just tired. I was not harmed, *m'ijo.*"

I was trying to be strong, but tears came to my eyes and spilled out as I totally sobbed with relief. As we walked into the house, I think Mom was supporting me more than I was supporting her.

"Are you hungry, Mom? Let me make you something."

"Just some hot tea."

I went to fill the teakettle, when I heard a faint sound of shouting.

"Armando! What's happening?"

Mom looked at the phone on the counter. "Were you on the phone, Armando?"

"Oh, I forgot, it's Connie. Here." I handed Mom the

phone and she spent some time reassuring Connie she was well. Then she reached Dad at his office.

I listened as Mom told Dad her story. Mom had been ambushed by three men in masks, on the side road that led to the Country Club. She was blindfolded and taken to a house and locked in a bedroom. The kidnappers had been very business-like and had "acted like gentlemen." They had taken her cell phone to make the calls to Dad. Just before sunrise, two men came into the room, blindfolded her, and drove her around, finally dropping her off in a canyon outside of downtown Tijuana. Her Lexus was there, and she drove straight to the border.

"I am so sorry you were worried last night," she told Dad. "I didn't realize they gave you the impression they would release me last night.... I knew you would pay the money, Orlando.... Yes, I admit, when they didn't come to my room last night, I was afraid something had gone wrong.... No, I'm glad you didn't go to the police.

".... No, I couldn't, Orlando.... Yes, of course, I would have called you as soon as they let me go, but my cell phone was dead. Once they let me go, I didn't think about anything but getting myself safely across the border as soon as I could. If I'd been thinking straight, I would have realized I'd be caught in border traffic and it would be another couple of hours before I could let you know I was all right.... I know, I know. I am so sorry."

After she hung up, Mom looked at me with exhaustion in her eyes. "Your father is on his way."

"Oh, Ma," was all I could manage.

Ma went upstairs to shower and change her clothes. I followed her and stood outside the bathroom while she showered, afraid to let her get too far away.

By the time Ma had showered and done her hair and make-up and dressed, Connie and the kids had arrived. Then Dad showed up with Gaby. Chuy was going to pick up his family and be there soon.

After an hour with my family, I needed a break. Mom went to her bedroom to take a nap, and after a few minutes Dad went in to be with her, closing the door behind him. Although I hated to leave Ma, I really didn't want to spend the whole afternoon in the bosom of my family, especially after Chuy arrived with his loud and obnoxious wife and kids. I took off for the office, saying I'd be back later.

So happy and relieved was my mood, even Lucy's usual heinous Saturday attire of velour sweatsuit (today, powder blue) and Teva river sandals on her long bony feet, failed to bring me down. I filled her in on Mom's return home.

"Did she have any idea who the kidnappers were?"

"No. They didn't mention any names in front of her. She says the men didn't hurt her. I just hope she's not lying about that to protect us."

Lucy shook her head. "Listen, you really didn't need to work today. Don't you want to be at home?"

"Not really." I explained the family gathering situation. It would have been nice to think Mom's kidnapping and return would somehow make Dad change his mind about disowning me, and we could all be one big happy family like when I was a kid, but that wasn't going to happen.

"Well, Armando, you've had other things on your mind, but we did have Domingo's preliminary hearing yesterday. The judge refused to dismiss the case, but I think he'll end up excluding Paolo Sanchez's testimony. At first, I was afraid he was buying Paolo's 'reformed gangster' act. But Paolo started to look bad on cross-examination, as soon as I tried to pin him down on his testimony. Weiss was taken aback when Paolo couldn't say where or when he heard that Domingo was associated with the gang. He looked at the DA with an expression like, 'what are you trying to pull?' He'll have a ruling by the end of next week.

"You were right about Christine. She came across very well on the witness stand. She'll be an excellent witness on our suicide theory."

***

When I got home, the whole family was still there. Gaby and Mom were cooking dinner with the kids in the kitchen. Connie and Chuy and their spouses were having drinks in the living room with Dad. After greeting them, I spent a few minutes hanging out with Mom and Gaby and playing with my nieces and nephew.

We joined the others in the living room for cocktails. Dad stood and walked Mom over to sit next to him on the couch, and put an arm around her and pulled her toward him as she sat down. The room suddenly fell silent and we looked around at each other nervously.

Mom leaned her head briefly on Dad's shoulder and then smiled at all of us. "Thank you all for helping me this week. I am so sorry to have caused so much trouble and worry for all of you. Not to mention the expense, of course," she said, addressing Dad. "I'm grateful to be home."

Ma looked striking, with her gold-frosted hair, and her dark, wide-set eyes luminous in her classically beautiful face. With his thick, iron-grey hair cresting back from his sensual, heavy-featured face, his gold watch and ring standing out against his dark, hairy arms, Dad reminded me of a male lion.

"I am glad I was able to recover you," Dad said. He looked around the room. "It is good to have the family together again. This is how it should be."

My heart started to pound. If I got out our old set of dominoes, could the family gather around and play a game together?

While I was wondering, Chuy and Dad started talking about a business deal they'd had to put on hold to arrange Mom's ransom.

"Our little delay may work in our favor, Dad," Chuy said. "I think they got nervous we were going to back out."

Dad threw back his head and laughed, squeezing Mom closer to him.

Connie and Chuy's wife, Elena, started talking about their problems with the help, ignoring cries and thumping sounds as my nieces and nephews ran in and out between the living room and the downstairs bedrooms. Gaby slumped in a corner, glued to her iPad.

A few minutes later, Mom disengaged herself from Dad and said, "I'll just check on the dinner."

I stood up to join her, but Dad raised his palm to stop me, and followed Mom into the kitchen.

Despite my concern for Mom, I just couldn't be there. I walked toward the kitchen to say goodbye to her. When I got to the doorway, I heard raised voices.

"Gloria, *mi amor*, I know it's hard for you to talk about. I only asked about it because I want to know if you are really all right. You may require medical treatment."

"Of course, Orlando. But you have to believe me when I tell you the men did not touch me."

"All the same, a medical examination and some kind of counseling could not hurt. I'll make arrangements with Horacio. He's on the Hospital Board with me and will know the best place for you to go. I've already put a call in to him. And when you are ready to cross the border again, I'll be sure we have bodyguards to protect you."

"Thank you, Orlando," Mom said. "I'm so sorry you have been put through this. I was afraid for you, too. I thought you might try something risky, and...." She started sobbing. "These past few days have been a nightmare."

"Hush, *querida*," I heard Dad say softly. "*Eres mi tesoro por siempre.* You are my treasure. We don't need to talk about this now." Her sobs became muffled.

I backed away and returned to the living room, giving my niece Raffi a noisy airplane ride to cover up any sounds from the kitchen. A few minutes later, Mom and Dad came out and Mom announced brightly, "Dinner's ready, everyone."

Since dinner had been announced, it was a little harder for me to make a discreet exit. As I left, I heard Dad saying, "What does *he* have to do that is more important than being with his mother at a time like this?" and my mother's voice shushing him in low tones.

16

The following week, I didn't get to see much of Ma, because Dad was staying at the house with her. I spent some evenings hanging out with Slim and ignored two calls from Justin. Thursday, I had another good therapy session with Christine, which helped me start to recover from Mom's kidnapping.

Now that Domingo's preliminary hearing was over, Lucy was catching up on other cases. I spent the whole week plowing through mountains of paperwork.

"It's been too boring around here, *Abogada*," I said, early Friday afternoon. "I'm thinking of applying for a job with the County Mental Hospital. I know I'd make a great therapist," I went on. "Unfortunately, you have to go to school for years and years and then work for free for a couple more years."

Lucy raised her eyebrows. "Do you think you would like it?"

"I think so. I mean, most of the time, all you have to do is listen to people's problems, right? You don't actually have to solve them, like a lawyer does. It seems much less stressful."

"Really?" She put down her legal newspaper, and I could see I was in for one of her lectures, which she likes to give regardless of her actual knowledge of a subject. "In my opinion," she said, "people end up being one of two kinds of therapists: the saintly, or the sociopath. If you're sensitive, you become emotionally consumed with your clients' problems, lose your effectiveness, and end up as a burn-out. If you're more tough, you become a controlling sociopath who loses the ability to sympathize with others.

"There is a possible additional type, the Freudian/Jungian types of psychoanalysts and their progeny. They've made psychotherapy into a sort of religion. Instead of burning out or becoming cynical, they plow happily along, keeping the faith their form of therapy will eventually cure their patients, even if it takes a lifetime. Hmmm, yes. I would call that type the shaman, or the mystical type of therapist. You know...."

As she paused for breath, I interrupted, "Why couldn't you say the same thing about what you do? You try to keep your clients out of jail, and it's emotionally upsetting when you're not successful. Lawyers have to toughen up or burn out, too. Maybe with the exception of someone like you—the true believer, who has faith in the fight for truth and justice."

"Oh, no, no. Watch out, Armando. There's a big difference. Think about how you feel after a half-hour interview with one of our more difficult clients, especially if they're in custody. Picture doing that all day, every day."

"You wouldn't always be with people like that," I said defensively. "There are regular people who just go to therapy for a little help. Didn't you tell me your sister was seeing a therapist for her hoarding problem?"

"Try spending half an hour with my sister and listening to her problems," Lucy said.

"Oh, well, OK, I don't know your sister. But she's functional, has a good job and everything, right? Wouldn't she be an interesting patient?"

"My sister is a neurotic who avoids her own problems by reading about other people's. She would have spent her life as a perpetual student, if the local community college system hadn't finally hired her to teach history and literature survey classes. Really, she is one of the few people I've known who actually enjoyed going to school all those years, instead of seeing it as a means to an end. I pity any therapist who tries to help her understand how her hoarding and sick relationship with her ex-husband are bringing her down. "

"Maybe it's hard for you because she's your sister and you don't know how to help her. There are some people who work as therapists who are really good at what they do. What about Christine?"

"Christine," Lucy said. "Our star witness. I'm sure she's very good at what she does. She has some charisma and inspires respect. Her patients probably become very dependent on her. I'd say she's not likely to burn out. Too cool and in control. She's her own number one concern, and everyone else is around to make her look good. She's probably a sociopathic type. Or possibly a mystical shaman type."

"You could be right about that," I said.

"Speaking of the Torres case," Lucy said, "Judge Weiss just ruled to exclude Paolo Sanchez's testimony. I need to let Domingo know. Let's go see him."

We took the trolley to the jail. Lucy told him the good news, and then told him we would be starting to prepare for trial. "We've been investigating who else might have had a reason to poison Patty. There is some evidence Frank Slattery, the attorney that Patty worked for, had been ah, bothering her. Did you see anything like that, or hear anything about it?"

Domingo's shapely eyebrows came down over his eyes. "Frank Slattery? What was he doing to Patty? How do you mean, bothering her?"

"Did she tell you anything?"

He frowned. "You mean, like touching her, saying sexual things to her?"

"That's the general idea, yes. Is there anything you can remember?"

"No. She said nothing to me. Slattery often interrupted our meetings to ask Justin or Patty a question. He was very rude. Once, he came in and asked Patty how much time she was spending on my case. Another time, he told her he needed to meet with her, so Patty had to cut our appointment short. He's not a nice man. I would have been very angry if Patty had told me that he was not a gentleman with her."

Lucy asked Domingo whether Patty had ever talked to him about Brad Fernwood. Domingo could not add anything to what he had told us before, that he thought Brad admired Patty.

"Was he bothering her, too?" Domingo asked. "My God! I wish Patricia had told me about all these men bothering her. I could have...ah, put a stop to it. Perhaps one of them did kill her. I may have been wrong to think that Cantara is involved in Patty's death. If Cantara did this, they will never be brought to justice."

Back at the office, Lucy decided to re-focus our efforts on the suicide theory.

"I want you to do an in-person interview of the victim's aunt, to find out if Patty had a history of depression. Book yourself a flight up to Oakland for next week. You can talk to Aunt Jill about how Patty's mood was the night she died."

She showed me a document she had recently received from the DA, which listed all of the items taken from the crime scene by the police. Item number 6 was "empty prescription medication bottle with label Fentanyl, for Martin, Patricia," with a date the medicine was prescribed.

"What's interesting," she said, "is that Patty got the prescription over three years ago, when she still lived in Oakland. It's still under her old name. Patty had this for three years, and still had enough to overdose. Maybe she was saving the pills because she was contemplating suicide. I'm hopeful about this investigation."

17

Saturday night, we were dining at Cocina de Frida, Gaby's choice for her last dinner out before returning to Berkeley. After a large pitcher of Margaritas, Gaby and I were starting to loosen up. Mom had drunk at least as much as we had but was cool and unaffected.

"Look what I have," Mom said. Mom's voice is high pitched anyway, and when she is excited or playful it turns into a charming trill. She got her purse and pulled out a pink piece of paper. For a second, I thought it was that horrible Mexico kidnapping joke flyer with the warning note written on it.

"It's the pink slip for the Lexus. I asked your Dad to bring it to me last night. He signed the car over to my name so I can go trade it in."

"That makes sense, Mom." Gaby nodded. "You had a bad experience with the Lexus. You should get a different car."

Mom blinked and brushed a lock of frosted hair back from her forehead. "Thank you, *m'ija*, for understanding. I do feel like a target every time I drive it. Shall we have another pitcher of Margaritas first, or are you ready to order dinner? After dinner, we'll go shopping, and get you the rest of the things you need for school."

Gaby ran her hands through her short black hair. "But Ma, I don't need anything more. All the stuff you bought me already isn't going to fit into my dorm room, let alone my luggage. Anyway, I'm trying to be more austere." She fingered the zipper on her O'Neill hoodie.

"I get it, you have a space problem. What can we do about that?" Mom's brow contracted in mock concern. Then her face cleared and she gave us a dazzling smile. "I know! We'll be more focused. I'll buy you a pretty little ring. Armando, come with us. Help your sister choose something. I want to buy you a jewel, too. A gigantic diamond earring? A ring? I saw a band with tiny emeralds, very simple, your favorite color. It spoke to me. I think it will speak to you."

Ma makes shopping an art form, caressing fine fabrics as she walks by them, cocking her head to one side and squinting her eyes to critique a new style of jacket, and holding up expensive leather shoes to see the rich glow reflecting off the buttery surfaces.

By the time we got to the jewelers, Gaby and I were totally into it, too. Boris, the grey-haired jeweler, was so happy to see my mother walk in the door, he clasped his hands in front of his heart. We spent an hour of pure sensual pleasure chatting with Boris, who ignored the other customers who wandered in and out while he brought us beautiful pieces to look at and try on. We got drunk on the different colors of light that flickered deep within the rubies, emeralds, garnets, sapphires, topazes, amethysts, and diamonds.

Mom's eyes glittered as she insisted on buying me the ring that had spoken to her. It was a narrow silver band with three small emeralds inset to let the blue-green light show through the stones. Gaby chose an emerald ring with a round flat stone and tiny diamonds embedded in a delicate gold design on each side. Ma got a flashy necklace with several large green stones.

"Emeralds! All beautiful green emeralds!" Ma cried, pulling out her Tiffany's card. "Marvelous! Like the ballet by Balanchine! What fun we are having, my children."

"Thanks, Mom," said Gaby. "This was transcendent."

"*Mamacita*, you are too much," I said, kissing her on both cheeks.

"Thank your father. He's the one who'll pay the bill." Mom smoothed a lock of lightly frosted hair back behind her ear. "Now, how about a drink? I want an Irish Coffee."

***

Sunday evening, I was sitting at the little kitchen counter at Justin's crib, watching him open some boxes of frozen food to microwave for our dinner. When he'd called that morning and asked me to come over, I'd told him I wasn't sure I should.

"Come on, 'Mando. You know you want to."

"All right, but we won't talk at all."

"Really? Is that what you want? 'Cause that's not what I'm looking for. Not with you."

What could I say? So there we were, having dinner and talking about *P. v. Torres*. I told Justin about the judge's ruling to exclude Paolo Sanchez's testimony. "So maybe our problem will go away. We can forget about the whole drug cartel angle to this case," I said.

Justin looked at me in surprise. "You think so? Did Lucy say that? I would think it would still be an issue. Paolo may still be active in Cantara. Maybe Patty had learned something about his activity, so he decided she had to be killed. I wish she'd taken me with her; I wish she'd told me what she was doing. I wonder whether she interviewed anyone else."

I couldn't tell Justin I was backing off from Cantara because they'd kidnapped Mom.

"We're looking into other angles right now," I said.

"What angles?"

I shook my head. Lucy had Claude looking into Frank Slattery's alibi, but that was another thing I couldn't tell Justin. I told him I'd be going to Oakland to look into Patty's past and meet the aunt she'd Skyped with the night she died.

Justin took the last container out of the microwave, peeled off the plastic top, and set it on the counter. There were two dinners in their microwave boxes, one for each of us. He opened a drawer and put out two forks.

"Dinner is served," he said.

I sighed and walked over to his cupboard and took out two plates, ripped two paper towels off of a roll, folded the paper towels, and put the forks on top of them. Then I got a big spoon out of the drawer, spooned our food onto plates, and threw out the microwave boxes the food had come in.

Justin watched me. He went and got two glasses and filled them with water, placing them neatly at the corners of our plates. "There. Better?"

I picked up my water glass and gave him a toast. The water was good, but I couldn't eat more than a bite of the glutinous microwaved mass. Justin polished his off, and then ate mine.

When he finished, I asked, "How could Paolo have known to poison Patty with her own medicine? It just seems improbable. And would she have let him into her apartment?"

"It's a bit of a stretch," Justin said, "but it's possible. Paolo may have had other plans to dispose of Patty, and adapted them when he got to her place. Patty would have let him in if he said he had information to help Domingo. She wanted to win Domingo's case."

18

Monday lunchtime, Justin and I sat sunning ourselves in the outside food court at the top of Horton Plaza. It was the first day of a heat wave. Families of tourists strolled around, wearing shorts and flip-flops, licking ice cream cones, and carrying big bags from mall shops. The work force, on its lunch break, blinked in the bright sun and seemed to carry with it a protective aura of air conditioning and fluorescent lighting. In the hot light, the sky and surrounding buildings almost matched the garish blue and peach colors of the mall.

Justin's freckles stood in sharp relief against his white skin and his heavy mop of hair. I stared at his refined face, slender frame in the cheap blue suit, and long sensitive hands. He looked so beautiful to me, like a creature from a different planet than that of all the sloppy tourists and greasy, puffed-up business people. I turned my face into the sun and felt the hot Santa Ana wind.

I hadn't planned to see him again this soon, but Justin had asked me to meet him so he could give me a file with some of the legal research he'd done on the specialized immigration law that was the basis for Paolo Sanchez to become a US citizen. Lucy might be interested in seeing the research, he said. I'd told Justin to meet me at the food court at the mall, hoping I could get him to come do a little shopping with me after we ate.

"Hey, why don't we go walk around Nordstrom's for a few minutes?"

He shook his wavy mop and stretched his legs out in front of him. "Hmmmn. Go walk around a cold, sterile department store looking at overpriced, useless stuff, or sit here basking in the sun before we have to go back to our offices. That's a tough call. Why don't we sit here and think about it for a while?"

"They got a huge sale going on. I was there with my mom and my sister on Friday night. There's some shirts that would look great on you."

Justin took my hand and looked at the emerald ring Mom had given me. "Is that where you got this?"

"No." I told him about our spree at Tiffany's.

"Your mom sounds fun. What does she do?"

"She never worked. She raised us four kids, she loves to cook and work in her garden, shop, dress up, go to dinner, to the opera. She used to take care of my niece and nephew while my sister was at work, but she just quit doing that so she could take an English literature class at City College."

"Why's she doing that?"

"Why, why, why. You are so curious." As I talked, I got up and pulled Justin's chair out from under him. "Let's just walk this way," I said, steering him towards the stores. "We can walk and talk."

"OK," he said. "But let's walk down the street, towards my office. I have to get back to work, but I also have a surprise for you."

I gave up and followed him. As we got to the corner where our paths back to work diverged, Justin stopped me and pulled me over to a doorway. "Here, come stand over here for a second." He opened his wallet and took out two tickets and held them up.

I took a look. "Rudolfo!" I cried. "At the fairgrounds! This is so cool," I said. "I have his latest CD. I'll burn a copy for you."

"I already have it."

"You?"

"Sure. I've been a fan for a while."

"Wait a minute," I exclaimed. "How did that happen? He's big in Mexico, but not really big here. What's a gringo from the Bay Area doing listening to Rudolfo?"

Justin smiled.

"Well?" I asked. He didn't speak. I remembered the picture I'd seen taped to the computer in his office. "Ah, of course. I'm not your first Mexican boyfriend. Right?"

"We can talk about it later. I gotta go. Here." he handed me the tickets and closed my hand around them. "You take care of these. See you around."

Lucy glanced at her watch when I appeared at her office door.

"Have a nice long lunch?" she asked.

I had been gone like an extra five minutes. "I'm sure it was not nearly as exciting as whatever you did," I said breezily. "What did you do? A nooner with Dr. Six Martinis?"

Just before it was time to leave work, I called Brad Fernwood at his office and reached him on his direct line.

"Brad, Armando Felan here. Glad I've finally caught up with you."

"What do you mean?"

"Oh, I mean I left you some messages last week. I hear you were out of town."

"Yes. I had to go out of town for work. I got your messages when I returned, but I figured you wouldn't need to talk to me any more. You know, since the preliminary hearing is over and you didn't need to subpoena me after all." There was a note of triumph in his voice.

"True, the hearing is over. Now I have to follow up on a few details for the trial. We can do that now, if you want to, then we don't have to bother with an in person interview. Is now a good time, or do you want to schedule something?"

"Uh, no, it's alright, I can talk now if it won't take too long, but I don't think I could tell you more than Chris already has."

He gave short unhelpful answers as I took him through his first meeting Patty (at a party, with Christine) to the night of Patty's death. Finally I asked, "So, Brad, do you think Patty was serious about Domingo?"

There was a silence on the other end of the line.

"Brad? Are you there?"

"I'm here. I can't answer that question. I only saw them together once or twice. It wasn't easy to read Patty's feelings. She wasn't open, that way. I sometimes got the feeling she didn't know, herself, what she wanted from life."

"Really? Interesting. You and she were pretty close, weren't you? Did Patty ever give you anything, like a birthday gift or something?"

"What are you talking about? No, she didn't. She was the friend of my wife, not of me. My wife."

"Just one more question," I said. "Your office told me you weren't working last week. Where were you? Why did you say you were working?"

"OK, this is bullshit." Brad responded. "Can't a person take some time off, just to get away and breathe, without people making a federal case of it?"

"So, you just went on a vacation, to get away from the stress," I said. "Buddy, that's totally dope. I wish I could. Where did you go? Hawaii?"

"As a matter of fact, no. I drove up the coast for a few days. I needed to get away. That's all you're going to get from me. If you want to ask me anything else, I'm going to get a lawyer." The line clicked as Brad hung up on me.

***

When I got home, Mom was at the kitchen counter, chopping onions. She smiled and brushed her hair back from her forehead with her elbow. I could hear the olive oil starting to sizzle in the iron pot on the stove, releasing the scent of garlic and chile.

"Hey, Ma, what are you doing cooking? I thought I was taking you out tonight."

"I felt like cooking. Do you know, I haven't really cooked a nice dinner since the night I...came back home. You don't mind?"

"No, I'm happy. It's nice to see you cooking again." I sat down at the counter and admired her economical movements as she stirred the spices while preparing the meat and vegetables and taking out the greens for the salad. Maybe I could get her to talk to me about why she'd been crying the other night.

"I have help today," Mom said, pulling the salad bowl out from under the kitchen counter. "Italia is going to join us."

As if on cue, a short, plump woman walked in from the living room, took the salad bowl from her hands, and placed it on the table.

"Armando!" Her arms stretched out and she hugged me to her huge bosom. "Let me look at you. Gloria, your son, he's *muy bien* fine!"

Italia had a plain, cheerful face, with a hint of a dark mustache on her upper lip that I had always found very becoming. The last time I had seen her, she had worn her thick black hair in long braids; now it was expensively cut in a short style, slightly teased at the crown, with the straight and shiny look of a Brazilian Blowout.

"Hi, Italia. It's been a long time. How's Clara doing?" Italia's daughter Clara is the same age as me and we'd hung out as kids, when our families vacationed together.

"Very well, very well," Italia said in her rich deep voice. "She's just gotten her license as a CPA, and she's been hired by her Dad's bank. Arturo is worried because she hasn't found a husband yet. Don't tell Arturo this, but I tell her, no rush. She should take time and have fun *antes de suicidarse.*" Italia drew her forefinger across her throat in a graphic gesture.

Italia put her arm around Mom and said, "Look at your boy. Grown up and watching his mother cook. You made this same meal for me at my house recently. You make the best *pozole.*"

"Yes, my great achievement in life."

"It's no small thing, *amiga,*" Italia said, spinning the lettuce in the lettuce spinner. "You are too modest, Glo'."

I rocked back and forth on the bar stool, watching Italia using her bare hands to shred the lettuce leaves and toss them into the salad bowl. "Ma's the best. I'm happy to see her cooking again. That means she's feeling more like herself."

"Does it?" Ma said.

"Well, I thought so. What do you mean? You're not feeling better?"

"What I mean is, I hate cooking," she said. "It's fun sometimes, especially with a friend over to help, but there are usually things I'd rather be doing."

"Oh, wow, Ma. I thought you loved to cook. You're, like, an artist of cooking." The bar stool suddenly felt unstable beneath me, and I stopped my rocking.

"*Ai, pobrecito,*" Italia said. "Gloria, dear, you have shocked your son. Poor Armando. Your mama doesn't love cooking, and there ain't no Santa Claus, either." The two women laughed raucously.

An hour later, I was on the phone with Slim. "Slim, does your mom like to cook?"

"I dunno."

"Go ask her."

"OK. Hang on." I heard his footsteps, then the opening and closing of a door, then his voice, "*Mamacita,* do you like to cook?" I heard a short reply but it just sounded like a grunt over the phone line. I heard the door and Slim's footsteps again.

"Yeah, man. She says she likes it."

"Well, get this. My mom just said she hates to cook."

"No way."

"Can you believe it?"

"That's a shocker. I'm really sorry, *amigo*. You wanna come over for dinner? Mom's making carnitas. We could play games after. I'm not going to go out with Daniel 'til like eleven o'clock."

"I just ate. Mom made *pozole*."

"Your mom makes the best *pozole*. I thought you said she hates to cook."

"I know. It's weird."

"So you want to come over?"

"I'll call you back. I need to call Justin."

"Justin, does your mom like to cook?"

"Oh, Armando, hi. How are you?"

"OK, I guess. So, does she?"

"What? My mom?"

"Yeah."

"Well, she and my dad both work, so they share the cooking. He probably likes to cook more than she does. She's got a sweet tooth, so she likes to make cakes and cookies."

"Oh."

"Why do you ask?"

"I'll tell you about it later. What are you doing tonight?"

"Studying. I got behind in my reading last week. You're still going out with your mom, right?"

"We already ate. She made *pozole*. Her friend Italia came over and they're going to go out to a chick flick." I pronounced it like Ma had, with an exaggerated accent, *'cheek fleek.'*

"You weren't interested?"

"I wasn't really invited," I said.

"Come over tomorrow night?" He asked.

"You come here," I said. "I'm leaving for Oakland the next morning, and I can drop you home on my way to the airport.

"I'll bring a cake." He hung up.

19

I slept on the short flight from San Diego to Oakland. The evening before, Justin had installed himself in the Jacuzzi, taking short breaks to dive into the pool to cool off. The heat wave was still on, and the cement radiated heat even after the air cooled off.

"You didn't tell me you had this set-up." He leaned like a cat, so one of the strong jets hit him between the shoulder blades. "I'm going to stay here forever."

"Any time," I said, not realizing until I'd said it that it didn't make sense. "I didn't know you were such a lizard." I cupped my hand and flicked a cannonball of hot water at him with a little more force than I'd intended. He tightened his eyes shut and turned his head away as the water sprayed his face.

"When are you taking me out to the desert?" Justin asked, sinking deeper into the hot pool until his head rested on the cement rim.

I watched his wet hair fan out on the concrete and stain it black. "We'll go when it cools off. You don't want to go right now."

"Alright. Did I tell you I'm back on Domingo's case? Frank's hired a new attorney, a guy who has a lot of experience with asylum cases, and he wants to get the case moving again. We might even go to Juarez, Mexico, to meet Domingo's uncle."

"Frank hired a man? I thought he always had woman attorneys work for him."

Justin opened his eyes and narrowed them at me. "Not this time. So, have you guys learned anything new on the cartel angle?"

I looked up at the wide-open sky where the last daylight was still half-bright against the dark silhouettes of our neighborhood's pines and palms. The warm Santa Ana winds rustled the palm leaves. The little cottonwood tree Mom had planted behind the pool house made clapping sounds with its round flat leaves. Santa Ana winds sometimes bring smog into our air, and that night, the raw fuel smell made me think of Mexico.

"Be careful," I said, not exactly answering him but echoing what Domingo had said to me before Mom was kidnapped.

Justin's hair had dried just enough to show glints of dark red. I found a way to distract him from the subject of Cantara.

Lucy had sent me on this trip to Oakland because she thinks I have dumb luck at finding out random important things that help her put together her cases. Today I didn't feel lucky. I was distracted by thoughts of Justin putting himself in danger investigating Cantara, maybe even getting himself killed, or kidnapped like Mom. That reminded me of my sessions with Christine, and that I needed to call her and cancel that week's therapy appointment since I would be in Oakland.

Expecting to leave a voicemail message because it was still early, I dialed Christine as I was waiting in line at the car rental desk. I was surprised when she answered on the second ring.

After we said "hi," she said, "You sound flustered. Do you have an emergency?" It cheered me up just to hear her voice.

I laughed. "'Help, I've fallen and I can't get up,'" I squeaked. Then I felt bad, like Christine might think I was making fun of her clients. But Christine just squeaked it back at me, and we giggled like twelve-year-olds.

"Actually," I told her, "I'm calling because I have to reschedule my appointment."

"No problem. Thank you for being thoughtful and calling me ahead of time. You want to reschedule now?"

"No, I'll call you."

There was a hesitation on the end of the line. "Armando, while I have you on the phone, is there anything you can tell me about how Patty's case, I mean, Domingo's case, is going?"

As Christine talked, I watched the family in front of me get called to the desk. The husband stalked up to the counter, taking out his wallet and some paperwork and putting them on the desk. Behind him, his wife struggled with a stroller occupied by a restless toddler, two rolling suitcases, and a big duffel bag that looked as heavy as a dead body. When she looked at me as if to apologize for moving out of my way so slowly, I covered the phone and said, "No worries."

"No real developments." I told Christine. "I'm off to Oakland to follow up some leads."

"Really? That must be stressful for you after all you've been through. Take good care of yourself, and don't work too hard."

When I hung up, I thought the truth in this case was not in Oakland, or with Frank Slattery's office, or with Brad and Christine, but with the Cantara gang. Why would Cantara have kidnapped Ma and told me to back off, if they hadn't been involved in Patty's death? As Domingo had told us, if it was Cantara we'd never be able to pin them down. Our only hope was to introduce other suspects or scenarios to the jury, to raise a reasonable doubt that Domingo was guilty. Maybe Patty's former employer, or her aunt, would provide information to bolster our suicide theory.

***

Patty's former workplace was in a mid-rise glass building, in what looked like one of the more upscale suburbs in Oakland. The top story of the building was labeled Gosmore and Huskins, LLP," in ugly, square red letters. A quick Internet search had revealed Gosmore was one of the largest law firms in the state, with its main office in San Francisco and satellites in Oakland and San Jose. The firm occupied the top three floors of the building

The seventh floor was set up with a rectangular block of shoulder-high cubicles in the center and offices along the outside walls. A high-fashion model sat at a glossy dark-wood desk and offered me coffee or tea while I waited for Ms. Penny Chandler, Patty's former supervisor. Within two minutes, a very tall, well-dressed man, who looked like he might play a lot of tennis or water polo in his spare time, walked me back across the thick carpet to a corner office at the far end of the floor. Before opening the office door, he renewed the offer of refreshment, which I again declined. Then he tapped on the door and let me in.

Ms. Chandler was a polished blonde in her early forties, wearing a boxy, dark-green power suit with a Hermés scarf. We sat in comfortable chairs around a shiny oval conference table. Through a wall-to-ceiling window, I could see the Oakland skyline in the background. In the foreground was a big grassy park with large trees and tennis courts.

"Has someone offered you something to drink? Tea, coffee, water? I can have Randy order you a sandwich, if you're hungry."

"I'm fine, thanks."

"I've asked Don Baker, to join us. Don started working here at the same time as Patty, and they knew each other fairly well. He should be here in a moment."

She sat back slightly in her seat and gave me a friendly smile. "Did you fly up from San Diego this morning?"

"I did. I took the six a.m. flight."

"How was your flight?"

"Very smooth, and I had a window seat so I got a great view of the sunrise. Then I got an early check in to my motel and had a swim. Nice way to start the day."

"Oh, you're a swimmer? I've been doing master swim this year. The firm has an arrangement with the local country club for us to use the facilities, and they have a pool that's very well heated. That makes it easier to get into the water at five thirty in the morning."

There was a tap on the door.

"Come in," Ms. Chandler said. "Don, this is Armando Felan, the attorney defending the man accused of killing Patty Martin. Mr. Felan, this is Don Baker, the attorney I was telling you about. He'll be the best person to answer any questions about Patty's personal life."

A square-jawed man in an expensive suit bounded forward to shake my hand. Like all the other people I had seen at the firm, he brandished an aura of physical and mental fitness.

"I should clarify, I'm not actually an attorney," I said. I got out my cards. "I'm the investigator for Attorney Sanders in this case." I tried to make it sound like Lucy had a full-time investigator for each case.

"Don, Mr. Felan is a swimmer, too. I've been telling him about our master swim program."

Attorney Don Baker was also a swimmer, as well as an avid racquetball player and body builder. After the right amount of chitchat, Ms. Chandler shifted gears.

"Well, Don, how did your deposition go this morning?"

White teeth flashed in his tanned face. "Short and sweet. They fell for it, just like we planned."

"Excellent." Chandler smiled like a cat. "Sorry, Mr. Felan, this is a case Don and I've been working on, and we hadn't had a chance to talk this morning. Now, how can we be most helpful to you? We were, of course, shocked to hear of Patty's death. Can you tell us more about what happened?"

"Sure." I gave them a quick summary of the circumstances of Patty's death, including the possibility Patty had taken her own life. "It's possible her death was related to something that happened up here or someone from her past. I'd like it if you could tell me how long she worked here, what she did, who she knew, and what her...mood was like."

Ms. Chandler said, "Patty worked here a little over a year. I had Randy pull the dates for you, in case you need them." She handed me a sheet of paper. "She left us in February of last year."

"Why did she leave?"

The two attorneys exchanged glances. Then Ms. Chandler said, "Officially, Patty resigned from our firm. After she completed her first year, we'd had to tell her that her work was not of the quality and quantity to keep her on track for a partnership with the firm. That's not uncommon, as most of our associates do not make it to partnership. They can stay on as associates, although many of them choose to explore other options at that point. What made Patty's situation a bit unusual was that we did not offer her the choice to stay on."

"Oh?"

"Several of the attorneys who worked with Patty noticed conduct that wasn't...consistent with our high standards. We asked her to resign, and gave her a generous severance package. I'm telling you this now, because our firm wants to cooperate fully. If Patty were still alive, the firm would never divulge Patty had not left here voluntarily."

"What kind of conduct are you talking about?"

Ms. Chandler thought for a moment. "Patty was, well, brilliant, in some ways, but erratic. She was impatient with the details and stringent ethical requirements that are essential to good law practice. At first, we were very impressed with her ability to grasp the big picture and plan a strategy in a complex case. But when it came to doing the day-to-day work of a new associate, she would ah, overreach. A couple incidents occurred where it was her word against another's, but I believed she was at fault. Don, I recall you had to call one of her mistakes to my attention.   On one occasion, she came to me and made some rather improbable accusations of sexual harassment against one of our well-respected attorneys. I advised her of her right to follow procedures for making a formal complaint. She never followed up."

"Patty wasn't happy here," Don said, running his finger under his collar. "It wasn't a good fit. She was glad to take the severance and leave. She told me she was going to take some time off, maybe go into business for herself or find a small firm. I think she'd met a man and was focused on him."

"Oh? I hadn't heard about that. Was it a serious relationship?"

"I don't know. I'm just telling you an assumption I made at the time. The only thing I can tell you for certain is that shortly before she left, Patty told me she'd met a guy she really liked," he said. "I never met him, but she seemed very happy."

"Did she tell you anything about him?"

"No, I don't think she even told me his name. She met him at a party, or a bar, I can't remember. He might have been well off, because before she left she told me she didn't think she'd ever have to go back to work if she stayed with him."

"Do you think anyone else here at the firm might know more about this man?"

"I doubt it," Don said. "Patty knew she wasn't going to be asked to stay on. The last few weeks, she spent more time hanging out at the Club swimming pool than in the office."

After our interview, Don walked me out. As he waited with me in front of the elevator, he said, "I think I should tell you this, in case it can help you find the truth. There was something really off about Patty. She could be bright, even brilliant. But I saw her really flip a couple of times, once when a senior attorney criticized her work, and once when a law clerk she was close to suddenly quit and left her with a lot of unfinished work and a short deadline to meet. Both times, she came to my office and vented, saying she thought they were trying to sabotage her. It was hard for me to calm her down."

"Are you saying she was paranoid?" I asked.

"Paranoid, short fuse, I don't know. I'm not a shrink," Dan said, "but I knew she wasn't to be trusted. It was too bad. I liked her."

Looking at the flush on his hard, chiseled face, I wondered just how much he'd liked her.

***

The front desk of the Oakland Hills Country Club was manned by a friendly Latino kid, whose badge told me his name was Leo. His fresh intelligent face told me he was probably finishing up his summer job there before going off to college. He seemed cool, so I just showed him my card and told him the truth.

"Wow, you're trying to find out who really killed this lady so your client doesn't get executed?"

"Sort of. He might just get life in prison, but you never know. It's my job to look for other possible suspects, since the police are not doing so. We think they're prejudiced against my client because he's an immigrant."

"I got you. So, you just want to know, do we have records of this attorney coming here, and the names of any guests she brought?"

"Right. There was a new guy in her life, and I'm trying to get his name." I told him the two months I needed to look at.

"Those records are kinda old. I'm not sure we still have them. We have a guest sign-in that gives the name of the guest, the date, and the name of the member who brought them. The Gosmore firm people, the ones who aren't members, can bring guests only to the pool and the gym. They all use the same sign-in."

"Can you check if you still have the records for those months?"

"Yeah, but they'd be in a filing cabinet in my boss's office. I don't think she'd let you look at them without some kind of a court order. She's really, uh, *muy delicada*."

"Got it. What can we do about that, Leo?"

The kid smiled. "I know." He looked me up and down and nodded. I had on my grey Armani slim-fit blend, with a classic white shirt and slightly wide tie with stripes of plum, ivory, and pale green. "You're thinking about working for Gosmore, and their recruiter sent you over to check out the facility, OK?"

He walked me to a side door, down a short hallway, and knocked. "Ms. Curlew? I have a Mr. Felan here, he's here from the Gosmore firm to get a tour. Do you want to take over the front desk while I do it, or do you want to take him?"

Ms. Curlew was a very old lady who, thanks to a large amount of plastic surgery, appeared to be merely late middle-aged until she stood up and started to move. Her mummy face cracked a grin at the mention of Gosmore. "I'll take care of him, Leo. You go back to the desk."

"Thank you, Leo," I said as Curlew guided me out into the lobby.

"You're most welcome, sir. Enjoy your tour."

Compared to the Tijuana Country Club, where I'd once run a golf cart into the lake while my Dad played a round, this joint was small and understated. It had a rustic veneer (all signage on irregular shapes of varnished wood with "burned on" letters), but luxurious amenities (state-of-the-art weight room, heated towels). The pool was ni-iiiiice, probably half of an

Olympic in size, with a high-dive over the deep end. Would they let me come back tonight for a swim?

My scary mummy guide was lecturing about the number of Gosmore attorneys who had, after many years, risen to the rock-star heights of full membership in the Club. Her voice had a surprisingly youthful ring and hints of a high-toned east coast accent. Membership here, she advised me, meant something more than it did at most clubs. It was truly like joining a family. Members celebrated family occasions together in the home-like but spacious dining facilities, and often took group vacations to exotic destinations.

I had figured Leo would find whatever he needed within twenty minutes. When that time was up, I cut the Curlew short as she completed the tour of the gym and started to steer me towards the dining room.

"I really think I've seen enough," I explained. "I'm afraid if I see any more, I'll be seduced by the beauty of this place and it will affect my judgment. You know, I still haven't decided whether to take Gosmore up on their offer. I wouldn't want to end up stuck in the wrong job, you know, by getting hooked on an affluent life-style. I'm sure you understand."

The crack in her face twitched in response, and she turned back. I'm usually good at reading faces, but this was like looking at an egg.

"Here we are, then," she said, when we got back to the parking lot. "Best of luck in finding a suitable position, Mr. Felan. It is to your credit you are taking a thoughtful approach. I see many young people whose ambition blinds them to their true metiér. If I may say so, I hope you will not sell yourself short, dear. Do you need directions back to your hotel?"

I let her drop me off at my car, got in, and then waited while she tottered back through the entrance. While I waited for Leo, I practiced Curlew's high-toned accent so I could imitate her when I called Justin that night. "Oh, I, Ahi dew hope yahw will nahat sell yoahself short, deah." A couple minutes later, Leo came out with a handful of papers. He handed them through my car window.

"Here you go, *amigo*. All the guest logs for the time you wanted. It was faster to copy them than go through looking at the names."

I gave Leo a generous tip. "*Gracias, compadre,*" I said.

Putting the papers on the seat next to me, I typed my motel address into my GPS and said, "Home, James."

My motel's version of room service was an ice machine and two vending machines on the second floor outside the laundry room. I looked down at the sad little kidney-shaped swimming pool as I walked over to get some Hot Cheetos and a Coke for my late lunch. Maybe if I'd played my cards right, the Curlew would have comp'd me to the Club's lunch buffet as part of my tour. I could be eating lobster salad and watching the privileged classes stroking golf balls or clocking laps in the pool. I sat by the pool and used a motel towel to wipe the orange shit off my fingers as I consumed the Cheetos.

When I finished eating, I fished the papers Leo had given me out of my briefcase and leaned back in my lounge chair to review them. After two minutes, I found what I'd been looking for.

"Oh, yeah!" I said out loud.

I almost called Lucy. Then I thought it would be more fun to write up a full report and e-mail it to her. I brought my laptop down by the pool and typed. By the time I was done, it was starting to get cool even though the summer sun was still high.

I went inside and accessed the motel's wifi to e-mail my report with a cover letter that said:

Hi *Abogada*: Patty and Brad Fernwood got busy in Country Club pool. See report for details.

Am going to celebrate at 4-star restaurant on generous per diem. Armando

20

SimCo's office was a thirty-minute commute from Oakland, in a business park towards San Jose. I pulled into a parking space right on time for my five o'clock appointment with Patty's brother, Sam.

"Excellent, James. Tip-top." I said to my GPS.

This SimCo office building was much larger than the satellite where I'd visited Brad in San Diego. The youth and ethnic mix of high-tech workers was similar. I went up the elevator with a young Indian man and woman, and decided I would try their accent on when I got back in the car with James. "James, you are tooo brill-yent, isn't it?" I practiced in my head, and slightly waggled my head side to side.

As he faced me across his desk, Sam cocked his head at me and smiled. On his own turf, he looked much happier and more comfortable. He reminded me of those kids you grow up with who are baby faced class clowns and you know they're going to look and act exactly the same when they're all grown up. His office was cluttered with tools and pieces of equipment I didn't recognize, including a metal device the size of a shoebox, with red and blue wires spilling out like guts on Sam's desk.

"Hey, buddy," he'd stood up to greet me with a handshake. "Good to see you again. Welcome to my lair."

"Thanks. What do you do here?" I asked.

"This is where we test and refine the hardware parts of our medical-equipment products. If I hadn't gotten into this kind of work, I probably would have worked as a car mechanic. This work isn't as dirty, and it pays a lot better."

"I take it Brad doesn't do the same kind of work as you do?"

"Oh, no. Brad is a brain and a half. He works on the software and interfacing aspects of the design. Highly theoretical. He's like a design genius. I'm just a construction and mechanics guy," Sam told me.

"Brad's a computer genius?"

"Let me put it this way. He does the creative stuff you get paid big bucks for. But he's kind of clueless about some of the basic, practical aspects of how things work. That's where hacks like me come in."

"I'm sure you're too modest. I bet you have an engineering degree and know a lot about computers yourself."

"Actually, I don't."

"Don't what?"

"Have a college degree. I took some classes, but never finished. I got what I needed to know, taught myself some stuff, and then I got this job."

"Wow, good for you. So, do you know a lot about computers?"

He turned his head a little so the light reflected off of his eyeglasses. A self-satisfied smile played over his face. "Just what I need to know for what I need to get done," he said.

We went over his alibi, and a few other questions I hadn't gotten around to the afternoon we'd shared a couple of six packs together at Patty's condo. The night Patty was killed, Sam had gone home and spent the evening alone, and been back at work for a meeting at eight thirty the next morning. If his story checked out, he would barely have had time to drive to San Diego and back between the time he left work the night before and the time he signed in the following morning. He could have flown down and back, though, if he'd gotten an early flight back, like the one I'd taken that morning.

I said, "Didn't you see anybody after work that night? You don't live with anyone?"

He hesitated for a moment. "No. I mean, I'm seeing someone. But I didn't see her that night."

I knew from the DA's investigation that Patty's savings had been a little over $6,000.

"Did she leave anything else of value?" I asked Sam.

"Not really. I brought back a few little things I thought Aunt Jill might like. Patty didn't have anything valuable."

"You never found her wallet, did you?"

He shook his head. "No. Strange, huh?"

I said, "Your Aunt Jill isn't returning my phone calls. Do you know when would be a good time for me to drop by her place?"

Sam hesitated. "Aunt Jill's a little, um, uncomfortable with strangers. Let me call her first and set something up. It'll be better if I prepare her for your visit."

After he set up the appointment, and I was turning to leave, I asked him, "I heard Patty had a new boyfriend, someone she met while she was still working at Gosmore. What can you tell me about him?"

"Really? A boyfriend? I don't know. If it was anything serious, I would have known about it."

Sam escorted me to the elevator. While we were waiting, he said, "I don't understand why this case is still going on. She took those pills. She was depressed. I know your boss is supposed to be a good lawyer, but why isn't she getting this case dismissed? It's really stressful for all of us."

"I get you, man. She's trying, believe me. It's even more stressful for our client," I said, as the elevator pinged and opened behind me.

The next morning, my first task was to see Patty's reclusive aunt, Jill Crenshaw. James, my trusty GPS, directed me to a dispirited 70s-era apartment building south of downtown Oakland.

The door of her apartment had a sign on front next to the apartment number, which said "Manager." After I knocked, I heard footsteps, and the sound of the television being turned down. The door opened a few inches and a stocky woman in a lumberjack shirt, sweats, and bedroom slippers peered out at me nearsightedly. Her hair was iron grey and stringy, and her soft skin was covered with wrinkles, which creased as she squinted at me.

"Hi," I said, holding out my business card to her. "I'm Armando Felan. Your nephew Sam called you yesterday to say I'd be coming by?"

She took my card and looked at it for a second. "You're from San Diego?"

"Right."

She opened the door and backed away to let me in.

"So you've come all the way up from San Diego. I would never live there myself. Don't like the politics."

"Oh?"

"That's right," she said. "I know I like it here. Actually, I don't really like to leave my apartment at all. That's why this job managing these apartments works for me."

"Good for you. Why mess with a good thing, then."

"That's right." She shuffled over to a recliner that was dead centered in front of the TV, and motioned me towards a couch next to the chair, which also had an excellent view of the giant screen. The TV stayed on.

Aunt Jill's face turned towards the TV. The sound had been lowered, but it was still very audible. I saw I would be competing for her attention with a History Channel program on the Crusades. Maybe this was her way of avoiding having to talk about her niece. What the heck. We watched the show for a minute.

"You have a nice television," I said, angling myself sideways on the couch seat so I could see her profile and not have to conduct the interview side by side like strangers on a park bench. The TV was state of the art, with a flat screen as big as Mom's kitchen table, and so new the label was still stuck to the frame.

She peered at me. "What?

I raised my voice. "I like your TV!"

"Why shouldn't I have a nice TV?"

"No reason."

"It's a good use of money. There's nothing wrong with TV, if you watch educational shows." She gave me a sudden wide smile, revealing a space where an upper tooth was missing halfway back in her mouth.

"Good point," I said. I might have put my priorities elsewhere than a TV screen that was right in my face. For example, in dental work, or a couch that didn't have springs popping out of it, but I wasn't going to judge her. Maybe she was afraid of dentists. She had the same forest-gnome quality as her nephew Sam. Patty must have taken after her father's side of the family, I thought.

While I had Jill's attention, I added quickly, "Listen, I'm very sorry about your niece. Her death must have been a shock to you."

"Oh, it was, honey. When Sammy called to tell me she was gone, I couldn't believe it. I'd just talked to her the night before, on Skype."

"What time did you talk to her?"

"The usual time. She'd call me once or twice a month, usually around the same time. She knew I like to watch the Discovery channel every night from nine to ten, so she would call me some time after that. I remember her call was a nice surprise, because we'd just Skyped the week before. Sam came to see me the very next day, the day they...found her. I said to him, how can that be, I just talked to her."

I looked around the cluttered room and saw a small laptop on the kitchen table. "Is that the computer you used?"

"Yes. When Patty moved away, Sammy gave me one of his old laptops, and set it up here for me so I could use the Skype to keep in touch with Patty. I don't think much of computers, but it sure has been nice to see her and talk to her."

"What did you talk about, the night she died?" I asked.

Her gaze turned back towards the television, which was showing an advertisement for weight-loss medication. The list of side effects, in small print on the screen and speed-read in a low, mildly apologetic male voice, was long and alarming. I saw that Ms. Crenshaw's eyes had reddened and one of her hands was trembling. She suddenly seemed much older than she'd looked at first. It took so long for her to answer me that I was getting ready to repeat my question when she spoke.

"We talked about anything and everything, like we always did," she said in a quavering voice. "That's what made our relationship special. We didn't talk about our lives so much as the bigger things. History, nature, science, legal cases, you name it. I remember this last time I told her about a show I'd just seen on whales. I asked her if she knew the biggest kind of whale, and she did. But she didn't know how long whales live. Did you know a female Orca can live to be eighty years old? She was surprised at that. I asked her how was work, and she said fine, like she always did. She asked me how was my work, and I said fine, like I always did. After we talked about the whales, she told me about a place in San Diego where they have lots of sea animals, and she'd been there and thought of me, that I would like it.

"I can't remember anything unusual in our conversation. The only thing I've thought of is, when we signed off, she said, 'Aunt Jill, you take care of yourself. I love you.' Usually she just said, 'take care,' not, 'I love you.' That was nice of her. I wonder now if she knew she was going to die."

"Did she look worried or unhappy?"

"No, not that I noticed at the time. She looked a bit tired. She'd been working hard."

"What did you see in the background, last time you talked to her? Was anyone there with her?"

"Someone with her? Oh, no, I don't think so. I didn't even know she had a boyfriend until Sammy told me they'd arrested that man. No, I recall she was sitting, with a pillow or something behind her back. She had a laptop, like mine, and often she'd take it in her room so she could relax on her bed while we talked. Patty was an early riser, and I'm a night owl. She'd often call me right before she went to sleep."

Ms. Crenshaw didn't seem to remember anything else of use from her recent conversations with Patty. They had talked about many things, but it appeared the conversations frequently consisted of Aunt Jill summarizing the nature program she had just seen for Patty.

"Patty and her brother Sammy are the only family I had left, since my sister died." She looked vaguely around the room. "I used to have a lovely picture of her, but I seem to have misplaced it."

I scanned the room, but did not see any photographs. The room was rather cluttered. While Aunt Jill was wiping her eyes, I got up and looked around, looking under papers and sweaters and other objects that might be hiding the missing photo. "Sorry," I said. "I don't see it."

"I'll ask Sammy to get me another one," she said.

I asked her about Patty's life before she moved to San Diego.

"I didn't see much of her when she was growing up," Ms. Crenshaw said. "Her mother and I, well, like a lot of sisters, we had an intense relationship. We were estranged for many years. When Marie, got the Alzheimer's, I started to see more of Patty and Sammy. They would sometimes come together to see me after visiting Marie in the nursing home. I do remember when Patty was young, Marie told me she was quite a handful."

"Oh?"

"Yes, quite a handful."

"How so?"

She frowned in an effort to remember. "I couldn't tell you any specifics. It was so long ago. My sister was not the easiest person to get along with, herself. My general impression is Marie spoiled Patty when she was young, and when Patty hit her teenage years she started to rebel and act out. Later, it was boy troubles. She grew out of that phase, though. Still had a bit of a wild streak, but these last few years I couldn't have asked for a nicer niece."

"Do you know whether Patty ever suffered from depression? Did she ever get any mental health treatment?"

"Not that I ever heard. But her mother might not have told me. She was always a moody girl, though, I can tell you that."

"Did you ever meet any of her friends, boyfriends, people she worked with?"

"I met her friend Christine a few times. A sweet girl, came over with Patty to visit me a few times when they were going out to the movies here in my neighborhood."

"What about boyfriends?"

"She did date someone that summer before she moved. I remember her telling me she'd met a nice boy, and I said, just teasing her, so that's why I never see you."

"Do you know his name? Would you recognize him if you saw him?"

"No, I'm afraid not. I never met him."

"Did you ever meet Christine's husband, Brad?"

"No." She turned back to the TV screen, which displayed a Crusades reenactment, with a small number of Christians wielding heavy shields and waving swords at an unseen enemy. I was guessing it was a low budget show. I wondered if I could come back that night and get her to put on MTV. ABDC was getting down to the final six dance crews tonight, and I'd probably never get another chance to see the show on such a big screen.

When I could get her attention back, I asked, "You said your niece still had a wild streak. What did you mean by that?"

She watched the screen another minute and then turned to face me. "A wild streak? Yes, I guess she did."

"Can you give me an example?"

She was watching the screen again, so I wasn't sure if she'd heard me. I waited to see whether she would answer. A minute later, she said, "Well, I'll tell you something she did once. Once, when she and Christine were over, Patty took out her cell phone. I don't approve of cell phones. I think they're rude." She paused and looked at me suspiciously, like she'd seen the bulge of the cell phone in my pocket.

I scratched my head. "Is that why you said--?"

"Oh, no, dear. Let me finish. Patty took out her cell phone and made a call to the law firm where she worked. I was impressed at how she was able to disguise her voice. She asked to speak to one of the attorneys, and she reached his secretary. She told the secretary she was calling from the court and the judge wanted this attorney to file some paperwork with the court by that afternoon. I don't remember the details. Well, it turned out, Patty had had a meeting scheduled with the attorney that afternoon and she wanted to go to the movies with Christine instead. She made up this story so the attorney would be too busy to meet with her. When she hung up, she laughed so hard!

"Her friend Christine was a little shocked, I think. Patty said the attorney had tried to make her look bad in front of her boss, and, she said, 'It's him or me.' It was like she was just getting even. Christine said something to Patty like, 'honey, you're really in the wrong job.' Then they both laughed a little."

"Wow," I said. "That's a funny prank." I wondered if I could use it to get Lucy out of the office some time. "I heard from people who knew Patty in San Diego, that she was very quiet and sweet."

Aunt Jill had turned back to the screen and was watching some kind of pretty shots of old cathedrals with gargoyles and other ornate decorations. I watched with her. A minute later she spoke again.

"Quiet and sweet? Yes, she is, was, very sweet. But quiet? Oh, no, she was a dear, but I wouldn't have exactly called her quiet. She had a salty tongue when she wanted to. I can't repeat the names that she called some of the attorneys that she worked with. Patty was a lot of fun." Her eyes swiveled back to the TV.

Fighting the TV for Aunt Jill's attention was starting to get on my nerves. After saying goodbye, I let myself out, my head spinning slightly.

The apartment where Patty had lived while she worked at the Gosmore firm was not far from Aunt Jill's apartment building. By the time I drove to the address and parked, I was ready for lunch. It wouldn't hurt to get a feel for the neighborhood and grab a bite to eat before I went in to interview Patty's old neighbors.

The neighborhood was in a marginal area. It was close to a good part of downtown with high-rise office buildings, high-end shops and restaurants, and an indoor mall, but if you walked the other direction you hit project housing with broken windows and people doing business on the street corners. I wandered into the mall, grabbed a Subway and a coke, and ate at the counter looking out at the shoppers. The Oakland lunchtime crowd was dressier than San Diego's. A lot of guys were wearing these black pants with almost-skinny-fit legs and a subtle sag at the hip. They looked so good. If I got some, would they feel all wrong in San Diego? I could see myself in them late night clubbing, or maybe at the Rudolfo concert, like with a black net tee, or a solid tee and the platinum chain Ma had given me.

A few hours later, a little after five o'clock, I walked out of the mall and dropped off my shopping bags in the car. It really hadn't made sense to try to talk to Patty's neighbors until after work hours.

Patty's former apartment was in a rundown high-rise, filled with unfriendly people who seemed desperate to get into their apartments and crash after their workday. The door to Patty's second floor apartment was on an indoor cement walkway above a cement slab with a small round swimming pool staring up like a blue eyeball. It did not surprise me most of the neighbors either didn't remember Patty or had moved in after she left.

Finally, at an apartment across the indoor courtyard on the same level, I found a neighbor who remembered her. He was a grey-haired man in his sixties, wearing jeans, high-tops, an Oakland Raiders football jersey, and holding a bottle of Budweiser.

"Sure, I remember them," he said. "They moved in about a week after I did. I took them a six-pack as a welcome present."

"They?"

"Two girls, right? Good looking. Especially the one with the long legs." He gave me a comradely leer.

"But just one of them actually lived here," I said. "Maybe you saw her with her friend?"

"Huh? Oh, yeah, maybe they did tell me it was just the one girl renting the place. I kind of forgot, because I saw both of them there all the time. Sometimes, they'd go out jogging together in their shorts. Uh-huh."

"Did you ever see any men visiting?"

"One of them had a boyfriend coming around, after they'd been there a while. Nerdy guy with a square forehead."

"Which, uh, girl, did you see him with?"

"It was the one who lived there. The shorter one, the girl with short brown hair and the big...."

"No," I interrupted, "the one who lived there was Patty, the tall one," I said.

"Really? Oh, right. Well, anyway, it was the other girl who had the boyfriend."

I didn't get anything else out of the neighbor. Patty apparently had the good taste to avoid him after his first overture with the six-pack. I gave him my card in case he remembered anything significant.

Back at my motel, I completed and e-mailed my detailed report to Lucy. Then I slumped on the saggy bed, with my laptop on a pillow on my lap, looking for the best bars and clubs in the area. My cell rang and I saw it was Justin.

"Hi, baby," he said. "How's your investigation going? Can I tell Domingo his attorney's going to get him sprung so we can get cracking on his asylum case?"

"I wish. I keep learning little things which could mean something, but to me they add up to nothing," I replied. "Maybe Lucy will make something of them. Sometimes I feel like I'm just her camera."

"Well, you must be a damn good camera, or she wouldn't keep you on. There's a lot of people out there who would kill to work for her. Hey, I talked with our new attorney, Dave Rosen, about Paolo Sanchez. Dave thinks Paolo may be key to Domingo's immigration case. Have you got any more information on Paolo?"

"I haven't. Our investigator, Claude, is planning to do some surveillance, but I don't know if he's found out anything yet."

"Oh. Can you let me know what he learns?"

"Sure," I said, clicking on one of my search results for clubs in the Oakland area. "Hey, do you know of any good clubs up here?"

"Yeah, of course, especially if you don't mind going into The City. Wish I could go with you."

"Me, too. I hope Lucy lets me come home early tomorrow. I'm so lonely and bored, I'm having a close personal relationship with my GPS."

Before we hung up, Justin asked, "You will be home for Saturday night, won't you, Armando?"

"Of course. I have our Rudolfo tickets. Slim is going, too, with your friend Daniel."

"Oh, really." Justin sounded surprised. "I didn't hear about that. Pete just told me he and Rodrigo were going. Shit. I wish it was just you and me. I don't need the drama right now."

"Well, what can we do?" I said. "I agree, your friend Daniel is bad news, but Slim can handle him. Slim doesn't believe in getting too attached to anyone."

"Yeah, a lot of guys say that, but you never know. I couldn't do that."

I was scrolling down these sample pictures on the Internet dating site I had somehow ended up on: "Oakland Daters." A few of the guys were really hot.

"Sorry," I said. "Do what?"

"Never mind, 'Mando. I'm just missing you. Let me tell you the clubs I like best, and then I can go have a hot date with my Corporations text while you're out having fun."

Justin had given me good leads on the club scene. I didn't get back to the motel until almost four a.m., and forgot to turn off my cell phone before I crashed between the cool sheets. The first attempt barely woke me, only enough where it's like, OK, I'm kind of awake, but just enough to be happy that I'm in this delicious soft bed and I know it'll only ring a couple more times and then I'm going to slip right back into…. The second attempt got me up enough to pull the pillow over my head and whisper, "no, no, no, go away." The third time, I picked up, knowing she wouldn't stop. I checked the time. Eight a.m. I cleared my throat.

"I'm not on the clock for another half hour," I greeted her. "Early morning costs triple overtime."

"You've probably done all you can up there," she replied. "You've gotten what you could, and I need some help. Get an earlier flight home and come on in to the office. You don't have anything planned for today, do you?"

"Oh, my God, did you even read my reports? Did you see what I found out about Patty and Brad?"

"Yes. I read your email and your report last night. This relationship between Patty and Brad is unexpected. It appears you were right about the engraving on the Napoleon statue. I may need to talk to Brad Fernwood myself. What was your impression of him? Could he have done this?"

"I don't know," I said. "I can't see him committing a crime of passion. What I don't get is how Patty and Christine could both be attracted to him. He's arrogant, obsessed by his work, boring, and not at all good-looking."

"Well, that's no head scratcher, Armando. He probably makes an extremely good salary," she said. "Ah, this case has too many odd things about it. Why didn't Brad or Christine mention Patty's romance with Brad? Now if Christine didn't have an alibi.... But she does, because Patty was alive and Skyping with her aunt when Christine was on her way to Santa Barbara. Aunt Jill told you Patty was moody, that will support our suicide theory. But then, why is Patty's wallet missing? The gang might have taken it. But if it's a gang killing, would the gang really use the victim's own medication to poison her? They might have improvised.... Maybe there's another angle altogether. God, we have so much to do."

"Is there anything else I can do up here?" I asked.

"No, Armando, as I said, you should take the next flight back. I've got five court appearances today, and things are piling up rather badly here. Your flight doesn't leave until this evening.

I'm not going to pay you to lie around the pool all day, or barhop, or ride the ferry, or whatever else there is in Oakland for tourists to do."

"Barhop?" I said. "The ferry?" Seriously? I hung up on her.

I turned off my cell and went back to sleep for a few hours, which is really the best cure for a hangover. Then I had a nice swim in the motel pool, and went out to lunch at a cute restaurant on the waterfront near the ferry landing.

Gazing across the bay at the skyline of The City, I called Justin. I told him about my night out, and he told me a long, funny story about one of the clubs I'd been to. We made weekend plans. After I hung up, I nursed my second Bloody Mary and smiled as I replayed parts of our conversation. Yeah, there was a freaking cold wind, reminding me again I wasn't in San Diego any more. But Mama Sun was kissing my face and my shoulders and my thighs and I felt real fine.

21

As I wheeled my bag to my car in the long-term parking lot in San Diego, the sky was dark but the air was warm and loving. I was debating whether to call Justin, or go home and spend some time with Mom, when my cell phone rang.

"Hi, Connie."

"'Mando, are you back? Are you back in San Diego?"

"Just leaving the airport."

"Oh, good. Marco's dying to talk to you. Here he is."

"Uncle 'Mando?"

"Marco! Hi buddy! Howyadoin'?"

"My tooth fell out today. I'm going to put it under my pillow. Can you come over and see my tooth before the tooth fairy takes it?"

"Sure I can. Let me talk to your mom."

"Hi, are you coming over?"

"Yeah, but I can't stay too long. I haven't seen Mom yet."

"Don't worry about that. She's going to the opera with Italia tonight. I just talked to her, 'cause I needed her to babysit. Thank God, you can do it instead. Enrique's taking me to dinner for our anniversary."

As Marco climbed all over me, Connie shared her servant troubles. Not only was the new babysitter chronically unavailable, but the cleaning lady was also starting to disappoint.

"She leaves the clothes in the dryer too long and our clothes get all wrinkled. Mom never let that happen."

I had been walking Marco around the room with his little feet on top of mine. I stopped and looked at Connie. She was brushing Rafaela's hair, which was so fine and sparse that it stood in a crest like meringue on top of her head.

"Are you telling me Mom does your laundry?"

"Well, when she was here babysitting all day, she didn't have anything else to do. I didn't ask her to do it."

Marco started lifting his feet on top of mine, like that was going to make my feet start stepping again. It worked.

The front door slammed and Enrique walked in. Enrique is a pouchy ex-jock who works in management at the same insurance company as Connie. He gave Connie a kiss, turned the channel on the big screen TV to a sports station, and sat on the couch.

"Hey, Armando. How's the law business?"

"Thrilling and chilling, as always, Brother. How's the insurance business?"

"Great. You and Connie been talking about our family vacation?"

Connie handed Raffie to Enrique and stood up. "Not yet," she said. "You tell him, while I get dressed."

Enrique changed the channel to another sports station, where three big ex-jocks sat at a table and moved their mouths. Their TV is always on, and the sound is always turned just above the subliminal hearing range. I felt like I was back at Aunt Jill's apartment in Oakland.

"Are you guys going somewhere fun?" I asked politely. Marco had walked me over to the couch and sat in my lap with a picture book.

"You mean us guys. Connie and your Dad are cooking up a big family get-away to Acapulco. You're supposed to come, and Chuy and Elena and their kids and your mom. We'll bring the kids so your mom can have some quality time with them while Connie and I go scuba diving."

"Does Mom know about this?"

"It's going to be a surprise. You know, me and Connie went there for our honeymoon. You can go parasailing, jetskiing, sportfishing, anything you want. There's a great sports bar, too. It's got six big screens and full satellite…."

I nodded and tried to grin heartily. "Can't wait," I thought to myself. But I was already casting back in my memory for what I'd heard about the nightlife and the boys cliff diving in Acapulco.

***

The trolley whined to a stop, and a wave of high-school kids spilled out the doors on to the sidewalk in front of us, shoving and yelling with youthful exuberance. A group of girls were literally screaming at each other, hoping to attract the attention of some nearby boys. By the time we got in and were seated, there were two pinched lines between Lucy's eyebrows.

"Remind me," she said, "to wait until after school has started next time I decide to take the trolley downtown."

I yawned. It had been late by the time I finished babysitting the night before, as Connie and Enrique had taken the opportunity to go clubbing until the early morning hours. I was having trouble switching into work mode.

"Has Claude found out anything about Paolo Sanchez?"

"No. He's been checking up on Frank Slattery this week."

"Oh?"

"You know, after reading your reports from Oakland, I can't imagine Patty would have been so uncomfortable dealing with Slattery's harassment. She doesn't exactly sound like a delicate flower. Your reports changed my idea of what she was like."

"Right? I'd been picturing this sweet, gentle, idealistic lady. After talking to people at her old law firm, I had to adjust my view of her, too. Either everyone at the firm was lying about her, or she was a bit of a twister. And her Aunt Jill even said the same thing. I wonder if something happened that made her change when she moved down here."

"Possibly." Lucy said.

"What?"

"I don't know," she said. "Do people change so?"

"Sure," I said. "Maybe Brad changed her. Maybe she felt guilty for having an affair with her best friend's husband. No, wait. I think the affair with Brad was over. She fell in love with Domingo, and became the woman he wanted her to be, quiet and sweet."

Lucy nodded. "She may have been less assertive in fending off Frank's advances, because she was feeling guilty about her involvement with Domingo. He could have seen her with Domingo or Brad, and had a fit of jealousy."

"But, remember she made false accusations of harassment when she was at Gosmore."

"We don't know they were false. And we know Frank was harassing her. Her co-workers were witnesses."

"Only to some of it. Patty might have made up the part about his coming to her house with champagne. She probably exaggerated the harassment."

"Why would she do that?" Lucy asked.

"Well, before I talked to her old firm in Oakland, that wouldn't have occurred to me. But now it makes sense, 'specially if she was unhappy with her work. Maybe Frank had been criticizing her work and she wanted to get back at him. That would fit with her behavior at Gosmore. I really don't think Frank was involved in her death."

Lucy gave me a questioning look, but the trolley stopped and we got off and headed for the jail.

Lucy and I told Domingo what we'd learned about Patty's prior relationship with Brad. Domingo seemed oddly elated by this news. "I should have known it!" he said. "Brad was in love with her, I'm certain of it. He killed her because he knew she loved me. I was so afraid it was Cantara, that my involvement with them had caused her death. But I know it was Brad. I don't believe she ever really loved him. She told me she never loved anyone until she met me. Of course, it was a crime of passion. You can prove it, and they will execute him. Thank God, your fine country still has a penalty of death."

Before we left, Domingo asked, "When are you going to see Francisco? He told me you would be going to Juarez."

Lucy looked at me blankly. I shook my head. Then I remembered.

"It's Slattery's office," I said. "Justin told me Frank's hired a new attorney, who's going to take over Domingo's immigration case. They plan to go to Juarez to investigate the case."

Her eyes got hard as I spoke. She looked over at Domingo and said calmly, "Ah. Well, we'll have to coordinate with them over this."

Lucy started to ream me out as soon as we stepped out of the jail. I report all of my investigations to Lucy in detail, either in person or in writing. Unfortunately, I hadn't remembered to tell her about my recent conversation with Justin, since it had taken place kind of outside of work. But I couldn't tell her that.

Lucy was quiet during our trolley ride back to the office. When we walked in the door, she said, "Come sit down for a minute. I want to talk about how to handle this thing with Slattery."

I sat and fidgeted while she got herself settled. Did she suspect something about my relationship with Justin?

Lucy cleared her throat. "Justin seems like a worthwhile young man. He's smart, and he's gone out of his way to help us in this case. I'm concerned his working for Frank Slattery is going to do a lot of damage to his resume, if Frank ends up being our guy and all this comes out. But we can't warn Justin without jeopardizing our investigation of Frank."

"You think he would tell Frank we suspect him?"

"Of course he would. Even if he doesn't respect Slattery very much, he's going to feel a lot of loyalty towards him. He'll want to protect Slattery."

22

When Rudolfo finally came on stage, and started singing "*La Trampa de Oro,*" Justin and I looked at each other and smiled and started singing along. I had to fake the high notes, but Justin hit them high and long, closing his eyes and smiling. The night was warm, with a cool, salty breeze coming from the ocean, which borders the racetrack. I looked up to the blue-black sky and saw a flock of seagulls flying over the infield, and the first stars coming out, and the glow from the big stage spotlights disappearing under that dark, magically infinite blanket which was the universe above us.

Justin had brought the binoculars he uses for birdwatching, so he could see the stage better. I could tell Slim thought he didn't look very cool, but I was beyond caring. I let myself go and watched my beautiful red-haired boy holding the binoculars, his long fingers straight and parallel to the ground, bobbing his head to the music as he scanned the stage.

The first half of the concert went by fast. Then there was an intermission, during which we noticed our friends behind us were engaging in some D.

"Hey! He asked you to back off!" I heard Rodrigo say loudly. I looked behind me. Rodrigo was standing between Pete and Daniel. Daniel was trying to get around Rodrigo to grab at Pete. Rodrigo was in his cop stance, legs spread apart and arms hanging ready at his sides.

"I just want to buy him another drink. Drinks on me, for everyone. I just want to talk to him." Daniel lurched forward against Rodrigo.

Pete started making his way in the opposite direction. Rodrigo shoved Daniel back down in his seat and followed Pete.

Daniel started to get up to follow them, but his knees buckled and he sat back down. Slim pressed on his shoulder, and Daniel finally relaxed and shook his head.

"Ah, fuck it," Daniel said. He crossed his arms and legs and slumped down into his seat.

Slim crawled awkwardly over the back of the seat next to me. "Can I have some of your beer?" he asked, grabbing the half-full paper cup and downing it.

"In case you haven't noticed," Slim whispered, leaning towards me confidentially, "my date has gotten himself pretty waxed."

"So I see. How long has he been like this? I wasn't paying attention to you guys back there."

Slim smiled and peeked around me at Justin, who was using his binoculars to track some seagulls flying overhead. "Yeah," he said. "I noticed."

I looked back up at Daniel, who was beginning to mutter something under his breath. His pomp was windblown, a clump of white-blond hair had blown over his forehead, and his jacket fell open at his sides.

"What are you going to do with your naughty boy?" I asked Slim.

"Oh, he'll be OK, now." Slim was still whispering. "I expect Rodrigo and Pete'll go hang out somewhere else. If he starts to act up again, I'll load him in my truck and take him home."

"Are you sure you can handle him?"

"What?" Slim frowned at me, as if the bright lights from the stage in front of us were hurting his eyes.

"Can you take care of him by yourself? What if he turns mean?"

"Oh." Slim put his arm on my shoulder. "I see what you're sayin'," Slim continued to whisper to me, switching to Spanish. "What I don't understand is, he just had the one drink, and he didn't seem drunk when I picked him up to drive here tonight. This came on kind of sudden."

I looked over at Daniel. His head had kind of lolled to one side and his long legs had uncrossed and manspread out in front of him. Slim shook his head.

"I should prob'ly drive him home right now. But I want to hear more music. Plus, I don't feel so much like driving, yet."

Slim was whispering so I could barely hear him, and I noticed his eyes were unfocused.

"Slim, are you OK?" I raised my voice, causing Justin to put down his binoculars and look at us.

"A little dizzy," he whispered.

"Sit down." I got up and eased him into my seat.

I turned to Justin. "He says he's dizzy."

Justin came closer to Slim and looked at his face. Slim stared back with round eyes. "Slim, do you feel like you're on something?"

"I don't do drugs, man."

"OK. But do you feel funny, like you're seeing things?"

"More like things are kinda moving around."

Justin touched my arm. "Sit here with him for a minute."

I kept my hand on Slim's shoulder and watched as Justin climbed over the back of his seat and sat next to Daniel, who was still sprawled in his seat. He shook Daniel's arm, and Daniel turned to look at him.

"Hey, Justin, my friend. Are you having a good time? I'm having a good time."

"Hey, Daniel. Sure, we're having a good time. Listen, did you take something tonight?"

"Just a little XTC, man. You want some?"

"No, thanks. Did you give Slim some, too?"

"I put it in our drinks. Me, Slim, Rodrigo. Even that rat Pete, I gave him some too. Nice of me, huh?"

"Just Ecstasy? Nothing else?"

"Nothing else. Why, you want something else? You know I can get it for you."

I looked at Daniel. "You shithead," I said. "You gave them drugs without telling them."

People were starting to return to their seats around us. Daniel kept looking at me. "You want something, too, Armando?" His voice got louder. "I can get you some weed, coke, reds, yellow jackets, you name it. Just ask Justin."

"Shut the fuck up," Justin said.

I stood Slim up. "Let's go get you a drink of water, baby."

Justin followed us out to the aisle, and he and I walked on either side of Slim. As people went back to their seats, the hallway inside of the grandstand was clearing out, and we found a drinking fountain. As Slim took a long drink, I got out my iPhone and punched in an Internet search for "ecstasy overdose."

"Nice friends you have," I said to Justin, as I waited for my search results to come up.

As the second half of the Rudolfo concert started, Justin and I were walking Slim around the deserted hallways behind the Grandstand, past bored-looking bartenders and popcorn sellers, up the stairs on one side, down the other side, hearing the music and the crowd in the distance. Slim is petite, and he had not been expecting this experience, so the drug acted powerfully on his unaccustomed system. When he said he needed to go to a hospital, I came close to calling 911. We talked him down, gave him some water, and fed him a hot dog to dilute the drug in his system. After about twenty minutes, Slim had calmed down and was starting to enjoy the effects.

"I feel so much love for you guys right now, Armando."

"I love you, too, baby," I said. "You're going to be OK."

"Let's go hear the rest of the music."

Justin and I looked at each other.

"C'mon guys. I'm much better. That dizziness is gone, and I'm just feeling kind of happy and calm. I want to go back to Daniel. Don't worry, I won't let him give me any more drugs."

Back at our seats, Pete and Rodrigo were still gone. Daniel was still in his seat, zoned out. As Slim slipped back to his seat, I heard Daniel say. "I missed you, Slim."

"You're bad news, Pomp-head," Slim sat down next to him. "Sit down and stop causing trouble for a while."

After Rudolfo's second encore song, Justin and I turned and saw Slim and Daniel walking towards the exit.

"Do you think Slim's OK to drive?" I asked.

"He seemed a lot better," Justin said.

"Let's catch up with them," I said.

As I started to walk towards the exit, Justin touched my arm. "Wait a minute. I have a surprise for you."

"A hit of speed, maybe? Some roofies?"

He stood and looked at me, his face pale and intense under the grandstand lights. "You're pissed at me?"

I thought about it. The whole second half of the concert had been wrecked for me. Slim drugged and frightened, Rudolfo's haunting *narcocorridas* narrating grisly stories of the cartels' activities, had all given me flashbacks to childhood times in Mexico, my troubles with my father, mom's kidnapping. The beautiful bright night had turned dark and nightmarish.

The exiting crowd bumped around us as we stood on the stairway. "How did you know Daniel had drugged those drinks?" I asked Justin. "Has he done this kind of thing before?"

"No, of course not. Uh, not that I know of, anyway. Pete told me Daniel uses Ecstasy sometimes. I thought maybe he'd gotten Slim to try something. Believe me, Armando, I never thought Daniel would do something like this."

"Then, I'm not mad at you. But if we ever have to go out with Daniel again, I'm going to make you taste my drink before I have it. To see if it's poisoned."

"Deal. Follow me. We should hurry." Justin turned and scrambled down towards the stage, weaving against the flow of the crowd. I followed his red head down to the rail of the racetrack, and over to a temporary fence set across the racetrack. Security guards in suits were stationed along the fence, making sure the crowd didn't try to sneak back towards the tents and trailers set up in the infield.

When I got to the fence, Justin was standing next to one of the guards and smiling at me. The guard was holding the fence open, and I followed Justin through. The guard closed the fence back behind us.

Justin and I walked to the door of the biggest tent, which was located right behind the stage. Another guard at the door checked for Justin's name on a clipboard, checked his ID, and waved us through. The tent was huge, with couches along the walls, a few small tables and a lot of folding chairs, and a long table stocked with drinks and food. Members of the band lounged around sipping water and liquor, and around them chattered groupies and personal assistants and security guards in suits. At the far end of the room, sitting on a couch, was Rudolfo.

"Justin, how did you...."

"Come on, let's go say 'hi' before this room becomes a zoo."

Rudolfo had exchanged his flashy costume for an oversized fleece shirt, baggy jeans, and a thick scarf wrapped around his throat. With the rock star vibe gone, he looked like a regular guy you'd like to hang with. He was drinking water from a metal bottle with his logo on it, and sitting next to a middle-aged Latino man in jeans. In a chair across from them sat a black man in a military uniform, whose profile looked familiar to me. As Justin moved forward to greet Rudolfo, the military man turned and looked at me.

"Hey there, Armando." And there was Claude, our star investigator.

"Claude! What're you doing here?"

"Long story, girlie. What about you?"

"My friend just brought me back here."

We turned and listened to Justin greeting Rudolfo and his security guard, Hector. They were speaking fast in Spanish, so I summarized what they were saying for Claude.

"Justin's asking Rudolfo about how Rudolfo's family is doing. They're talking about Rudolfo's brother, Miguel." I lowered my voice. "Hey, Claude, did you ask Rudolfo about Domingo?"

"I did, as a matter of fact. Rudolfo owes me a little favor, and his security guard, Hector, is gonna get me some information. Rudolfo don't got nuthin' against Domingo, he says."

I heard Rudolfo laugh out loud at something Justin was telling him.

"*No me digas!*" Rudolfo cried, slapping his knee. He looked at me curiously, his humorous face lit up with amusement. Clueless, I just grinned back.

"Rudolfo, this is my friend Armando," Justin said.

Rudolfo shook my hand and said it was a pleasure to meet a friend of Justin's. I babbled something about the honor of meeting him, and he nodded graciously and turned back to Justin.

"Armando, I'm gonna split," Claude said, from my other side. "That little shit Paolo Sanchez and his buddies are in the house, and they're in with Rudolfo's man, Hector. I don't want to run into them." Claude pulled the brim of his hat a little further down over his eyes, and slipped out of the room.

I turned back to Justin and Rudolfo. The room was getting more crowded, and some people were lining up behind Justin, waiting to see Rudolfo. Justin shook hands with Rudolfo, pushed back his chair, and took my elbow. "Want to go?" he asked me. "Or you want to hang out for awhile?"

"Let's get a drink."

"Yeah." We made our way through the crowd to the long table. "Who's that soldier guy you were talking to?" Justin asked.

"Lucy's investigator, Claude. I'm guessing he trailed Paolo Sanchez here tonight. Not sure how he got to come backstage."

Justin and I hung out for an hour in the VIP lounge, talking to musicians and crew. I spotted Paolo Sanchez coming in with two men and two women. I turned away to avoid his seeing me. Paolo and one of his companions went over to Rudolfo's guard, Hector. Hector shook their hands and took them out one of the side doors. I was tempted to follow them, but I became distracted having to help Justin fend off a couple of groupies who kept wanting to play with his red curls.

When we were ready to leave, we went to say good-bye to Rudolfo. He was still in his seat, surrounded by a small crowd, and looked cheerful but tired. As we left, he winked at me. "You watch out for the Borgias! Ha, ha!" He and Justin laughed.

"What was that about?" I followed Justin outside to the grassy infield where there were a couple of big buses and a small trailer. Security guards were still stationed around the perimeter of Rudolfo's tent, and roadies were folding up equipment and packing it into big black cases. A few musicians strolled around enjoying the night air.

"I told Rudolfo about Daniel drugging people's drinks tonight," Justin replied, "and then I told him what you said about my tasting your drink first whenever Daniel is around. Rudolfo thought that was funny."

As we turned back towards the Grandstand, we heard a loud thump come from behind one of the buses. I crouched down to look underneath the bus, and saw three sets of legs moving around.

I felt a tap on my shoulder and almost jumped out of my skin.

Claude's deep voice said behind me, "'Mando, go stand on this side of that bus. There's two guys talkin' to Paolo in Spanish. I want to know what they're saying."

Justin put a warning hand on my arm, but I crept quickly over to the side of the bus and listened. I heard another thump, not as loud this time, and the bus vibrated next to me.

"Ow! Watch my jacket!" said Paolo's voice.

"We're gonna wrap it around your neck and choke you with it, if you don't give us a straight answer. You got some mileage out of that job in Juarez, but that doesn't make you the boss. Now, let's try this again. Tell us what the fuck you were doing messing with Torres."

"OK, man. I knew we didn't want a hit on this side of the border. When he was arrested for killing his new girlfriend, I thought of another way to get him. I thought I was helping out. That's all, man."

"Your job is not to think. Your job is to remember you're a piece of shit and people give you orders to do their shit work so they don't have to get dirty. You got that?"

"Yeah, sure."

"Ask him about the DA," another voice said.

"Paolo. What kind of a deal did the DA offer you to talk to them? Don't give us the same story or you'll be sorry."

"OK. They told me if I didn't help them, they'd get the ICE to mess up my green card and get me deported."

"And you believed them?"

"Fuck, man. They brought a fuckin' Border Patrol guy with them. He parked his white truck in front of my house. Half the people in my building was running out the back door."

There was a brief silence. Then a humorless laugh.

I heard the men start to move, and I darted back to join Claude and Justin, who were standing and watching me from the edge of the turf. We walked together back towards the parking lots and I translated what I had heard.

Claude's hard gaze skimmed over Justin, standing at my side. "All right, then, I'm out of here."

"Tell me how you got in to see Rudolfo," I said.

"Some other time. I'll catch you guys later." Claude peeled off towards the VIP parking lot, pulling out his cell phone.

"You going to call Lucy and deliver your report now?" I called to him as he started to turn away. He pretended not to hear me and walked off into the night.

Justin and I walked the half-mile back to the overflow parking lot. He was analyzing the implications of what Paolo had told Hector and the other Cantara gangsters, but I couldn't listen. My head was spinning with the fear I might have endangered Mom by appearing backstage. Had Paolo seen me, or would Rudolfo tell him I'd been there? Were these the people who had kidnapped Mom? I remembered Rudolfo's curious look at me.

"Hey." Justin broke into my thoughts, as we arrived at the car. I leaned against the hood, and looked up at the dark sky. The moon had gone behind a cloud, and a few stars were visible behind the murky atmosphere. Justin sat on the hood next to me, but not too close, like he could sense my jagged mood.   His feet in their worn hi-tops rested on the front bumper. I felt my breath deepen and I let out a sigh.

"Sorry," I said. "Having some morbid thoughts."

"About what?"

"I don't know, exactly," I told him. "Mexico, maybe. My past, my family. People doing bad things."

Justin's profile was still and dim in the damp ocean mist that had drifted over the coast. Even his red hair looked dark and dull. "Yeah," he said. "People do bad things."

23

Justin kept me well distracted the rest of the weekend, and I didn't think about Cantara or Paolo Sanchez until Monday afternoon. Lucy had asked Claude to join us to talk about the Torres case. As Claude and I sat on the couch and waited for Lucy to finish a call, I probed again.

"What're you doing here, anyway? Didn't you already give Lucy your report, in person? Saturday night, after you left us? You know, after midnight?"

Claude shook his head. "Get yourself a life, girlie."

"Well, how did you get in to see Rudolfo?"

"You can wait for my report."

"But Lucy's already heard it, riiiiiight?"

He was silent. Lucy was still on the phone. I decided to change the subject.

"So, did I tell you, I'm going to Acapulco with my family?"

"I thought you didn't get along with your family."

"Well, it's kind of a surprise for my mom. I get along with her and my sister's family OK. I don't have to hang out with my dad or my brother and his wife." I chatted away, enjoying the look of boredom on his face, until Lucy came in and joined us.

Claude reported he'd been tailing Paolo, as I'd suspected. By pure chance, Claude had possibly saved Rudolfo's life. Claude had been mingling in the crowd in front of the stage, which gave him a good view of Paolo and his buddies. He'd spotted a B-A gang member with a gun approaching the stage, and worked with security to remove him. Rudolfo's security staff had wanted to 'interrogate' the guy on their own, but Claude had insisted on calling the police. Still, Rudolfo had been grateful enough to bring Claude backstage and thank him.

At Claude's request, I repeated the conversation I'd overheard between Paolo and Hector, where Paolo admitted he'd tried to help the DA incriminate Domingo.

"It sounds like Cantara was not involved in Patty's death," Lucy said. "Unless you think Paolo killed Patty and is lying about it to his bosses."

"I agree, Luce," Claude said. "I talked awhile with Rudolfo's bodyguard, Hector. They said they owed me a big favor, and I asked them to tell me straight up if Cantara killed Patty or messed with Domingo's case. Hector promised me Cantara had nuthin' to do with Patty's death. He said they didn't put Paolo up to making those accusations against Domingo, either. I believe them. I think this angle is a dead end."

Lucy sighed. "Probably." She turned her blue stare on me.

"Now, Armando, please tell me that the red-haired young man named Justin you went to the concert with is not the same one who is a potential witness in the case we're investigating. Because when Claude described your date to me, I'm afraid I had to wonder. I know that even you wouldn't have such bad judgment, but I need to ask."

Shit. "So what if he is?" I told her. "He invited me. We were doing research on the case. You should be glad I was working free overtime for you."

Claude said, "Kind of a coincidence that Justin knew Rudolfo, and Rudolfo turns out to be involved in the Torres case."

Lucy added, "How did he get you backstage?"

"Justin spent a summer in Guadalajara, working on his Spanish. He made friends with Rudolfo's little brother, Miguel. He got close to the whole family, including Rudolfo."

Lucy snorted. "Close? Maybe he was close to Rudolfo, and to his gangster bodyguards. Dear God, Armando, your friend Justin's involved in this case every which way you turn. .... Blah, blah.... You've reached a new height of recklessness.... Blah, blah, blah, ... 'unprofessional' doesn't begin to describe your behavior. Blah.... description sounds .... something more than just a date. How far has this relationship gotten?"

I glared at Claude. He gave me a hard stare back, but I could see the corner of his mouth lift a little. Suddenly I felt like I was ten years old and my parents were punishing me for taking Dad's catamaran out by myself without permission.

"This is bullshit," I snarled. "You guys are both way out of line."

"Promise you won't see Justin again until this case is over."

"Fuck that. You don't own me. I'll do what I want, when I want, with any boy I want. I'm not going to give you any of the details about my personal life when I'm off the clock. If you need to get yourselves off, go rent a movie. Or fuck each other. Oh, I forgot, you're already doing that."

I really didn't slam the door on the way out. It just closed quicker than I expected.

***

Tears ran down my face. "It's been going on for almost five years, now. I was only nineteen when I started working for her. I must have quit or walked out at least fifteen times, but I always end up going back for more of her abuse. She's cold and intolerant and controlling. Just like my father. Oh, my God, I left my home, I left my father, and ended up with Her instead.

Why do I keep having these sick people in my life? It is so unfair."

"Of course, it's unfair." Christine's motherly face radiated sympathy. "That's your starting point, Armando. Unlike...some people, we don't need to name them, you have a beautiful free spirit which lifts the spirits of others. Some people want to pin you down. They want to make you follow petty rules and conventions, which have no real moral foundation. What you need to realize is that these people don't intend to hurt you, they just want to harness your beautiful energy and use it for their own benefit. Of course, that's not fair to you. Do you understand this?"

I nodded and hiccupped. My breath started to come easier.

"Good," Christine continued. "Now, I have a sense.... May I go out on a limb here, Armando? I have a sense of you as a gifted artist. Does that resonate for you?"

I stared at her in wonder. "How did you know?" I told her all about my aspiration to become a professional dancer, which I'd had to give up after high school when I had to go work for Lucy to support myself.

She nodded. "It's hard to have a gift, a God-given purpose, if you will, and not be able to use it fully. I'm going to make a couple of suggestions. First, I want you to think about whether your job is really such a bad fit as you think. Having seen you in a work context, I get the sense you enjoy the interactions you get with some aspects of your job, and are very good at what you do. Ms. Sanders must respect your work highly or you wouldn't be working for her. I see you as strong enough to give back to her what she dishes out. On the other hand, maybe you do want to consider making a change. Have you considered law school?"

"Lucy keeps telling me I should go. I'd have to go to college first. Truthfully, it all seems like too much work, for something I'm not even sure I want to do. Did you always know you wanted to be a therapist?"

"Me? Oh, no, Armando, it took me a while to find my passion. You have plenty of time to find yours. Now, my second suggestion for you is: you mentioned you are still doing some dance. Can you find time to do more?"

After concluding our session, Christine asked me about our progress on Domingo's case. I was still stinging from Lucy's attack on my professionalism, and I suddenly felt a twinge of guilt at discussing details of the case, even with Christine.

"Nothing really new," I told her. "It's a tough case."

She nodded, and her mouth twisted in sympathy. "I know it is. You must have been quite disappointed when the court failed to dismiss the case at the preliminary hearing. I mean, the case for suicide is so clear, it shouldn't be rocket science to get the case against Domingo dismissed. See, even your big bad boss isn't a miracle worker, right?"

"Oh, girl, you're so right," I laughed. "Thank you."

The session had worked its magic. My anger at Lucy had turned to compassion, and Christine's gentle support had cleared my head and restored my confidence. We made an appointment for the following week. I walked out of the building ten feet in the air.

***

"Hey, Justin?" I was having trouble concentrating on my *Vogue*, and was lounging on Justin's bed, thinking about the photo I had seen taped to his computer monitor. Justin lay across the other side of the bed, frowning into his Corporations textbook.

"What?" He looked up at me with red eyes. I enjoy a couple of hits of weed now and then, but as we spent more time together I was beginning to realize Justin's use was more than occasional. He could study intensely for several hours straight, after taking in a quantity that would have reduced me to staring into empty space and saying, "wow," until I came down a couple hours later. This night, I had declined his offer to partake.

"How did Patty get Domingo's case?"

"How did she get it?"

"Yeah. How'd he end up coming in to your law office?"

He put down the book and rolled over. "Why do you ask?"

"You got the case first, didn't you?"

"Good guess." Justin slowly edged his body to lean up against the wall next to me. His calm bloodshot gaze warmed when his eyes met mine. He began to stroke my arm with his hand, using the oh-so-light touch I was getting to know so well.

"I met Domingo last summer, when I was studying Spanish in Mexico. Rudolfo's brother, Miguel, and I joined Rudolfo on the tour for a few days, during the same time as Domingo was interviewing Rudolfo for his article.

"When Domingo was leaving, Rudolfo had a party for him and people were all giving him their numbers, and I gave Domingo my card. I was surprised he kept it, but when he got to the US it was in his wallet and he called me for help with his asylum case. Patty had already told me she was interested in doing some *pro bono* work, so I asked her if she wanted to work on it."

"Why didn't you tell me you'd met Domingo before?"

"I don't know. It seems like a long time ago."

"One year is a long time?" My face was starting to feel hot.

"Hey. Armando." He pressed my arm gently. "What is there for you to be upset about?"

"Gee, I don't know. What do you think?"

"Miguel? He's not exactly any competition for you. He lives in Guadalajara. I haven't seen him since last summer." His reddened eyes and intelligent gaze focused on me as if from a long distance. I felt a stab of wild attraction and something else that was more painful.

"But you're in touch with him." I hated how I sounded. "That's how you got the passes for us to go see Rudolfo backstage."

"Yes, and I told him about you and that I was taking you. He's happy for me."

"OK. No big deal. I was just surprised you hadn't told me the whole story." I pulled myself together. I'd only known Justin for a short time. Maybe I should back away for a while, I thought. Not because Lucy told me to, but because jealousy is a blinding sin.

***

The following night, Mom was hanging out at the pool with me and Slim. We were all lying in adjacent lounge chairs like passengers on the deck of a cruise ship, holding our stomachs and waiting to digest our Thai food feast before getting into the pool.

"Thank you for buying dinner, Armando," Mom said.

"Now I know how to bribe you to spend time with me, Ma. You're so busy nowadays, I have to make a date to see you."

"Tell me all about your case. The one with the handsome client."

I updated her and Slim about our investigation of the Torres case, finishing with the bit of excitement at the Rudolfo concert.

"Ah, Rudolfo," Ma sighed. "What a voice. And you got to meet him, and your friend saved his life. Wow." She deliberately pronounces "wow" with an exaggerated American accent, like wah-oh.

"It was fantastic," Slim agreed.

I gave him a look. He and I hadn't yet talked about the night of the concert.

He looked back at me with his Aztec eyes half closed, and a small cat-like smile turning up the corners of his mouth.

Mom drummed her red nails on the arm of her lounge chair. "If your client Domingo is innocent, who killed his girlfriend? Could it be this boy, Paolo?"

"We don't think so," I said, without giving her details. Although Cantara had apparently not killed Patty, I still believed their kidnapping of Mom was intended to keep me from probing into their other activities.

"They say poisoning is a woman's crime," Mom said. "Not so bloody. Perhaps it was one of her girlfriends."

I thought about it. "There's her old friend, Christine, but she's really nice and has an alibi. The only other girlfriends we've found are a couple of women she worked with, Annie and Linda. Claude is supposed to be following up on their alibis. Annie and Patty were friends outside the office. I don't know why either of them would have done it, though. Except Annie has a monster crush on Domingo."

"There you are," Mom said. "A woman, consumed with jealousy. This Domingo, he's a real bomb, right? He leaves a trail of broken hearts and broken lives in his wake. Possibly one of these friends of Patty fell in love with him, and killed Patty out of jealousy."

"Maybe Annie did it," I said. "But Christine didn't even like Domingo, and she was at a hotel up in Santa Barbara."

"What about Christine's husband?" Slim said. "You said he liked Patty. If Patty was in love with Domingo, maybe the husband was jealous. A jealous man can be very dangerous, too."

"Brad seems like such a zero, though." I said. "He was at home with the baby that night. He's this super-quiet, nerdy guy who's kind of a shadow of a man. Where's the passion?"

"Sounds like a poisoner to me," Slim said.

"Yeah, I guess. I don't know what Christine sees in him," I said.

"At this point, even if she doesn't love him, she sees a father for her child," Mom said.

"There's another possibility, but I don't think it's likely. Patty's boss was after her, and might have gotten out of control."   I told them about Frank Slattery's aggressive temperament and history with women.

Mom nodded. "If he doesn't take rejection well, he would have been upset.   Usually men who are sexually aggressive like that get used to rejection, though. Of course, if he found out she was seeing Domingo on the sly, that could have set him off. That would be a reason for him to kill her. However, the style doesn't fit. Your killer is subtle and patient. This Mr. Slattery sounds like the kind of man who would hit her over the head with a baseball bat."

I laughed. "So, Ma, enough about my case. How's your school going?"

She smiled. "I love it. I just added a computer class."

"What kind of computer class?"

"A bookkeeping program. Very practical. I used to be good with numbers."

"Hmmm. That doesn't sound very fun, though."

"Ah, *m'ijo*. I have been feeling like a dinosaur. The computer age, it was passing me by. I want to learn. Time to join the new world."

That night, after Mom went in to do her reading for school, I had a chance to talk to Slim about Daniel. We were in my pool house, playing video games and listening to my Rudolfo CD.

"What happened after you and Daniel left, *amigo*? You should have told us. Were you OK to drive?"

"No worries. That XTC was some weird shit, though, man. After I went so crazy and you and Justin walked me around, then I started to feel goooo-ood. My brain was intensely focused on every note of music, like it was the best thing I ever heard. I fell in love with the band, and the crowd all singing along to Rudolfo. Then, Daniel put his arm on my shoulder and my whole body got electric. It was so intense, I mean, you know...."

"You don't need to spell it out. I read about what Ecstasy does."

"Well, yeah. So, anyway, me and Daniel decided to go somewhere more private."

"You drove home while you were still high?"

"Actually, we didn't go that far."

"What? Oh, God, your truck?"

"Guess again."

"Oh come on. I don't know. What, the men's room of the fairgrounds?" I joked.

He kept looking at the video screen. I looked over and saw he was smiling.

I put down my video control. "Get out!" I said.

Slim took advantage of my change in focus to blast some fireballs at my avatar.

"Hey! Stop shooting! Look at me."

"What?" He turned his head to face me.

"Slim!"

"Hey, what?"

"Daniel is bad news, man. You know that."

"I can handle him."

"I thought you could. Now, I don't think so. After he drugged your drink, you should be doing nothing but running the other way as fast as you can. Man, I should have kept an eye on you."

"Lighten up, 'Mando. You've done the same kind of thing."

"Not with someone who just poisoned me. Daniel's only real love affair is with trouble. You'll get hurt."

"Hey, honest, I won't. You know me. I'm just having fun."

"You know he's been stalking Pete. He could turn around and start it with you."

"He's not 'stalking' anybody. If you knew him, you'd see that. Daniel acts tough, but he really isn't. He just wants to see how people will react to him. He's curious."

"Yeah, right."

"'Mando, stop. I don't talk about your friends like that."

"What's that supposed to mean?"

"Forget it, baby. We're just going to piss each other off." Slim handed me my control. "Here. New game."

24

On Friday night, I sped up Highway 15. Justin rolled down his window and put his sneakered feet up on the dashboard. It had taken some talking to convince him we needed a getaway together, and that our relationship was more important than his Saturday study group. Finally, he'd agreed. "I can get Pete's notes from him next week," he said. Half an hour later, he was packed and waiting for me at the curb when I pulled up in front of his apartment.

Justin and I got into the groove as soon as we took off, bombing up the highway at ten o'clock that night, headed for my favorite Palm Springs resort. He was playing one of Rudolfo's older CD's for me, and waving his hands gently side to side as if conducting the music.

"You realize it's going to be like a hundred and ten degrees," I told him.

"What's the matter, you can't take the heat?"

I glanced over at him. He was looking at me, his eyes glittering in the dark. It was so-oooo good to be alone with him, and on the road.

"Me?" I said to him. "I'm gonna bloom in the sun like a fuckin' flower. I was just worried what you can take, baby *gringo*."

"You'd be surprised what I can take, baby *vato*. Hey, look who I work for."

"How long have you been working for that asshole, anyway?"

"Let's see. Since my first year of law school, so, almost two years. I work full-time in the summers and part-time during school. I think I told you, he's helping pay my tuition this year."

"Nice. Do you have to pay him back, or work it off, or anything?"

"No. He's always done this for his law clerks who, well, who do good work for him. When he was in law school, someone helped him the same way."

"Lucy might help pay for law school if I went," I said. "But I'd have to go to college first."

"You should do it. You're lucky to work for her. Frank has taken good care of me, though."

Justin reached into his jeans pocket and pulled out a baggie.

"What the fuck are you doing?"

"Hey, we're on vacation. What's the problem?"

"Are you nuts? I don't want that shit in my car, man. What are you thinking?"

"Hey, relax. Just don't smoke any while you're driving and it's no big deal. Look, I only brought a little."

"What's wrong with you? Can't you do anything without getting high?"

Justin took the baggie, threw his head back, and poured its contents into his mouth. He threw the bag out the window. I watched the bulge in his cheek as he chewed for a minute, then he leaned out the window and spat.

"How's that?" he asked, as we sped through the black night.

"You better not have got that shit on my car."

***

"*Ah-bo-gah-dah*," I chanted, balancing my double cappuccino in one hand over my head and swaying my hips like a waitress in a musical, as I dumped my briefcase on my desk.

She was lounging by the fireplace, reading the daily legal journal. "How was your hot weekend?"

"Very rewarding. I drove up to Julian to the annual retreat for the American Association of University Women."

"Oooh, that sounds naughty. Did you get lots of sweet girl kisses?"

"There was the usual solidarity and stimulation. I feel refreshed."

"That makes two of us." I smiled happily, daring her to try and ask me anything about my weekend.

"Claude has gotten some more information about Frank Slattery's possible involvement in the Torres case," she said.

I froze in the act of sitting down at my desk. "What?"

"Frank and one of his employees claim they spent the night of Patty's death together, at Frank's apartment. Both of them have motives to kill Patty."

"Which employee?" I asked.

"Patty's friend, Annie. The one you'd already interviewed." She looked at me reproachfully. "Claude's report is on your desk, ready for you to read and file."

I picked up the report and sat down to read it. Claude's scary stare had clearly gotten better results than my friendly interview with Annie and my abortive attempt to interview Frank. He'd confronted Frank with the evidence of his history of sexual harassment of Patty and others, and convinced Frank he needed to provide an alibi or be subpoenaed to testify at trial. An hour later, Frank had called and agreed to be interviewed again about his alibi. When Claude arrived at the office, Frank and Annie met with him and told them their story. They had attended a monthly dinner for local Immigration attorneys, and then gone back to Frank's place, where Annie had spent the night. They had been together until they both left for work in their separate cars.

"Does Claude believe them?" I asked.

"Clearly there is some major dysfunction in that office. Everyone who works for Frank Slattery is still under suspicion, as far as I'm concerned. I'm going to have to renew my request that you stop seeing Justin until this case is resolved. It shouldn't be long now, Armando. Last night I re-read the file, including your reports on your trip to Oakland. I think it's all going to come together soon."

"Really? What's your theory?"

"I don't have a theory. It's more of a feeling that there's a key piece we haven't put together yet. Inconsistencies.... The answer's here, in the back of my mind. It just hasn't come to the front yet. "

As I left the office that afternoon, I felt at peace with Lucy's request I temporarily stop seeing Justin. Our weekend in Palm Springs had been amazing, but the relationship had been moving faster than I was used to. Hopefully I could figure out the right way to tell him and he would understand.

I had an appointment with Christine that evening, and I realized what was really on my mind was all the conflicting feelings I had about our family trip to Acapulco. The scent of lavender massage oil wafting into the waiting room, the sleek, comfortable couch and soothing atmosphere of Christine's office, and Christine's warm greeting and empathetic expression, all worked to ease my mind before I even started talking. The fifty-minute process worked its magic.

"Wow. How could I not have known that this Acapulco trip would bring up so many old family issues for me? I mean, I've hardly spoken to my dad in so many years. Why did I think I could just forget all that for this trip?"

"Tell me if this sounds right, Armando. It's possible you weren't thinking of yourself, you were thinking of how the trip would be part of the healing process for your mother."

"Yes," I sighed. "Yes, that's right."

"You're a kind, loving person and you care deeply for your mother. But sometimes you also need to think about yourself."

"Yes. Thank you so much."

***

I flinched as Justin laid a light hand on my shoulder. After my appointment with Christine, I'd decided to get our temporary break-up over with. It had seemed wrong to have this conversation over the phone, so we were meeting at the Bar Bar, but now I felt nervous. To make things worse, Rodrigo and Pete were there sitting in a booth and I'd felt I had to join them. Justin slid into the booth beside me.

"We need to talk," I said to Justin.

"Let's walk over to my place."

When we got up to leave, Rodrigo was talking on his cell phone and he motioned to us to wait.

"It's Slim on the phone with Rodrigo," Pete said. "They're at Daniel's place and Daniel's flipping out. Slim's locked himself in the bathroom."

Rodrigo was listening, his head bent forward to hear in the noisy bar. He looked up at me and I held out my hand for the phone. Rodrigo covered the phone with his hand and shook his head at me.

"He sounds paranoid, Armando. Now he's saying something about Daniel putting drugs in his drink at the concert. I think we should go over there."

"Ask Slim if he can get out of there safely."

As Rodrigo got back on the phone, I turned to Justin and Pete. "Have you guys told Rodrigo what Daniel did at the concert?"

Pete said, "I didn't tell Rodrigo because I didn't want Rodrigo to get into it with Daniel."

"You'd better tell him now."

"Maybe it's not the right time for that," Justin said. "We need to make sure Daniel and Slim are safe."

"I agree," Pete said. "Rodrigo could really hurt Daniel."

I stared at him. Justin stood next to him and looked at me with his eyebrows raised.

"You don't know Rodrigo very well if that's what you think would happen," I told Pete.

As we argued, Rodrigo nodded at me and held up the phone. "Slim wants to talk to you."

"Good. These guys have something to tell you."

"Slim?" I spoke into the phone rather loudly. The noise in the bar was getting worse. "Can you hear me?"

"Hi, Armando. Can you and Rodrigo come out here? I'm worried about Daniel. I don't want to leave him here alone. He won't stop drinking and he threatens to hurt himself if I try to take away his bottle. I tried sitting on him, but he's, like, supernaturally strong, and he pushed me off."

"Give me the address. We'll be right there."

When I hung up, Rodrigo was standing up looking questioningly at Pete and Justin. Pete was shaking his head and Justin was watching me.

Rodrigo said, "What are they supposed to tell me, Armando?"

"Never mind. I'll tell you in the car. You and I need to go help Slim with Daniel."

"I'm coming, too," said Pete.

"You might set off Daniel," I said. "Let us take care of this."

"Rodrigo," Pete said. "I want to come."

Rodrigo looked at me and I shook my head. "He's right, Pete," he said. "You should wait here. I'll call you when we get there."

Justin had been watching quietly, his face pale under the bar lights. "Come on, Pete. Let's hang out here. They'll call us, OK?"

I grabbed Rodrigo's arm and pulled him outside before Pete could come after us.

As I drove, I told Rodrigo about Daniel's lacing the drinks with Ecstasy at the Rudolfo concert.

Hurt flashed across Rodrigo's face, like it always does when something disillusions him.

"Screw these guys," he said.

On a weeknight, the streets in the Gaslamp District were still active, with the late dinner crowd carrying their take-out boxes back to their cars and the dressed-up club crowd just starting to pull up in limos and nice cars. Turning east, I located a space about a block from the address Slim had given me.

After I was parked, Rodrigo looked at me and put a hand over mine. Compared to Justin's, his hands were square and muscular. "I still miss you," he said. "What's with you and Justin?"

"It's complicated, *amigo*." I removed my hand and opened the car door. "Let's go rescue Slim."

"Holy shit," Rodrigo said. "Twenty-fourth floor. Baby, we're going to the penthouse."

The elevator shot us directly up to the top floor, half the distance of a football field, in a few short seconds, giving no sensation we'd even been in motion. When the doors opened, we walked into a hallway with two doors with numbers written in script on brass plates. The far door had the number Slim had given me, and the door was ajar.

Rodrigo kicked into his cop mode, putting his body in front of mine. "Let me go first." He balanced on one leg and used the other leg to push open the door. Then he cautiously put his head inside the door. "Oh, for Chrissake," he sputtered.

"What?" I asked. After pushing the door open, he had straight-armed me behind him.

Rodrigo snorted and dropped his arm down to his side so I could peek around him inside the apartment.

They were both there, across a broad expanse of thick, creamy carpet, on an oversized sectional couch. I froze for a second while I registered what I was seeing. Then I watched for another few seconds, feeling Rodrigo breathing next to me. Finally, I pulled myself back into the hallway.

Rodrigo joined me, closing the door quietly behind him.

"Wow," I told Rodrigo. "I've never actually, uh, seen that before."

"You mean this is the first time they asked you over to watch?"

"I mean, I've never seen that particular--" I saw he was smiling. "Shut up," I said. "Let's get out of here."

"Slim is totally right about one thing," I said, as we stepped into the elevator. "Daniel really is strong. I mean wow, right?"

"I don't know," Rodrigo argued. "Slim's light, and he has good balance. Like you. But how did they...."

Our discussion became technical and we were both pretty stimulated by the time we got back to Hillcrest. Rodrigo's hand was moving up my leg as I parked the car. When I started to open my door, he grabbed my arm.

"Wait." He slid on top of me and kissed me. "Don't go back to the bar. Forget those messed-up law students. Come home with me."

I let myself go and lost myself in the familiar contours of his mouth and body. I tried to remember if there was a spot in his apartment where we could achieve the acrobatics we'd just witnessed. I could tell by the way he was moving his body he was thinking the same thing. Finally, my hip bumped the steering wheel hard enough to bring me back to myself for a moment.

"I can't, honey. I have to talk to Justin about something."

Rodrigo looked at me. His blue-green eyes pulsed light in his dark face. "You're sure?"

"Yeah."

"OK." He moved back into his seat, and patted the stiff spikes on top of my head. "I like your new hair style." Then he reached back to open the car door. "Thanks for the ride."

Justin and Pete were still at the booth where we'd left them, absorbed in a discussion of whether our country's involvement in Libya constituted a violation of international law.

"You have a very narrow interpretation of the concept of a nation's right to self-determination...." Justin was arguing heatedly, when they saw me standing at the edge of the booth.

"Armando! That was fast! What happened?"

"Where's Rodrigo?" Pete asked, at the same time.

I glanced briefly at Pete. "Rodrigo split. I told him I'd fill you in. Let me just say, they uh, made up. They didn't even see us." I smiled meaningfully at Justin.

Justin raised his eyebrows at me, and I nodded. His face broke into a wide grin. He started to laugh. "Guess Daniel wasn't as drunk as we thought."

The Bar Bar was filling up. Justin bought me a mojito, and we danced, and then he bought me another mojito. Everyone else in the place seemed to disappear. We danced some more. I told Justin I needed to talk to him, so he invited me to his apartment to talk. As we walked inside, Justin kept distracting me, brushing against me and laughing and pressing me for details of what Rodrigo and I had seen inside Daniel's apartment. It somehow didn't seem like the right time to have a complicated discussion about our potential conflict in *P. v. Torres*. Tomorrow, I promised myself.

25

The next morning when I got in, Lucy was parked in the leather chair in front of the fireplace, with two large file boxes and piles of papers at her feet, frowning at a transcript open on her lap. Reviewing appellate records is one of Lucy's least favorite tasks, and she would be looking for some kind of distraction, most likely involving nagging me about something. Like, for example, whether I had told Justin I couldn't see him until the Torres case was over.

"Good morning, *Abogada,*" I said, dumping my briefcase on my desk. "Let me pour you some more tea. Hey, it looks good, I think I'll have some too. Man, what a night I had last night." I told Lucy the story of my rush to rescue Slim the night before. She relaxed enough to smile, especially when I gave her the details of what Rodrigo and I saw through the open door of Daniel's penthouse.

"I swear," I told her, "all my friends are crazy. It's like, I'm the only normal one."

"Do you still want that new career as a therapist?" she smirked.

"Sure, why not? I could practice on my friends so they wouldn't be so nuts. The only thing is, I don't want to go to school 'til I'm thirty years old just to get my license. If they would just give me my ticket, right now? I'd go for it."

Lucy had been about to take a sip of tea. She put her cup back down on the coffee table and looked up at me. "You'd do what? Say that again."

"I'd just do it, you know? Put my license up on the wall, and start delivering some kick-ass therapy to all my wacked-out friends. And to anyone else who would pay me. Of course, I would totally miss the righteous quest for justice and...." My words trailed off when I saw she had stopped listening to me.

Her eyes widened and she stared at my face like she wasn't really seeing it. She stood up and paced to the office door, then back to her seat, then over to my desk.

"Armando, I've got an early lunch set up with Dr. Bibber today. Call him at his office and tell him something's come up and I'll need to reschedule. His daughter, Stephanie, is coming in this afternoon at 3:00 to sign a retainer. I'll be back by then. I'm going over to Claude's office to follow up on something. Oh, and put away this mess," she said, gesturing at the transcripts she had strewn across the coffee table and on the floor.

She pulled out her cell phone, grabbed her purse, and headed for the door.

Justin agreed to meet me for lunch at the mall. I got there early so I could think about what to say. Did I really have to do this? If Lucy'd just solved the case, was it even necessary? Yes, it was, until the case was over. Maybe it wouldn't be that long, now.

From the food court on top of the mall, I leaned down over the rails to watch out for a mop of red hair. I was watching the big stairway that connects the mall to Broadway, when I jumped at a soft tickling on the sides of my ribs.

"Got you!" He laughed, springing back with that lightness of movement that had become so enchanting to me.

"You asshole."

I looked at him laughing in the sun. He looked happy and carefree. Part of the wave of love I felt for him was seeing the happiness animating his face and body and knowing without any doubt that it was there because of me. Maybe that's not the best basis for a relationship. Some people might say it's egotistical to love someone more for the power you feel in making him happy. I could hear Lucy saying, "I can get that kind of love from my dogs." I was afraid that in a few words, if I didn't handle it right, I could smash the beautiful spirit in front of me. I found myself twisting the emerald ring Ma had given me up and down on my finger, testing to see if I could slide it over my knuckle, until my skin started to burn.

"Hey, *Loco*," I said. "Let's go sit down. I have to talk to you about something."

We found a tiny table next to the rail, and sat down across from each other.

"What's up?" Justin asked.

"Lucy thinks I should stop seeing you until Domingo's criminal case is over. I don't want to do it, but she's my boss and I agree it's the right thing to do. It'll only be a few weeks, I hope."

His eyebrows rose in surprise, and then his brow knitted as he focused his intelligence on the problem.

"Because of the conflict while Frank is a suspect," he said. "Right?"

"Pretty much, yeah."

"I respect Professor Sanders as an attorney, but she's being unreasonably cautious about this." He frowned. "Is there something you're not telling me?"

I realized I couldn't even tell him Lucy and Claude had identified Justin himself as a suspect. When the case was over, I could tell him and we could laugh about it.

So I tried something I'm not very proud of. "Well, Lucy, she can be kind of a control freak." Which, of course, was very true. "It can really affect her judgment sometimes." Not so true.

"I doubt that," Justin frowned. "Anyway, you said you agreed with her. Tell me why, Armando. I have to know what you're thinking about me."

"That's the whole point, Justin. I can't tell you. You must get that."

"Sure I get that you can't talk about the case. What I'm having trouble with is I feel you're just going along with this and not being straight with me."

"It wasn't my idea. You should be able to understand what this is like for me. I have to show some loyalty to my boss, too." As soon as I said it, I knew I'd made a mistake.

Justin jumped on it. "Loyalty to my boss? As in, me helping my boss get away with murder? And why did he do it? Just because Patty wouldn't fuck him?"

"Come on, Justin."

His brain was still working. "You'd need a better reason than that, wouldn't you?"

"Nobody really thinks you did anything…."

"They think I did it for money, perhaps? Did you tell them Frank's helping me pay for law school?"

I flushed. "Well, I thought if I told Lucy, she might want to help me, too," I joked lamely.

"Yeah, right. Like you'll ever go back to school."

I stood up. "I thought you'd be grown up about this. Maybe all your fine schooling still has a few things to teach you."

***

I trudged back to the office and kept myself busy with a stack of mindless paperwork. Lucy was back in her office with the door shut, emerging once, briefly, to get herself a cup of tea and ask me a question.

"Did Justin ever tell you whether Patty planned to go to Mexico to investigate Domingo's case? Did she have a passport?"

"I have no idea," I said. "And I can't ask Justin. He's not speaking to me. Well, I guess I could call him. Why do you want to know?"

"Never mind," she said. "I'll call Justin myself."

"What's going on?"

She walked back to her office and closed the door.

Once, my cell phone rang and I checked to see if it was Justin, but it was my sister Connie. She probably wanted me to baby sit, I thought, turning off the ringer and sticking the cell back on my belt. I wondered if Lucy had reached Justin. Did she suspect Patty of planning to flee the country? Had Patty been involved in some illegal activities that had gotten her killed?

Lucy's three o'clock client, Ms. Stephanie Bibber, showed up fifteen minutes late and shit-faced. I hoped she hadn't driven to the appointment that way. Maybe she'd tanked up at the Pink Phink on the corner before coming to our office. The way my day was going, if I'd known she was there, I would have joined her for a few. She declined my offer of coffee. As I showed her back to Lucy's office, I murmured, "Were you able to find parking nearby?"

"Yesh, I wash. Right on the corner." She lurched into the couch and I steadied her with my hand under her elbow. She grabbed my arm with her other hand and pulled herself a little closer to my body than was necessary. I guided her firmly away and forward towards Lucy's office.

"That's good you found parking," I said. "Sometimes it can be tight around here. You sure I can't get you some coffee?"

"I don't drink coffee. Shtains my teeth." She smiled to show her teeth, which were indeed quite white. Although she must have been no more than forty years old, the teeth had the solid white perfection of dentures, which looked kinda scary standing out in her tanned, horsy face. She'd put her blonde hair in a messy pony tail that had taken hours and a lot of hairspray to achieve, and wore a pink velour sweat suit that said "hottie" in big white letters across the ass. Her hand caressed my arm when we stopped at Lucy's office.

I knocked on Lucy's door and opened it. "Here is Ms. Bibber," I sang, wiggling my eyebrows at Lucy behind the client's back.

"Thank you, Armando." She looked at the client, and raised her eyebrows back at me. I made a little drinking gesture with my hand, over Ms. Bibber's fluffy blond head.

"Ah." Lucy looked displeased. "Do you have that retainer ready?"

"The paperwork's on your desk." I closed the door behind me.

Five minutes later, my phone line buzzed. "Armando, can you get Dr. Bibber on the phone for me? Try his office, first." Lucy's voice was calm, but slightly slower and higher than usual, which signaled about a three out of ten on her annoyance scale.

I called the number and, by using Lucy's name, got through to the doctor at his office in less than three minutes. I forwarded the call to Lucy. A minute later, Lucy buzzed me again.

"Listen, Armando, Ms. Bibber, er, needs a ride home. Her father's not available to come get her. I'd take her myself, but I have a critical meeting with Claude this afternoon."

"Jesus Christ. Does she need to be carried?"

"Not at this time."

"Sure," I said. "I'll take her. My day already sucks."

26

After dropping off Ms. Bibber, I made it back to the office, ready to pack up and leave. Lucy's face was flushed with excitement.

"Armando, can you stay for a few minutes? Dr. Bibber will be compensating us at your hourly billing rate for the last two hours, so I can pay you overtime."

"So Daddy's paying her legal bills, huh? Did she sign the retainer?"

"No, she did not sign the retainer," Lucy said irritably. "Think about it, Armando. She was too drunk to understand what she would be signing."

"Occupational hazard for a DUI attorney," I remarked. "So, what are we doing? Have you cracked the Torres case?"

"It's looking promising. Claude is checking some records for me. I have a technical question for you. Is it possible to tell, from some kind of telephone tracking records, where someone was when they were making a Skype call?"

"I'm not sure. Do you mean where they were, like geographically? You would at least be able to tell what computer they used, I think, because of the cookies. I don't know if there would also be some tracking, like if the GPS was enabled on the device...."

"Cookies?" Lucy interrupted.

"Yeah, it's a record on your computer that shows what Internet sites you've been on. I'm pretty sure Skype has them."

"Are cookies on all kinds of computers? Like a laptop, or a cell phone? Can they be erased?"

"I think so. Why? Did Patty go somewhere to Skype with her aunt that night? Do you think she was poisoned somewhere else?"

"I hope we'll get the answers when we find the cookies, among other things. I'm going to ask the DA to get a search warrant."

"For whom?"

Lucy told me, and I felt like I'd been punched in the gut. To cover my reaction, I asked, "Do you need me to do anything more tonight?"

"Let me think. I've set up a meeting for us tomorrow afternoon with Alan Shaw, the deputy DA in charge of the case. It would help to have someone at the DA's or the cops on our side," Lucy said to me. "Didn't you make a contact with someone on the investigative team?"

"Only my friend Rodrigo at the DA's."

"Track him down." She went into her office and shut the door.

Rodrigo picked up his cell after two rings.

"*Hola, guapo*, did you change your mind about coming over?" Rodrigo's *Espanol* is *muy suave*, the words all slurred together so you can barely understand them until you get used to it, a legacy from his Cuban father.

"Oh, my," I minced, in a high treble. "This is Lady Justice speaking. My goodness, you have a very sexy voice, sir. Are you inviting me to your home?"

"Justice is always welcome in my home, Señora. Bring that sexy butterfly who works for you, and we'll have a threesome."

"Eeeew!" I cried. "Do-oon't!"

"You started it," he said calmly, switching to English.

We joked around for a while. Finally, switching back to his soft Spanish, he asked me, "Have you finished your fling with the skinny redhead?"

"*No se*." I replied. "We had a big fight."

"Then, why are you calling?"

"Business, *amigo*.   Righteous justice for our client, Domingo Torres. Only you can help us."

I told him Lucy wanted to have a police presence at our meeting with the DA. "What's the name of the cop who was first on the scene?   The one who thought Domingo was innocent?"

"His name is Eric. Don't know his last name. I didn't talk to him, I talked to a friend who works with him. Do you want me to find out?"

"If you think it would help. We need someone to light a fire under Deputy DA Shaw."

"Alan Shaw has the case?"

"Yeah."

"Maybe we can do something for you on this end, then. He's been known to listen to reason, especially if his ass is on the line."

Rodrigo called me back a short time later, and I relayed our conversation to Lucy.   She called Shaw back and told him she would like to include some of the officers from the initial investigation at the meeting.

"We'll see what good this does us," Lucy said. "Even if this Eric has doubts about the DA's case, cops always close ranks. Eric may avoid the meeting."

"He told Rodrigo he'd try to be there."

"That's something. But I can't tell you how many times I've thought a cop was going to tell the truth about something and they went south on me. You weren't here when I had…."

I interrupted her war story. "Tell me, what evidence did you and Claude get today?"

"Can't you guess? Well, you'll see it tomorrow. I want you at that meeting with me. Right now, I need to put together the paperwork for the meeting. Go home, Armando," she said.

"You can help me finish preparing tomorrow when I get back from court."

Looking back, I see if I'd stepped back and thought about what I knew, I might have seen what Lucy did. Even then, I doubt that I would have trusted what I saw. I wasn't as objective as she was.

Leaving the office, I felt light-headed. I'd forgotten to eat lunch after my fight with Justin. I stopped for fast food, and returned a call from my sister Connie.

"Armando, finally!" she exclaimed. "Have you talked to Mom tonight?"

"No. It's Thursday. She has a class."

"But she's not supposed to be going to school anymore. She dropped out."

"What? Are you sure?"

"Well, she told Dad her final exams would conflict with our trip to Acapulco. She said she'd have to drop all her classes."

"I hope she didn't do that. I told her not to. You can re-schedule the trip."

"You told her what??? Why did you do that, Armando? Dad says we can't change. It would cost too much to change the tickets."

"Well, he should have thought of that sooner. No one asked me whether I would be available during that time, either." I attacked my burger, and catsup splorked down my arm. I held the phone against my shoulder while I wiped myself clean with a bunch of napkins.

"What is wrong with her, Armando?" Connie asked. "It's not like her to be so selfish. She told Dad she couldn't go to a dinner party with him this weekend because she had a study group or something. It's important for his work. Dad has been so generous and patient with her."

"Gee, Connie, did it ever occur to anyone she might not want to go to Mexico, since the last time she was there she was kidnapped by masked men and held in a dark room for three days? Maybe a vacation in Acapulco wouldn't exactly be relaxing for her."

"Oh. But she'd be with family, this time. Dad got reservations at the Fairmont. She wouldn't ever leave the resort."

"Did Dad get the package deal that comes with armed bodyguards?" I asked.

Connie didn't laugh. "This is ruining my vacation plans. I need to tell my work the days I want off. Now I don't know what to do."

"Why don't you just go without Mom? Use Mom's ticket to take your other babysitter."

"I already asked. She's afraid to travel to Mexico right now, because of all the violence. Armando, you're still going to go, aren't you?"

"You mean, if Mom doesn't go?" Hmnnn. I'd been looking forward to the trip, if I could get the time off work. It would be weird for me without Mom there, though. Dad and Chuy would be doing their business or hanging out in the sports bar with Enrique, betting high on whatever sports were going on. Connie and Elena would be shopping and trying to get me to look after their kids. I could see myself sitting around the pool, playing lifeguard, for the whole vacation. I could still hit the clubs at night by myself, but how fun would that be?

"What about Gaby?" I asked. "Is she coming?"

"No, she said her classes wouldn't be over yet, so we didn't get her a ticket."

"I don't get this, Connie. Why didn't you guys just get tickets for closer to Christmas break, when everyone would be out of school?"

"Dad says the tickets cost a lot more then. You know, things are tight for him right now, after paying all that money to get Mom back."

"Then he shouldn't have invited the whole family. He could have just taken Ma."

"Well, he didn't do that. He wants the family to be together. Please, Armando. Mom will listen to you. Try to get her to come on the trip. Tell her it's for the family."

"OK, I'll talk to her."

When I got home, I put on the teakettle and took out some puffed rice cakes, the only snack Mom allows herself before bedtime. I found an antique serving plate Mom uses for special occasions: a flat, emerald-green glass platter with a wavy design etched along the border and little balls of green glass sticking out all around the edge. The refrigerator was kind of empty, but I found an old jar of big green martini olives stuffed with something red, and some cherry tomatoes, and made a design with the rice cakes on the plate. Then I sat down with my tea and my book to wait for Mom to get home from school.

When the garage door rumbled, I put the heat back on under the teakettle. Mom came in, carrying a large, colorful bag over her shoulder and raking back her thick frosted hair.

"Hey, Ma," I took her bag from her. "Nice bag. Not your usual style. Is it new?"

"You like it? I bought it in Tijuana, for my school things. I'm a little old to carry a backpack like most of the other students. It's very boho, no?" The bag was made from patches of woven fabric and covered with heavy embroidery of many-colored flowers, butterflies, and birds.

"Wait, you were in Tijuana? When?"

"It's OK, *m'ijo*. I was with Italia."

"Oh. Are you sure...?"

"Don't worry about me. Look at this," she said proudly. "My new laptop. This is the kind most people in my accounting class are using. What do you think?"

The teakettle whistled and I went over to the stove. "Have a seat, Ma."

She sat at the table. "What is this? *M'ijo*, how artistic! Green and red and white, the colors of the Mexican flag!"

"I thought you might be hungry after school."

"I'd forgotten about this plate." She ran her hand slowly along the little bobbles of green glass. "It's been a while since I've used it. How pretty."

I brought the tea to the table. Then I got small plates and paper napkins and set them on the table. We sat quietly for a minute, nibbling our snack and waiting for our tea to cool.

Mom's dark eyes glowed. "Do you know what we need, *m'ijo?*"

"Tell me."

"A little taste of sherry. In the nice glasses."

The glasses were like miniature wine glasses, with clear glass on the top and ruby-red glass stems. The clear glass part was etched with a tiny rose in the middle. I filled each glass halfway with the golden brown sherry, which took on a red glow at the bottom from the reflection of the red glass stem.

"*Salud!*" Ma said, and we clicked our glasses together.

"You know, Ma, it was sherry the killer used to poison Patty Taylor, the victim in the Torres case."

"Ah, poor woman. The young lady lawyer. It makes you think. She must have loved to sit and sip sherry, just like we are doing now. And now she's gone."

"Now she's gone." I realized that in the investigation of this case, Patty's character had seemed strangely elusive to me. Just hearing Ma describe her as a lady lawyer who loved to drink sherry, made her seem more real to me than all the other descriptions I had heard.

"What are you thinking, Armando?"

"I was wondering what Patty, the woman who was killed, was really like," I said. "People described her to me so differently. Domingo, our client, the man who loved her, described her as having a soft and sweet personality, highly principled, wanting to help people. The ladies she worked with here in San Diego said the same sort of thing. They said she was kind-hearted, idealistic, and good to work with.

"But the attorneys at her old job in Oakland let her go: they described her as unethical and temperamental, blaming others for her mistakes. I'm not sure I trust their opinions, though. Patty must have hated working with those puffed-up hacks. Her Aunt Jill loved her, but said she could be mischievous, even mean. It's like something happened, something that changed her."

"Hmmn. What kind of books did she read?"

I thought back to the books I'd packed in Patty's apartment. "She read mostly fiction," I said. "A lot of historical fiction. Psychological thrillers, chick lit. There were stacks of light-reading paperbacks spilling out of her bookshelves. There were some classics, too: *Oliver Twist*, and a lot of Dumas, including *Three Musketeers*."

"Interesting. Romantic, and socially conscious. A beautiful woman who liked to sip sherry and read, to escape the harshness of everyday life. She was highly sensitive, I think. *Pobrecita*. Poor thing. No books relating to her work?"

"Not that I saw," I said. "She probably kept the law books in her office.

"Yes, but...." Ma frowned. "She liked being a lawyer? It gave meaning to her life?"

"I don't know, Ma. She hated her first job. I think her new job was a better fit. Like she became a better person there."

Ma looked down, swirling her glass and tilting her head to watch the light reflecting on the last drops of sherry. "Being trapped in a bad situation could make anyone a little crazy."

Her face looked tense. I kept quiet, hoping she might be ready to share more about how her recent kidnapping had affected her, but the moment of opportunity passed. Mom looked at me, smiled, stuck her finger in her sherry glass, and licked the dark liquid off her finger. I followed suit, the sticky residue tasting sweet with only a hint of alcohol. The sweetness must have covered up the taste of the Fentanyl pills when Patty drank the fatal dose, I thought.

"Hey, Ma, I want to talk to you about the family trip to Acapulco."

"Must we?"

"No, it's good."

She arched an eyebrow.

"I've been thinking, Ma. You can't go on the trip as it's scheduled now because of school. Connie says they can't change the tickets because it would cost too much, and money is tight for Dad right now."

Mom pressed her teeth over her lower lip, but didn't say anything.

"So, I had an idea. I want you to be able to go, if you want to and would feel safe going there. Why don't we have Dad reschedule the trip for after your school semester ends? He can cash in my ticket, and use that money to pay for the cost of rescheduling. I don't mind giving up the trip, if it means you can go." I looked at her proudly, waiting to see her face light up.

Mom was shaking her head sadly. "My sweet boy."

"Really, Ma. I don't mind."

"This is going to be hard for you. Harder than I thought."

"What? It's not that big a deal, really. I can go to Acapulco some other time."

"Well, now I really am tired, *m'ijo*. Time for bed."

27

The following day, Lucy had gone straight to a court appearance in another case, and we had plans to visit Domingo when she was done. I shamelessly searched her desk for the new evidence she'd found in the *Torres* case, but she must have taken the file with her. I kept busy with other paperwork, waiting for her call.

At eleven thirty, Lucy called. "Armando, the court's in recess but I'll have to go back in at one o'clock. Can you get right over here?"

"Sure. Did you get the information you wanted?"

"Yes, it's just what I'd hoped. I must talk to Domingo about what we've found, then dash back here to court."

"I'll meet you in front of the jail."

"Hurry up, then."

I grabbed my messenger bag, and dashed out the door. Driving my car was slightly faster than if I'd run at a full out sprint, since I could park at the outrageously expensive lot right across from the downtown jail and courthouse. Lucy was waiting in front of the building.

She squared her shoulders. "Let's get on with it."

As we waited for Domingo, Lucy paced up and down the tiny interview room. "What a wasted morning. I didn't think I'd have to go back into court this afternoon. The judge had an emergency matter that set back the whole calendar. We barely got started with our settlement conference before the break."

"I checked your calendar," I said. "You have Ms. Bibber's arraignment tomorrow morning. Are you just going to have her sign the retainer at court?"

"Damn. You know I don't like to do that. You'll have to track her down and get it signed this afternoon, before our meeting with DA Shaw. Also, call her dad and make sure he's still on to drive her to court. Sober."

We heard a noise at the door, and turned to the now familiar sight of our client being escorted into the interview room.

"Sorry if you were waiting," Domingo said. "They had to come find me at lunch. If you can call it that." He smiled wryly, despite his extraordinary appearance just another ordinary prisoner complaining about the food.

Lucy shook his hand and sat down. "I need to be back in court on another case in less than an hour. So, please understand if I seem to be rushing you. Armando, can you translate the rest of this? Domingo, we have some new information about the case. The District Attorney's office is considering re-opening the investigation. I need to review some things you told us when we first talked to you."

"Of course."

"You had asked Patty to marry you. Is that correct?"

"Yes, I asked her, only a week before she died."

"Can you remember exactly what she said? Think back. This is important."

Domingo closed his eyes and then opened them again, staring at the wall behind us. "Yes. We were walking in the park, between the bay and the Convention Center. There was a band playing in the outdoor theater across the bay. It was a show tune, one I knew from watching American movies as a kid. I started to sing along.

"Patty started to laugh and said to me, 'Domingo, I love you. You are full of surprises.'

"I hadn't meant to propose to her, not until my case was resolved. But when she said that, I couldn't help myself. I told her I loved her, too, and that she was the only woman I had ever wanted to marry. I said, 'Patricia, would you marry me?'" Domingo closed his eyes again. "She looked very happy. She told me I was the only man she had ever loved. Then her face changed. She said, 'It might be complicated. I love you, but I am not sure I can marry you.'"

Lucy nodded. "Did you ask her why?"

"Yes, of course. I asked her why it would be complicated to marry me, if it was because of my immigration issues. She said, 'Sort of.' I asked her what that meant, and she said 'I can't tell you.' Then I got a little worried. I asked her if she had been married before, or if there was someone else and she said, 'No.' Then she said to me, 'Domingo, I love you. I will try to work it out so we can get married. Give me some time.' I told her of course I will give you time. Then I may have sounded impatient, because I told her I couldn't wait forever. But of course I would have."

As I finished translating, Lucy nodded. "That's exactly what I wanted to know, Domingo. You never had any other conversations about marriage?"

"No. How does this help you in my case?"

Lucy smiled, and sat back. "Let me tell you."

I could see a long story coming, and I knew she would have to leave in ten minutes to get her back to court on time. I nudged her and stuck my arm in front of her so she could see my watch.

"When we first started investigating this case, Domingo, I was surprised how little investigation the police had done before the charges were filed against you. Armando talked to a friend of his at the DA's office, who said that one of the officers on the case had doubts about their case. This officer had wanted to follow up by investigating Brad Fernwood, the husband of Patty's friend, Christine, and also Patty's boss, Frank Slattery. When this officer interviewed Brad at the scene of the crime, Brad had been unusually upset, which made the officer suspicious. But the investigation soon focused on you, perhaps the most natural suspect, as you were the victim's boyfriend.

"Unfortunately, you made things worse when you lied to the police about being at Patty's house the morning she died. As soon as one of Patty's neighbors said she had seen you there that morning, the police were convinced you were guilty. I can speculate about why the police were so quick to jump to this conclusion…"

I cleared my throat noisily and twisted my watch on my wrist.

"… but we don't have time for that now," Lucy continued smoothly. "Our office received your case, and Armando began to interview some of the witnesses the police officers had failed to follow up with. As you know, we discovered Brad and Patty had had a romantic connection."

"Then Brad did kill her?" Domingo asked, clenching his fists. "I should have stayed with her that night."

"I'm afraid she would have been killed at a later time anyway," Lucy said.

"She never loved that man," Domingo said bitterly. "I was the only one she ever loved."

"That's true," Lucy said. "The woman you loved didn't ever love Brad."

My eyes widened at Lucy before I translated this. She nodded at me and Domingo looked at me with wide eyes that mirrored my own as I confirmed what Lucy had said.

Domingo threw his big hands in the air. "But you just said…."

"The woman you loved was not Patty Taylor."

I was translating simultaneously now, on autopilot. Domingo was staring back and forth between Lucy and me.

"Of course, she was. I mean, she was my attorney," he sputtered. "What do you mean? Who was she?" He looked at me for support. I gaped at Lucy.

"The woman you loved, who loved you back, was Christine Delancy, who was a licensed therapist."

"Patty's friend?"

"The District Attorney ran a fingerprint check, and we got the results last night." Lucy smiled. "The victim's fingerprints matched prints on file with the State agency that licenses psychologists, for Christine Delancy, PhD. I feel confident when they fingerprint the woman who calls herself 'Christine', they will match the fingerprints taken by the State Bar for Patty Martin, now Patty Taylor, Attorney at Law. Most people don't realize these government agencies rarely have any coordination of their databases. Honestly, the incompetence.... And now, I must leave this second or I'll be late for court. Domingo, I can't promise anything, but this new evidence should convince the DA to re-open this case. I'll let you know as soon as we learn anything."

Lucy sped off to her court date, and I walked to the parking lot to retrieve my car. I sat in the car for several minutes, until I realized the sun baking on the black roof was roasting me.

I drove back to the office, got the retainer agreement for our new client, Ms. Bibber, and headed to her condo in Rancho Bernardo. It was a nice crib, in one of those big condo developments that calls itself a "Swimming and Racquet Club," with tennis courts and a couple of swimming pools. Fortunately, Ms. Bibber appeared to be sober, signed the agreement, and while I was there we called her father to confirm he'd drive her to her court hearing the next day.

By the time I got back to the office, Lucy was back in her office with the door closed. I knocked on her door.

"Come in, Armando. I'm just getting ready for our meeting. Make five, no, six, copies of these documents. Did you get the retainer signed?"

I took the stack. "Sure, I got Ms. Bibber's retainer signed. She invited me to go swimming with her. She says if I come over at night, they don't care if you go without a bathing suit."

"Charming."

I read the original documents as the copies were running. They included an affidavit from a private investigator in Oakland, signed the day before. I recognized the name as a woman Lucy and Claude sometimes used for process serving and investigations in the Bay Area. Yesterday, the investigator had received e-mailed copies of pictures of Patty Taylor and Christine Fernwood from Claude Washington, and taken the pictures to Patty Taylor's aunt, Jill Crenshaw, at her home in Oakland. Ms. Crenshaw had identified the picture of the woman known as Christine Fernwood, as her niece, Patty Taylor.

"This is incredible," I said to Lucy as she emerged from her office.

"Yes, I suppose it is. Let's hope the DA finds it relevant to the murder charge, and agrees to reopen the investigation."

"How did Claude get the idea to do this?" I asked.

"I asked him to, of course. I was suspicious of Christine and Brad from the beginning, but for the wrong reasons. When you found the inscription on that bust of Napoleon that Patty, the real Patty, gave to Brad, I thought there was a love triangle situation. But Christine had that strong alibi: if Patty was Skyping after ten o-clock that night, Christine was halfway to Santa Barbara, and could not have been there to administer the poison. Brad could have left his baby alone at home, and gone over to Patty's apartment that night, but he was hard to pin down.

"You're the one who gave me the idea, yesterday, when you talked about changing careers without going to school to get a license. When I put that together with Patty's wallet being missing, Patty and Brad being together in Oakland, and the very different descriptions we'd gotten of Patty's personality after she left Oakland, the idea came to me. Do you have the copies? Good. Let's get over to the DA's."

Alan Shaw was a thirty-ish guy with fluffy blond hair worn a little too long, and a head like an apple. Lucy had told me he was ambitious and politically astute, one of the rising stars at the DA's office. On his side of the conference table were Eric Parti, the uniformed cop who'd interviewed Brad and Christine at the scene, and Dan Burke, the homicide supervisor who had headed the investigation of Patty's death. Parti was a solid young guy with red cheeks. Burke was tall and bottle shaped, a few years from retirement, with a gut that probably would have disqualified him from working on the regular force. He glared at me as he came into the room, and I thought I would not want to be in an interrogation room with him.

When Lucy finished her short presentation of the evidence we'd gathered to support reopening the investigation, Burke was the first to speak.

"You're the lawyer, Alan, so correct me if I'm wrong. You guys always do, right?" His smile was ugly. "But I don't see any reason to reopen the whole investigation, when we've already got our suspect in custody and bound over for trial. I haven't heard anything new from Ms. Sanders that changes my view of the case. I think Torres is still good for it."

"You have to admit, Dan, she's come up with some very material information that, uh, was not there when we decided to file," Shaw said diplomatically.

"All I'm saying, and I could be wrong, is that I wouldn't want my ass hanging out there with the judge, explaining why the investigation is still open, even though we're still set for trial of Torres. The judge'll let him out and he'll head for Mexico and disappear."

Shaw looked at the paperwork that Lucy had given him. "I don't know. He's right, Lucy. Our position is still that Mr. Torres is the guilty party. We'll make an extremely generous plea offer, based partly on this new information you got about the, ah, apparent exchange of identities between the victim and her friend. That is certainly puzzling, but it doesn't *per se* incriminate anyone for this murder. I concede these facts may affect the strength of the evidence in our case. We still think Torres killed the victim, and if we get more proof, there will be no offer."

"I can't advise him to consider any offer seriously until our investigation of this case is complete. There are too many unanswered questions, and you know it."

Shaw stared at the papers in front of him documenting the identity switch between Patty and Christine. He shook his head again.

Lucy spoke. "Alan, I admit it's unusual to reopen an investigation after trial has been set. If you don't immediately bring them in for questioning, I'm going to ask Judge Weiss to lower Domingo's bail, based on this new evidence, and the need for further investigation. I'm sure my request will be granted. You have a giant question mark in your case that wasn't there when it was filed."

Shaw put the paperwork in a stack, and stood up. "I'm going to take this down the hall. You two can wait here, or go back to your office and I'll call you."

"We'll wait," Lucy said.

Shaw held the door for Parti and Burke and ushered them out of the room.

"What are they doing?" I whispered to Lucy.

"They're going to have to get it OK'd by the DA herself, or the assistant chief. This is good. He wants to go for it."

Within ten minutes, the three men came back into the room. Shaw was smiling his politician's smile. Burke's lizard-like eyes showed nothing except resignation, but his hands were clenched at his sides. The young cop, Eric Parti, walking in behind the others, grinned and winked at me before returning his expression to neutral.

Shaw sat down, folded his hands, and leaned towards Lucy. "We'll bring them in for questioning, and get some search warrants issued."

"Thanks, Alan," Lucy said. "It takes guts for you to do this."

"Yeah, well, better now than having you shred me in the courtroom," he said cheerfully.

"That young man will go far," Lucy predicted as we left the courthouse, where the DA's office occupied the fifth and sixth floors.

"I'm in shock," I told her. "Why would Patty and Christine switch identities? I never would have guessed."

"They must have done it simply in order to change careers. That was the benefit, for both of them."

"I can see that, now," I told her. "I wish we could be there tomorrow when they carry out the warrant."

"I know. I do, too. I'm glad Judge Weiss has this case. If he issues search warrants, they'll have to do everything by the book."

"What, you don't trust Shaw?"

"He was nice today, but remember he's the one who agreed to charge Domingo before the investigation was complete. He's the one who tried to put on Paolo Sanchez as a witness."

"Do you think Shaw knew Paolo's testimony was false?"

"I doubt it. My guess is that thug Burke and some of his buddies from immigration are the ones who intimidated

Sanchez into making the false statement. Shaw probably fell for Paolo's reformed gangster act."

"Then he's not so smart as you said. You made Paolo's testimony fall apart so easily."

"I didn't say Alan was smart. Really, Armando, sometimes I'm sure you don't listen to me at all. I said he'd go far. He can see which way the wind's blowing. And he has an effective smile."

When we got outside, the sun was still high in the sky.

"We're in limbo 'til we hear from the DA, *Abogada*."

"Yes. I can't get my mind around work. Let's call it a day."

28

When I got home, I hit the pool. After a dozen laps, I started to unwind. I let go of my anger at myself for getting involved in a therapeutic relationship with Christine. How was I supposed to know, when the woman had what seemed like a perfect alibi, that she would end up being one of the prime suspects? I had made a mistake in judgment, I'd been gullible and needy, but it was because I'd gone through the trauma of Mom's kidnapping, and dealing with years of Lucy's abuse, and I'd really needed the excellent therapy she had given me. Yes, I was sad, and shocked. But I wasn't going to keep beating myself up about it. Lucy would do that for me, anyway, when I told her.

Dragging my mind away from the Torres case, I started thinking about Mom and the Acapulco trip. I plowed through the glassy water, watching the bubbles come into being and rise to the surface with each stroke of my arms. Mom hadn't been herself lately: going back to school, ignoring her husband and her grandchildren, telling me she didn't like cooking, and now passing up an opportunity to travel to a beautiful place. I could understand her trading in the opulent, tank-like Lexus for a different car. The SUV had bad associations with her kidnapping experience, and, I had to admit, the sporty little Toyota looks really good on her. Suddenly there appeared before me an image of her waving the Lexus pink slip at me, but the pink slip turned into the pink "joke" flyer, with the writing on the back, "*no te ocupes.*"

"It looks good on her," I thought. With each stroke, I pounded out a word, "It...looks...good...on...her." I worked the mantra for several laps, gradually fading the words until I zoned into a mindless rhythm of strokes.

An hour later, I got out and lay on a lounge chair. The solar heat stored in the wooden slats flowed into my pool-cooled body. After the molecules in my body and the chair had equalized, and I felt the chair below me begin to suck heat back out of my body, I got up and went into my pool house to shower.

It was an Indian summer day, with warm Santa Ana winds teasing the tops of the palm trees around the pool and making the purple bougainvillea whisper outside my door. My little *casita* is tiny, but it has a really nice bathroom, and the dark little bedroom stays cool in the summer heat.

As I waited for the shower to warm up, I looked at the mosaic-like Portuguese tiles my mother had inlaid into the shower walls. She brought the tiles back from a business trip she'd taken with Dad to Portugal, Spain, and Italy. They're square, with geometric patterns made from small diamond shapes in grey-blue, tan, and cream, and outlined with raised grey lines as fine and organic as the strands on a spider's web. Each of the three tiles was slightly different, and inlaid at eye level, with the corners pointing down to make a diamond shape.

The main house is also full of my mother's touches: the giant arched picture windows she had put in to bring light and air into the dark Spanish style rooms, the cabinets she helped design using antique wood carvings, the beautiful fireplace and mantel made from a mosaic of old tiles and sheets of colored marble.... She'd told me, not long ago, that Dad was considering selling the house. I found it hard to believe he would do that to her. She would have to move in with Connie or move into Dad's house in Mexico.

I'd figured Mom was too strong to Dad sell the home she had made so much a part of her self. But how, really, could we stop him? I had saved a little money, maybe enough to buy a new car when I needed one. Ma had no money of her own. Her father had been a businessman who'd gone bankrupt and died while I was still in school. Her mom, my grandma, was a widow living in Mexico on a small pension. If Mom would just go back to her old self, I thought, Dad would probably let her stay here.

As I stepped out of the shower, I shivered in the cool room, and quickly dried myself off. Instead of dressing, I slid under my bedcovers so I could be warm and think. I curled into a fetal position, and soon fell into a deep sleep.

I woke up an hour later, lying on top of my bed having shed my cocoon of blankets. A musical splashing sound came from the direction of the pool. I threw on my shorts and went outside.

She was treading water in the deep end, her wet hair slicked back from her forehead and her eyes looking very large and dark in her face, like a sleek water animal. The outside table was set for two with the good plates, bowls, and silver, cloth napkins, a glass pitcher of water, and glasses for water and sherry. Plastic bags with the logo of our favorite Thai take-out were on the table. When she saw me, she swam to my side of the pool and gave me a radiant grin.

"You look happy, Ma."

"*Hola*, Sleeping Beauty. Yes, I have something to celebrate."

"So do I." I opened the bags and laid the containers of food out on the table. "We're about to solve the Torres case. What's your news?"

She got out of the pool and pulled her towel off of a chair. "Let's have dinner, first. Tell me all about your case."

Mom was fascinated by Patty and Christine's scheme to switch identities.

"Why would they do that, *m'ijo?*"

"We think they did it so they could switch careers. They hated their jobs and didn't want to go back to school and start over."

"Amazing! What a brilliant idea! How did they pull it off?"

"First of all, they moved from Oakland to San Diego, where nobody knew them. Christine, the real Christine that is, didn't have any close relatives still living. Patty had a brother, an aunt, and a husband. Patty's brother and husband probably agreed to go along with the scheme, because Patty told them it would make her happy. And they had the fake Christine take on Brad Fernwood's last name, so people who knew the real Christine under her maiden name, wouldn't recognize the name. Then, they just…started over."

"But how could they just start practicing such different professions, without all those years of education? Is our education system really so unnecessary?"

"Christine probably had some crash course in law, so she could understand legal terms and do basic legal research and writing. Maybe Patty taught her, or maybe she took a class or two somewhere. I could see that, 'cause I've learned a lot about the law, on the job."

"And what about the woman who was the lawyer, who became a therapist. What is she like?"

"I actually liked her, Ma. Just being around her, she made you feel like a good person. She is a born therapist. It makes me sick she might have had a part in killing her friend."

"But she has found her place in the world, doing what God meant her to do. I envy her that." Mom mused.

"What, killing her best friend?"

She waved her hand. "No, caring about her vocation enough to change her identity, maybe even to kill for it. It must have filled a powerful need, finally fulfilling her purpose in life, as a therapist."

"Well, Patty didn't have to give up her identity to work as a therapist," I replied. "She could have gone back to school for a few more years, and earned her own license."

"Don't be so literal, *m'ijo*," Mom said. "There is a powerful metaphor here. Patty and Christine were rebels. They rebelled against a system that creates too many barriers to realizing your true self. Patty had to give up her old self to save her new self."

"Kind of like kidnapping herself, hey, Ma?"

It had gotten dark around the poolside, the only light coming from the neighbor's windows next door. Ma's smile glinted in the darkness, exposing the charming little gap between her two front teeth.

"Exactly like that, *m'ijo*." She said softly. "Exactly like that."

We sat in silence for a minute.

"How long have you known?" Ma asked.

"I was slow on the uptake. You put that pink flyer in my room with the message, didn't you?"

"I didn't want you to worry. But when I came back, I realized you must not have gotten the message I wrote on the back of that flyer."

"No. You wrote 'don't worry', '*no te preocupes*', but the flyer tore, and I thought it said '*no te ocupes*', don't get involved. I thought it was a threat from the gang we were investigating. I was sure they'd taken you, because of me. I didn't figure it out until this afternoon." I started to feel angry. "Those days you were gone were the worst days of my life."

"I'm sorry you had to suffer." She crossed her arms over her chest, massaging her upper arms to keep them warm.

"Why'd you do it, Mom?"

"For the money, of course."

"You're going to leave Dad, aren't you?"

She sighed. "I'm sorry if this hurts you. That was my good news for you, that I've finally made my decision. I've wanted to leave your father for years, him and his mistresses and his money. When I've tried to talk to him about it, he's threatened me with selling this house and leaving me with no money. The last time I talked to him about leaving, that's when he decided to take out a second mortgage on this house."

"Why'd you sign off on it, then? You're a half owner of the house, right?"

Mom sighed. "Marriage is complicated. I don't know how to describe to you, I'm ashamed...." She stopped.

The night air felt heavy, laden with dark intricacies of my parent's marriage. There were details I couldn't bear to think about, and my head was filled with family-related words that I still didn't truly understand: seduction, betrayal, domination, submission; and words I already knew well: judgment, disgust, rejection.

"It's OK, Ma. I get it."

She continued, "The loan on the house was the last straw for me. After I signed the papers, I felt humiliated. Your father never gave me access to any of our money. I have charge cards to department stores and gas stations, and a debit account for things like groceries. Most of our assets on this side of the border are leveraged, and it's not easy to get the courts to award funds that are kept in Mexico. If I'd had more education or work experience, I would have left it all behind and tried to make my own way, but I was afraid of starting out with nothing.

"I felt truly trapped. Your dad was holding me hostage because he'd deprive me of all of our assets if I tried to claim my freedom. When I saw the pink flyer one day at lunch at the Country Club, that's when I got the idea. It seemed like poetic justice for me really to be kidnapped, so your father would get a taste of what he was doing to me. After lunch, I told Italia about my idea and she said she would help."

"I wish I'd known what you were going through. How long have you wanted to…to get away from him?"

"Off and on for a long time, *m'ijo*. There have been some happy times, or I couldn't have gone on for so long. Earlier, the threats were about keeping my children away from me."

"What? How could he keep us away from you?"

"He can't, now, but he will still try. He will convince Chuy and Connie to shun me, and force them to choose between him and me. I'll be the bad wife and mother, the homewrecker, and he'll be the abandoned father, who happens to have a lot of money to shower on the kids who take his side. The only way I might get Connie back is to become her nanny again. I'm ashamed I raised two such children.

"When your father…disowned you, six years ago, I almost left him then. He put you out on the streets. I'm so sorry I did not have my own funds to help you go to college or pursue your dream of becoming a dancer."

"Oh, no, Ma. There were friends I could stay with, most of the time. And I could have found a way to get through college. I made my choice to live the way I do now. Now I'm sorry I wasn't there to help you."

"You and Gaby will always be there for me, I know that."

"But we can't support you financially," I said. My face felt hot. "Not in the way you like to live. I should be able to support you better."

She put a hand on my arm. "Don't you understand? Between the one hundred fifty K, plus the extra money I got from selling the Lexus, and the money I can get for all the jewelry I've been charging to your Dad's accounts, I can make a new start. And I never told your father about the rent you've been paying me the past two years, which I've also saved. Italia's helped me set up some accounts that Orlando does not need to know about."

"But the house, and your jewels, and your whole lifestyle...."

"I would keep our home if I could, Armando. The other things mean nothing to me. 'Where your **heart is**, there will your treasure be.' I'll find my way."

29

The next day, Lucy got a call from Alan Shaw at eight o'clock in the morning, letting her know the warrant had been issued. Lucy left for court, to deal with the arraignment of Ms. Bibber. "I'll probably be back after lunch time," she'd told me. "Dr. Bibber will want to take me out to lunch after court."

Lucy stumbled in around three thirty. Her eyes were slightly unfocused, and she shook her head as if to clear it as she walked into the room. She hung up her jacket and eased herself onto the couch, smoothing her hair back into place with both hands.

"Are you OK?" I asked. "I was about to call you."

"I'm OK."

"Where have you been?"

"Where do you think? I've been knocking back drinks with my DUI client and her daddy. I'm getting old, Armando. I used to be able to have two martinis and not feel a thing. Now look at me."

"You look all right. Better than Ms. Bibber the other day."

"That's not saying much," she said tartly.

"I didn't mean…"

"Your friend Ms. Bibber was on her ass after one martini," Lucy informed me. "Her daddy, on the other hand, could have drunk me under the table in my best days. The man had five martinis, and yes I was counting. He didn't show any effect. Kept telling me stories of his fishing adventures in

Mexico. He's going to drive her home and then go back to his office this afternoon to perform surgery."

She looked up at me. "Well, too early to have news from Shaw, yet, I suppose?"

"Right. I haven't heard anything."

Lucy was asleep on the couch, and I was playing a game on my computer, when the call finally came in at seven o'clock.

"Hello, Mr. Shaw? Yes, this is Armando Felan. Yes, she's here."

I put him on hold, got Lucy, and put the call on speakerphone.

"The good news is, we found Patty's wallet," he said.

"Where?"

"It was in their study, behind some of Christine's files, in a drawer. It included a social security card and driver's license for the real Patty Acres."

"Was Christine there?"

"She was. We have them both down at the station for questioning."

"Is she talking?"

"Is she ever! That's the bad news. She's got an answer for everything. This is going to be a hard one to pin down. Hey, Brad's attorney says they're ready to talk to us. I've got to get back in there. You have anything for us?"

"There are a couple of lines of inquiry I can suggest," Lucy told him.

***

Transcripts
7:18 p.m., September 23

Shaw: This is an interview with Brad Fernwood, who is here with his attorney Patrick List. Present are Deputy District Attorney Alan Shaw and officer Eric Parti. Mr. Fernwood, we have advised you of your right to remain silent. Have you had a chance to confer with your attorney regarding your rights?

Fernwood: I know my rights.

Shaw: Very good. Can Officer Parti bring you a cup of coffee?

Fernwood: I don't want a cup of coffee. I want to talk to my wife.

Shaw: That's not possible right at this moment, sir. You may confer with your attorney if you need to do so."

Fernwood: No. Let's get this over with.

Shaw: Your statement to Mr. Parti, the afternoon the real Christine Delancy's body was discovered, states that you were at your home here in San Diego the night she died. Let's go over that again....

....

Shaw: Thank you, Fernwood.

[Pause and sound of papers rustling.]

Fernwood: Are we done?

Shaw: Just a couple more things we want to clear up. Mr. Fernwood, we believe you went to Ms. Delancy's apartment at about nine o'clock the night she died. Your wife was on her way up to Santa Barbara. Did you bring your baby with you that night? Or did you arrange for child care?

Fernwood: I wasn't at the apartment that night. I was at home all night, with my baby boy, Ethan.

Shaw: I'm sorry, Mr. Fernwood, I wish I could believe you. Especially because I worry about your having left Ethan home alone. The thing is, if you were at Ms. Delancy's apartment that night, as we believe you were, and you didn't arrange for coverage of your baby, then I'm afraid we'll have to have Child Protective Services take custody of him until we can clear this up.

Fernwood: No! Don't do that. I wasn't part of this. I want to confer with my attorney.

8:00 p.m., September 23

Shaw: This is the continuation of questioning of Patty Taylor, a.k.a. Christine Delancy Fernwood, a material witness in the murder of Christine Delancy, a.k.a. Patty Taylor. I am Deputy District Attorney Alan Shaw, and with me are homicide investigator Dan Burke and officer Diana Adams.

Ms. Taylor, we are back on the record. You understand we have previously cautioned you as to your rights and you understand those rights are still in effect?

Witness: Yes. Thank you so much for reminding me. You're doing an awesome job.

Shaw: Thank you. Let's review what you have told us. The wallet that was found in your home today, you took that from her home after you gave her the poison that killed her, is that correct?

Witness: Oh, no, that's not right. Believe me, I totally understand why you're getting confused. Yes, I know you found a wallet in my desk, but Christine gave that to me, when we changed identities. I became Christine, so I got possession of the real Christine's ID's. Of course, the picture on the license didn't match, so I wasn't using it. That's why it was put away. Now, doesn't that make sense?

Shaw: Excuse me? She gave you her ID's? Then, wouldn't she have yours? But you wouldn't be able to use them, so....?

Witness: (Laughter) It's very complicated, isn't it? I feel terrible, causing all of this confusion. Let me help clear things up.

Shaw: Good idea.

Witness: You want to know why I have Christine's ID's, but she doesn't have mine. Of course, you do. That's an excellent question. I really want to thank you for making me feel so comfortable here. I am so sorry our little subterfuge led to such confusion. It's the last thing I wanted to do. But I had no choice. I'm sure Patty took her own life, and there was no reason to confuse the issue of her death with our little plan. That was between the two of us.

I kept both ID's, because Christine said she didn't need hers. She didn't have a car, as she lived downtown and could take public transportation. She didn't need her license, but I did need mine, my real one, to drive, in case I got stopped. Simple, isn't it?

I'm sure my poor friend took her own life. During that last telephone call, at about seven that night, she told me that she was very upset over her fight with Domingo. She said she wished she was dead. Did I tell you before, she told me she was thinking of taking all those Fentanyl pills? Well, she did. She said that. I had lent her the pills, of course, a couple weeks earlier, because she was having problems with her back. I told her not to be overly dramatic, that I would worry about her. I even offered to skip my conference to come be with her.

Shaw: When exactly did you give her your bottle of Fentanyl pills?

Witness: About two or three weeks before she died. I remember I met her for lunch, and gave them to her. Her back was out, and she asked me if I had anything to help her. I told her I had some medicine I wasn't using, and I brought it to lunch. The date will be on my calendar, we had lunch at a little Mexican place near her office. How terrible do you think I feel about that?

Shaw: Why do you feel terrible?

Witness: I'm sorry. For giving her the pills she used to take her own life, of course. You see, this has been a case of suicide all along. I tried to make that clear to everyone who interviewed me. After I talked to Christine, I had that long drive to Santa Barbara. On the way up there, I was worrying about my friend. I couldn't help it, I'm like that. I worry too much about people that I care about.

Shaw: Why did you stop along the way and Skype with your aunt? It wasn't your usual day, was it?

Witness: Oh, no, it wasn't. That's very clever of you to know that. No, I Skyped with Aunt Jill precisely because I didn't want this confusion to come up. And now it has anyway. I'm so sorry.

Shaw: You didn't want confusion about…?

Witness: Well, I need to be more clear, don't I? Christine and I had exchanged our identities, as you know. If she did go ahead and try to take her own life, well, I wouldn't be there to save her. I was out of town. Once I suspected she might be about to do herself in, and I was too far away to stop it, then, well, I had to protect myself, and my family. There wouldn't have been any of these problems if the police had just realized Patty committed suicide.

Shaw: Er…. I think you mean, Christine, not Patty. And how do you know?

Witness: Oh, I'm so sorry, I know I'm not being clear. Yes, of course, I meant Christine. And how do I know? Well, I just do. I know her. In a way, I am Christine.

(Silence and sound of papers shuffling)

Shaw: You had killed your friend before you left San Diego. When she called you at seven o'clock, you went over there, had a drink with her, and put poison in her drink. Then you left for Santa Barbara. On your drive up, you stopped to call your aunt on Skype so that she could testify Patty Taylor was still alive when you were already on your way out of town. All that time, you knew that your friend was dead.

Witness: No. I can see how you would think that, but I didn't.

….

Shaw: She told you she wanted to have her old identity back, didn't she? She wanted to go back to being Christine Delancy. She was tired of the deception. She wanted to get her life back in order and marry Mr. Torres.

Witness: Marry Domingo? Oh, no. Actually, I think she was afraid of him. I remember now she said that she was. Yes, as she told me that night, she was disillusioned with their love affair. That was part of her depression.

Shaw: You told your husband, Brad Fernwood, the truth about how you'd killed your friend, didn't you? Did he actually help you with the poisoning part of this?

Witness: No, I didn't tell him about my early suspicion that Patty was going to take her own life, if that's what you mean. I should have called him that night, and asked him to go over there and check on Patty. That might have saved her life. But I didn't. I feel just awful.

....

Shaw: Ms., uh, ma'am, you realize what you and your friend did was illegal? You both practiced your professions without proper licensure.

Witness: I'm afraid I really shouldn't comment about that. I'd like to talk to an attorney before I answer any more questions. Thank you for being so understanding.

Interview terminated at 8:40 p.m.

9:00 p.m. September 23

Shaw: This is the continuation of the interview of Brad Fernwood, who is present with his counsel. Mr. Fernwood, you have consulted with your attorney, and we have talked off the record regarding certain issues. You have been informed of your rights and wish to proceed, is that correct?

Witness: Correct.

Shaw: Your wife, Patty Acres Fernwood, also known as Christine Fernwood, has confessed she switched her identity with her friend Christine. She admits she gave, or lent, her box of Fentanyl to her friend. Did you ever see a bottle of Fentanyl with a prescription to your wife?

Witness: Yes.

Shaw: When did you see the bottle of Fentanyl with a prescription to your wife?

Witness: I last saw it the day before Christine died.

Shaw: Where did you see it?

Witness: It was.... It was....

Shaw: Do you need to take a break, Mr. Fernwood?

Witness: No. Let's get this over with. I saw the bottle, the day before Christine died, in the medicine cabinet of our home.

Shaw: The home you share with your wife, Patty Taylor?

Witness: Yes. (Crying) And our baby, our baby.... God help me, I didn't know....

....

Interview terminated at 9:30 p.m.

30

For the past five years, Lucy Sanders has had the best-dressed clients in the trial courts of San Diego. Early on, I talked her into allocating a small budget so I could shop for courtroom attire for our clients. It appalls me how most attorneys let their clients dress for trial. As if the bad buzz haircuts and sloppy shaves aren't enough, they're tarted up in suits that are three sizes too large or too small, ill-fitting, starched, white button-down shirts which just serve to highlight the scary tattoos peeking out from their sleeves and collars, and ties that were once worn by junior attorneys sometime in the 1980s. What is the jury supposed to think?

As I walked towards the Hazard Hotel early on a sunny Saturday morning, I was feeling a bit sorry for myself. Even if Domingo's case had gone to trial, though, I probably wouldn't have gotten to do my favorite part of my job for him. He's the kind of guy who's gonna have really nice shit of his own, even when he's down and out. My only task today was to go through the box of Domingo's clothes that was being stored at his hotel, and get some fresh street clothes for him to wear for his release from jail.

I cheered up when I saw my friend's pumpkin smile across the front desk.

"Spanks, my man!"

"Armand-ino! You missed my show, man!"

"I know. Sorry, Spankster. I was going to go, but something else came up that night. My friend got us tickets to see Rudolfo."

"Who?"

"Forget it. Next time, for sure, OK? Listen, Lucy's worked her magic again. She got Domingo Torres off, and he's coming home. He need some clothes to wear out of jail this morning."

"Hey, that's cool man." Spanky leaned over the counter and gave me a high five. "Way to go!"

He pulled out his keys and unlocked a large cloakroom behind the desk, motioning me to come inside. "He didn't have a lot of stuff. I took the clothes from his drawers and put them in his big suitcase. His shoes and other stuff I packed into this box."

I picked up the suitcase first. Louis Vuitton, very nice. Mom had given me the exact same suitcase for our trip to Chuy's wedding in Germany. I pulled out a couple of shirts and shook them out.

"Too bad they're kind of wrinkled," Spanky said. "You know, the cops always leave everything a mess when they toss the place. You want to borrow an iron?"

It was the least I could do for Domingo, I thought. "Yeah, could I? This stuff is too fine for him to wear without a nice sharp crease."

The threads were indeed as nice as I had expected. I quickly zeroed in on a pale blue Lauren polo shirt and soft Hugo Boss dress pants. I dug out some underwear and socks and put them in a small compartment of the garment bag I'd brought with me.

I debated whether to get Domingo some extra shoes and a belt, since he'd have the ones he wore to the jail. The outfit I had chosen would look better with brown, although a soft black might be neutral enough to work.

"Oh, bam!" I pulled out a soft, distressed brown leather belt, not too wide or narrow, with quietly rustic stitching and a clean-cut brassy rectangular buckle. "Yes!" The inside of the belt was branded with the label, Dolce and Gabana. You couldn't get one for less than $300. Now for the shoes. As I went through the box with the shoes in it, I saw a stack of big magazines in Spanish.

The magazines turned out to be the Juarez weekly paper *Commoción*, which was printed in a flat, glossy magazine format, and contained the six-part series Domingo had written about Rudolfo. I'd never actually seen the notorious articles that had landed Domingo in so much trouble. I took the stack of papers out to Spanky's seat behind the desk and started to look through them.

I still had a little time before I had to be at the jail. I settled back to read, putting my feet up on the hotel counter and leaning back in Spanky's antique wooden office chair. Spanky came in and spoke to me a couple of times before I heard him.

"Sorry," I said.

"Watcha readin'?"

"Just some old Spanish newspapers Domingo had. See, here's a picture of Rudolfo, the singer I told you about."

Spanky peered over my shoulder. "Oh, I get it. He's one of them mariachis."

"Kind of. You like that kind of music, Spanks?"

"I like it all, man. Mariachi's real good when they have the big band sound, you know, with a lotta horns."

"Rudolfo's definitely got that," I told him. "OK," I tore my eyes from the paper. "You ready for me to iron?"

"Let me do it," Spanky said, taking the shirt and slacks I'd set out on the counter. "It's easier if I take it to my room."

"Thanks, man." I turned back to the papers.

It was clear why the series of articles had triggered Cantara's vendetta against Domingo. While Domingo's flowery prose painted a charming portrait of Rudolfo, capturing his humor and charismatic warmth, there were strong suggestions planted throughout the articles that Rudolfo might be an unwitting puppet furthering Cantara's illegitimate activities. *Commoción* had given the articles a lavish spread, with several full pages and a lot of large color pictures in each of the six parts of the series. I was disappointed the cover page of the earliest newspaper, which contained the first part of the series, was missing. The following page noted:

"On the cover: Philanthropist Jorge Arias and Francisco Torres open new Children's Museum in downtown Juarez. See page 7."

Was this an Arias as in the Bustamente-Arias gang? If so, what was he doing so brazenly on the cover of the newspaper, being chummy with one of the paper's editors? Curious to see the picture, I went back and rummaged through the box to try and find it, but it wasn't in the box. Maybe the cops had taken it? Or had Domingo torn it off for reasons of his own?

I went back and looked at the suitcase. The cops had probably gone through it pretty well when they searched Domingo's room. But maybe none of them had been familiar with Louis Vuitton luggage. If Domingo's was like mine, it had a special little pocket behind one of the zippered pockets on the inside of the lid. The cool thing is, you can't see this pocket easily, or feel it just by running your hand over the inside of the big zippered pocket. It's seamlessly velcro'd down behind the heavily quilted area on the inside lining, invisible but big enough to hold a pack of condoms, for example, without making a bump that you'd feel on a cursory search.

Sure enough, Domingo's suitcase had a little pocket just like mine, and inside the pocket was a folded paper. It turned out to be the missing cover page. A picture of two smiling businessmen, one of them a (much) shorter, rounder version of Domingo, who I assumed was his Uncle Francisco, covered the top half of the page. Below the picture of the other man, in blue ink, was neatly handwritten in a mixture of Spanish and English:

To Domingo: Buen trabajo, como siempre. La Carrera en la Politica de Rudolfo: Ultimada! I told you it would be your next big 'hit.' Viva B-A. Jorge

I carefully wiped the paper with one of Domingo's shirts, folded it back the way it had been, and replaced it, careful not to leave any of my fingerprints on it. I put the magazines back where I had found them.

"You saw nothing," I told myself. "Nothing."

Spanky was still in his little room off of the front desk, putting the finishing touches on Domingo's slacks.

"Thanks, buddy. I couldn't have done better myself."

I felt like I was moving in slow motion as I took hangers out of my garment bag, and hung up the shirt and pants. I made sure all Domingo's things were neatly packed up before Spanky put them back in the storage closet.

As I left the Hazard Hotel in a daze, Spanky called after me, "Tell Domingo 'happy freedom' for me, and I'll see him when he gets back here for his stuff. Boy, I bet you'll be glad to see your client back on the outside, huh?"

***

Lucy, Claude, and I stood on the sidewalk and watched our client walk out the door of the jail, squinting in the sunlight and breaking into a grin as he saw us. He looked bigger and better than ever in his street clothes. Personally, I would have worn the polo shirt out, but he'd used the brown belt I'd brought him and tucked the shirt in. His shoe collection had been a little ornate for my taste, but I had to admit the shiny brown Ferragamo loafers with the little chain across the front looked pretty OK on him.

He walked up to Lucy, threw open his arms, and enveloped her in a long bear hug. Lucy is above average height for a woman, but her head barely reached his chest. He bent his head to speak softly into her ear, so softly that I could not hear what he said. Claude and I lined up behind our boss. Before my find this morning, I would have been hoping for a hug, but now I was relieved that we each got a gigantic warm handshake instead.

"Armando, fantastic work! *Te debo por mi vida, mi hermano.* I owe you my life, brother." I'd done such a good job in erasing the note from my mind, I found it surprisingly easy to make eye contact and smile at him warmly.

"Can we take you out for coffee? Or drive you to your hotel?" Lucy asked.

Domingo smiled and shook his head. "No, thank you. What I would really like is to be outside. It's a beautiful day. I'll walk over to the park and then back to the hotel." He put his hands over his heart and smiled sweetly. "Thank you, again." He slung the white bag with his belongings from jail over his shoulder. Halfway down the block, he turned around and waved back at us, and took off.

"Hey, *Abogada*, what did Domingo say to you when he hugged you? I couldn't hear, he spoke so softly."

"Maybe he didn't want you to hear," she said primly.

"Come on, Luce." Claude said, squinting his eyes at her. "What was it?"

"He said it was a quote from *Don Quixote*, that reminded him of me. It went something like this:

'It is not the responsibility of knights errant to discover whether the afflicted they aid are reduced to these circumstances and suffer this distress for their vices, or for their virtues. The knight's sole responsibility is to succor them as people in need, having eyes only for their sufferings, not for their misdeeds.'"

"I guess that fits," Claude said.

The three of us went, client-less, to the Hob Nob Hill coffee shop, a short drive up the hill from the jail, for a debriefing. We all ordered the kind of giant breakfast you usually only get when you're travelling or after you've stayed up all night partying until you're totally starving.

"You were the one who gave me the idea, Armando," Lucy told me. "I had a feeling about Christine, as she called herself, from the beginning. She was close to Patty, and from your interview notes and her testimony at the preliminary hearing, I saw her as manipulative and disturbed...."

A wave of shame and dread went over me. How had I not seen it? How would I tell Lucy I had actually gone to her for therapy? Our big piled-up plates of food arrived, but I'd suddenly lost my appetite.

When the waitress left, Lucy continued. "But Christine's alibi was solid, because Patty was alive and well and Skyping with her aunt while Christine was on the road to Santa Barbara." Lucy continued. "Then, it was very strange how the Patty we heard about in San Diego was so different from the Patty who practiced law up in Oakland. One was sweet and rather weak, the other was manipulative and unscrupulous. I thought something must have happened to change her behavior, and that's where I was stuck.

"Then you, Armando, said to me that if you could just be given a therapist's license, you would change your profession. It hit me, that's what Patty and Christine could have done. It explained too many things: the missing wallet, which would have had the victim's real driver's license with her real name and picture on it, the unlikely apparent romance between Brad and the victim, the victim's personality change. Most of all, if the women had changed identities, then Christine no longer had an alibi. She killed Patty before she left for Santa Barbara, then Skype'd with her aunt to create the alibi."

"Good job, Luce," Claude said. "Here's to another brilliant piece of deduction." He toasted her with his coffee mug.

"Well, it was a group effort," she said. "I couldn't have done it without the two of you."

I started to feel better, and dug into my food as they continued to talk. After inhaling the hash browns and half the eggs, I asked, "You were going to ask Justin if he knew whether Patty had a passport. Did you find out?"

Claude said, "She didn't need to. I took a copy of her death certificate to Immigration, and they gave me a copy of her passport application."

"And the picture, of course, was of the woman we know as Christine," Lucy added. "That confirmed my suspicion, and that proof of the identity switch was enough for the DA to get a warrant to search Christine's home. Both women's passports as well as their driver's licenses were found in the home."

"Why did she do it?" I asked. "I understand switching identities to change professions. But why kill her friend?"

"I think Patty wanted her identity back. She was in love with Domingo. She may have believed the only way to keep him from being sent back to Mexico and being killed by the gangs, was to marry him so he could stay legally in the United States. It would have been risky to marry Domingo under her false identity. Or maybe she was just tired of the deception."

"But why would her friend have to kill her? They could just switch back." Claude said.

"It got complicated," Lucy said. "Christine is a sociopath. I think she'd been able to dominate Patty, until Patty fell in love with Domingo. She saw herself losing control over her friend, and she didn't want to give up her new profession. She probably feared if they switched back they would be discovered and prosecuted, and barred from their professions."

"I can see that," I said. "Christine loved her work. It was a big part of her identity."

"I dunno," Claude said. "Maybe, if you take all those things, and if she was in a strange mood and she just snapped."

"Oh, no, Claude, I don't think so," Lucy said. "She planned this for a long time, probably as soon as they decided to switch. I'm sure she suspected her friend was weak and wouldn't be able to sustain the façade. The murder might have been precipitated by events, but it was bound to happen. Christine kept that prescription of Fentanyl for a reason."

"Nah, I disagree, Luce. You wouldn't set up a plot to kill your best friend, just to get a professional license."

"Of course *I* wouldn't, Claude, but...."

As they argued, I thought about it. I was sure the Christine I knew would not have plotted in cold blood to kill her friend. Yeah, my judgment of her had sucked, because I liked her and she'd understood me. But she wasn't heartless. I remembered the look on her face the day I'd first interviewed her about her friend's death. Claude and Lucy continued to bicker, just for the sake of argument, not because they gave a shit. For them, the case was over. We'd never really know.

***

"Hello?" He answered like he didn't know who was calling.

"Hi, Justin. It's Armando."

"I know."

I waited for a second, sighed to myself, and pressed on. "Well, the reason I'm calling is, I have some good news for you, about Domingo's case. Domingo wanted you to know, and Lucy said I should call you."

"Lucy told you to call?"

"Well, I would have called you anyway, to tell you."

"It's not exactly breaking news anymore, is it?"

"What? What do you mean?" I said.

"Domingo's out of jail. That friend of Patty's has been arrested for the murder."

"How did you find out? Did Domingo call you?"

"No." His tone was still flat.

"So how did you find out?" I asked patiently.

"I went to the jail this morning. I thought I'd check in on Domingo. I got there around ten thirty, and they told me he was gone. They said the charges had been dropped. I went back to the office and got his old cell phone number, and the cell was out of service. Finally, I reached his hotel and they let me talk to him on their phone."

"Sorry," I said. "I should have called you sooner. I meant to, but I came home this morning and fell asleep."

"You could have called me last night."

I sat up taller against my pillows and pulled the covers over my lap. "I could have."

"Shit, are you still mad at me?"

"What do you think? I mean, after what you said to me and everything."

"I didn't know what to think, Armando. A few days ago, you tell me you can't see me because of this case. Then today I find out the case is over, and you haven't even called me to tell me. All I could think was, if it had been me I would have been on the phone the first thing. What do you think it's been like for me the past week?"

A wave of feeling rushed over me, washing away my position that I would wait for an apology before seeing him.

"Can I come over?" I asked.

When I arrived at his apartment, he blushed and pushed his hair back from his forehead, like he used to do when we first met. His amazing golden-brown eyes blazed into mine with an intensity I hadn't seen in him before.

"Armando, I'm so sorry. I was such a puffed up little prick. It makes me sick what I said to you, about school. No wonder you didn't call me right away."

"I didn't handle it well either," I said. "Anyway, you were right. I'll never go back to school. At least, not for anything practical."

"You don't need to go to school. You're perfect the way you are. I just said that about school because I was feeling insecure. I thought you were breaking up with me. God, I sounded like Daniel. I despised myself for saying it. What you said about me still having a lot to learn, you were right."

"I shouldn't have said that," I told him. "You just hit a sensitive spot with me."

His face cleared and he smiled. "A sensitive spot? Where exactly would that be?" His hands moved lightly down my back.

We had a late dinner at a little Chinese place around the corner from his house. The place is dim, with dark red booths that give a lot of privacy. We were finally free to talk about the Torres case.

It was after midnight when we finished talking. The row of red lanterns strung across the middle of the room seemed rosier and dimmer than when we'd come in. We could hear murmurs and occasional soft laughter coming from the other booths, and the two Chinese waitresses were still busy bringing big trays of food out from the kitchen.

I didn't tell Justin about the note I'd found in Domingo's luggage. That information still felt like a live bomb in my hands, hot and dangerous.

I watched as Justin opened my unused chopsticks, and started playing with them absently, sanding one edge against the other. After sanding, he tested the smoothness of the edge by gliding it delicately across his bare white wrist. His dark red hair glowed in the soft lamplight. He looked up and caught me staring at him, and his eyes flashed.

"Hey, Armando Felan. Let's go dancing."

31

"The Torres case was a lot of fun," I remarked to Lucy a few days later, as I wrestled with the reams of paperwork the government requires for payment to counsel in a court-appointment case. "Can we only represent innocent clients from now on?"

Lucy had Ms. Bibber's recently organized (by me) case file taken apart and spread on and around the coffee table in the front room. A stack of the client's medical records had just come in, and I sighed as I saw she was starting to look at the pages out of order and scatter them randomly on the table after she read them.

"God, I hate reading doctor's records, they're like a chicken walked across the page. A noble profession, but this illegible handwriting is a sign of arrogance and disrespect." She took off her glasses and rubbed her eyes. "Sorry, what did you say, Armando?"

"I was just blathering. I'm so happy to be getting back to client billing, after the overexcitement of last week."

"What a shame your job can't be one hundred percent action and entertainment. Some of us are mature enough to do the less glamorous tasks without complaining...."

I opened my mouth to interrupt her and point out she'd been whining worse than me, but clammed up at her next words.

"However, I admit I could use a pick-me-up, too," she said.

We got no work done the rest of the afternoon. We drank tea and then moved on to the bottle of aged single malt scotch Lucy keeps behind the tea canisters. Lucy bitched about her sister's pathological hoarding. When she's ragging on someone, I have to admit she's in there with the best of the queens.

"Can we have some attorney/client privilege?" I asked her, when she finally stopped to take a breath.

"Really?"

I nodded.

"Well, I suppose you are entitled to a few minutes of my services, as consideration for the past hour I've spent talking about my sister."

I told Lucy the truth about my mother's "kidnapping."

"Is this a joke, Armando?"

"No, I swear. Her friend Italia helped her. Mom stayed at Italia's house. They planned it for a time when Italia's husband was out of town."

"Then who made the ransom calls to your father?"

"Italia disguised her voice. She's a good mimic."

"Your mother came up with the whole plan?"

"Yeah. She cleared a hundred and fifty thousand bucks. Plus, she's gotten some more out of my dad on top of that." I told Lucy about Mom's trading in the Lexus, which netted her another $30,000, and about the expensive jewels she'd been stockpiling.

"So, she made a plan and it worked. Well." Lucy's blue eyes narrowed. "Good for her, I guess. I mean, she had to do what she had to do. But, well…."

"What?" I asked, after she had been quiet for at least a minute.

"I'm thinking about short cuts. Christine and Patty took an, ah, inappropriate shortcut to make their career changes, which, predictably, started their lives moving in a very bad direction. By engineering this kidnapping scheme, your mother took a shortcut to filing for divorce and fighting in the courts for a fair financial settlement. She must have been truly desperate, to put her family through that experience. I can understand her being angry at your father, but what about her children? What about what you had to go through?"

I thought about it. "Maybe she had a reason to be angry at all of us. Even me. We all used her and took her for granted. I really believed she just lived to take care of us all. I didn't see her as her own person. Anyway, she did try to tell me." I told Lucy about the note Mom had left for me, which I'd mistakenly taken for a warning from Cantara.

"Well, then, I'm happy for her. She's now left your father, I assume?"

"Yeah. Maybe she can afford a good divorce attorney, now," I said.

Lucy pursed her lips and poured some more tea. "You really want my advice? I wouldn't go in that direction."

"What do you mean?"

"With all due respect to my brothers and sisters of the bar, the attorney fees will devour her, ah, savings. Even if she gets a court order for your father to hand over her share of the community property, it'll be a nightmare enforcing it."

"So, what should she do?"

Lucy leaned back in her chair. "Listen. The legal system was not a good option for your mom, so she was smart enough to figure out another way of getting your Dad to fork over some of the money. Why not finish the job, with another shortcut?"

"Which is…?"

"Here's what I'd do. She doesn't want to marry anyone else right away, does she?"

I shook my head.

"Good. I'd file a simple separation statement so if hubby goes bankrupt or something, I wouldn't have any liability. Let him go through the expense and hassle of filing for a divorce, when he finally decides to marry one of his mistresses. By that time, he'll be more motivated to give me something if I agree to the divorce. I'd put all my valuables somewhere he can't grab them, like a safe-deposit box. Does she really want to keep the house?"

I nodded.

"Then I'd get an appraisal and the exact amounts of the loans on the property. It's half in her name, right? What do you think it's worth? In today's market, less than three hundred K, right? Find a friend, or set up a company, to buy it. Your dad'll think he's selling it out from under her, but she'll be getting it under a different name. It's the best investment she could make right now."

"Lucy, do you mind if I call her right now?"

She looked surprised. "Really? Sure."

I hesitated. "Uh. First, there's one more thing I need to tell you."

"What's up?"

I told her what I'd found in Domingo's suitcase when I'd gone to get his clothes. Her first reaction was a snort of derision.

"The incompetence of the police never ceases to impress me. Why am I even surprised? Can you imagine? Right there in a pocket of his suitcase. I love it." She threw back her head and laughed. "This is rich! Louis Vuitton! I love it! It was hidden right there, where even you could find it!"

I stared at her with my mouth hanging open, waiting for more.

She looked at me blankly. "What? Oh, did I insult you? I just meant, you're not a cop, you weren't conducting a search...."

"You're not even surprised, are you?"

She frowned. "You mean about Domingo? Oh, come on, Armando. Did you really swallow his 'I'm just a stooge' act?"

"I sure as hell didn't know he was a freakin' hit man for B-A. How did you know?"

"I didn't say I knew. I didn't want to know. Of course, I presumed he was innocent. But really, Armando, how you could be so surprised, after all…. Oh, well."

We spent another half hour discussing our former client. Lucy was convinced Domingo'd really loved Christine. In support of her position, she put forth examples of famous criminals and her own clients, hardened assassins and professional thugs, who compartmentalized humanity into "family and loved ones" and "potential victims." For example, Lucy argued, if Domingo did carry out the hit on the troubled Sabrina, he probably dismissed her as a whore, disposable, while categorizing the gentle-mannered Christine as a fine lady, worthy of his love and protection.

"Christine, I mean the real Patty, was right in her opinion of Domingo," I said. "She told me he was a user, just out for himself."

"Politics and business," Lucy said. "That's how they work. But I still think he really loved Christine."

Lucy was back on the police's failure to find the note in Domingo's luggage. "So, so, sloppy," she said, smiling sweetly. "Their prime suspect, and the evidence is right there in his suitcase. Bless their hearts."

"Yeah, bless their hearts," I said. "'cause it's good they didn't find it. You might not have got him out."

"Oh, well. Let's hope his future hits do continue to be journalistic. The pen is mightier than the sword, right?"

"Riiiight."

As I was pulling my cell phone out of my pocket to call Mom, Lucy fished her phone out of her purse.

"Who are you calling?"

She ignored me and speed dialed a number, walking towards her office and grinning.

I called after her. "Say 'hi' to Claude. I bet he'll be surprised when you tell him about Domingo."

The door shut behind her.

***

Christine (as I still thought of her) was convicted of second-degree murder by a jury, after several days of deliberations. She's already got her appeal filed. Without telling Lucy, I did go and visit her in prison, a few months after her conviction. Her resiliency was serving her well behind bars, and she seemed touched to see me.

"I felt like I had to come," I told her. "By the way, it was very cool of you not to bring up our relationship as part of your defense."

"Tchh. Like that would have gotten me anywhere, Armando. You and I always got along."

"I always liked you. I didn't expect things to…come out this way."

"I know you didn't. Well, some good's come out of this mess. I'm glad for your sake Domingo is free. You did an awesome job for your client."

"How are you getting along in here?"

"I'm trying to make the best of it. There are some interesting people to talk to in here. These ladies need a lot of help." Her face clouded. "So. We don't have that much time. Tell me how *you* are."

I told her some funny stories about my friends and family that I thought would entertain her. I wished I could have told her the real story about Mom's kidnapping, because she would have loved it.

A few minutes before it was time to leave, I asked her, "I know you can't talk about your case, but I'm so curious about your plan with, um, your friend to switch careers like that. My mom thinks it was a brilliant idea."

"Does she!" She looked pleased. "I'll tell you about it. Why not? It's the least of my worries right now."

She folded her hands and leaned forward, towards the hole in the security glass between us. At this closer range I became more aware of her orange scrubs and the jailhouse pallor of her motherly features.

"Chris and I were sitting around one day, a couple of years ago. Gosh, it seems like much longer. We both used to complain how we hated our jobs. She'd say, 'I'd love to do what you do, take legal cases and fight for justice in court. Being a therapist is draining, I feel like my clients are vampires sucking me dry.'

"I'd say, 'I'd rather do your job. You just listen to people's problems, you don't have to actually solve them. You don't have to wade through all this paperwork, or do boring research, or follow all these stupid rules.'

"We talked about what a nightmare it would be to have to go back to school to get another degree. So on this one day, it was a Sunday, we were sitting on my balcony and both feeling depressed about the upcoming workweek. Usually I could cheer her up, but that day I was really down, too. I hated my life and my ugly rathole of an apartment and my unrewarding job.

"That's when Chris said, 'You know, couldn't we just switch?' Isn't that funny, Armando? It was her idea, not mine. She hated being in a clinic around sick people. She pictured herself in a nice homey law office, with respectful, mentally healthy clients, whose problems she could actually solve. It was her dream. I just helped make it a reality.

"Sure, she needed a little convincing. But in the end, she was all for it. She truly believed, as I do, that our society's licensing and education systems are overregulated and unreasonable. We'd both chosen the wrong profession and discovered we had other callings. In a way, we were making a statement by doing what we did. And things just went on from there.

"We decided San Diego would be a good place to start over, far enough away from Oakland, but still in California where we could use our professional licenses. In case we ran into anyone from our past, I changed my name legally to take my mother's maiden name, and Chris took that name, Patty Taylor. Then I, as Christine Delancy, married Brad and took the last name Fernwood. It was easy to get new diplomas and licenses in the new names."

"You make it sound easy," I said. "What about changing professions?"

"Well, I think we proved our point, don't you? We both learned by doing, not by listening to boring professors and taking stupid tests."

"You're an amazing therapist, Christine, I mean Patty," I told her. "Maybe your friend wasn't so good as a lawyer, though."

"She would have been fine. She just needed more time and focus. Not to say anything against your client, but I blame him for this sad ending to our adventure. It wouldn't have happened, if Domingo hadn't come into the picture. Chris and I were a great team. Then she went with Domingo." Her eyes flashed as she glanced at me and then down.

I saw it all in that half second: the two women, the plan, the convenient marriage to the unlovely but wealthy Brad, the adorable baby to help keep Brad and Sam on her side, and then my irresistible client strolling into the picture and falling for Patty.

"You really loved...," I said, and stopped.

Christine blinked back tears and nodded. "Domingo disturbed her equilibrium and she destabilized. The depression got her and she took her own life. Such a waste."

She looked into my eyes for my agreement. With a shock, I saw the eyes of Lucy's paranoid clients when they tell me about the conspiracies against them or the plates the government had planted in their brains. Then, for an instant, I saw in her my own mother's despair as she struggled to free herself from the trap of her marriage. Quickly, her face cleared, and I saw only the familiar "Christine" who had been my therapist and even, still, felt like my friend, giving me her familiar wry smile.

"Such a waste," I agreed.

The End

Acknowledgements

Julie Brossy, Susan Duerksen, Elizabeth Fox, Jeffrey Wilson, and Abigail Padgett.

Made in the USA
San Bernardino, CA
09 December 2018